BEHOLD MY HEART

What Reviewers Say About Ronica Black's Work

A Love that Leads to Home

"If you love a slow-burn romance where the characters are carefully dancing around each other while being incredibly adorable, this story is for you. It was an emotional read for me, and if you want a good heart-wrenching story, read it."—*Hsinju's Lit Log*

Freedom to Love

"This is a great book. The police drama keeps you enthralled throughout but what I found captivating was the growing affection between the two main characters. Although they are both very different women, you find yourself holding your breath, hoping that they will find a way to be together."—*Lesbian Reading Room*

The Practitioner

"*The Practitioner* by Ronica Black is the angsty sort of romance that I can easily get lost in. I wanted to fill a tub and bathe in all the feelings. Hell, if I had one of those fancy, waterproof Kindles, I just might have."—*Lesbian Review*

"The beginning of this novel captured my attention from the rather luscious description of a pint of Guinness. I cannot tell a lie, I almost immediately wanted to be drinking it. …The first scene with the practitioner also pulled me in, making me sit up and pay attention to what was happening on the digital page. The relationship was like a low simmering fire, frequently doused by either Johnnie's personal angst, or Elaine's. This book was an overall enjoyable read and one which I would recommend to people wanting characters who practically breathe off the page."—*Library Thing*

Snow Angel

"A beautifully written, passionate and romantic novella." —*SunsetXCocktail*

"*Snow Angel* is a novella, and it flies by. It draws characters and scenes in large strokes, and it's good fun if you'd like a quick read that's particularly escapist."—*The Lesbrary*

Under Her Wing

"From the start Ronica Black had me. I loved everything about this story, from the emotional intensity to the amazingly hot sex scenes. The emotion between them is so real and tear jerking at times. And the love scenes are phenomenal. I feel I'm raving—but I enjoyed it that much. Highly recommended."—*Kitty Kat's Book Review Blog*

***"Emily" in* Women of the Dark Streets**

"A darkly disturbing brush with questionable magic that leads to an astounding one-eighty-degree turnaround after an apparent attempt at suicide. Mindboggling!"—*Rainbow Book Reviews*

The Seeker

"Stalkers, child kidnappers and murderers all collide in this fast-paced, dual-plotted novel. This is not Black's first novel, and readers can only hope it will not be her last."—*Lambda Literary Review*

"Ronica Black's books just keep getting stronger and stronger. …This is such a tightly written plot-driven novel that readers will find themselves glued to the pages and ignoring phone calls. *The Seeker* is a great read, with an exciting plot, great characters, and great sex."—*Just About Write*

Flesh and Bone—*Lambda Literary Award Finalist*

"Ronica Black handles a traditional range of lesbian fantasies with gusto and sincerity. The reader wants to know these women as well as they come to know each other. When Black's characters ignore their realistic fears to follow their passion, this reader admires their chutzpah and cheers them on. …These stories make good bedtime reading, and could lead to sweet dreams. Read them and see." —*Erotica Revealed*

Chasing Love

"Ronica Black's writing is fluid, and lots of dialogue makes this a fast read. If you like steamy erotica with intense sexual situations, you'll like *Chasing Love*."—*Queer Magazine Online*

Hearts Aflame

"Sleek storytelling and terrific characters are the backbone of Ronica Black's third and best novel, *Hearts Aflame*. Prepare to hop on for an emotional ride with this thrilling story of love in the outback. …Along with the romance of Krista and Rae, the secondary storylines such as Krista's fear of horses and an uncle suffering from Alzheimer's are told with depth and warmth. Black also draws in the reader by utilizing the weather as a metaphor for the sexual and emotional tension in all the storylines. Wonderful storytelling and rich characterization make this a high recommendation." —*Lambda Literary Review*

"*Hearts Aflame* takes the reader on the rough and tumble ride of the cattle drive. Heat, flood, and a sexual pervert are all part of the adventure. Heat also appears between Krista and Rae. The twists and turns of the plot engage the reader all the way to the satisfying conclusion."—*Just About Write*

"I like the author's writing style and she tells a good story. I was drawn in quickly and didn't lose interest at all. Black paints a great picture with her words and I was able to feel like I was sitting around the camp fire with the characters."—*C-Spot Reviews*

Wild Abandon—*Lambda Literary Award Finalist*

"Black is a master at teasing the reader with her use of domination and desire. Black's first novel, *In Too Deep*, was a finalist for a 2005 Lammy. …With *Wild Abandon*, the author continues her winning ways, writing like a seasoned pro. This is one romance I will not soon forget."—*Books to Watch Out For*

"Black has managed to create two very sensual and compelling women. The backstory is intriguing, original, and quite well-developed. Yet, it doesn't detract from the primary premise of the novel—it is a sexually-charged romance about two very different and guarded women. Black carries the reader along at such a rapid pace that the rise and fall of each climactic moment successfully creates that suspension of disbelief which the reader seeks." —*Midwest Book Review*

"Ronica Black has proven once again that she is an awesome storyteller with her new romance, *Wild Abandon.* With her second published novel, she has crafted an erotic, sensual and well-paced tale. …Black is a master at teasing the reader with her use of domination and desire. Emotions pour endlessly from the pages, moving the plot forward at a pace that never slows or gets dull. But Black doesn't stop there. She is intent on giving the reader more. *Wild Abandon* hints at a plot twist early on, and while we know who it involves, we do not know what will happen, and how, until the last minute, effectively keeping us spellbound."—*Just About Write*

In Too Deep—*Lambda Literary Award Finalist*

"Ronica Black's debut novel *In Too Deep* has everything from nonstop action and intriguing well developed characters to steamy erotic love scenes. From the opening scenes where Black plunges the reader headfirst into the story to the explosive unexpected ending, *In Too Deep* has what it takes to rise to the top. Black has a winner with *In Too Deep*, one that will keep the reader turning the pages until the very last one."—*Independent Gay Writer*

"…an exciting, page turning read, full of mystery, sex, and suspense."—*MegaScene*

"…a challenging murder mystery—sections of this mixed-genre novel are hot, hot, hot. Black juggles the assorted elements of her first book with assured pacing and estimable panache."—*Q Syndicate*

By the Author

In Too Deep
Deeper
Wild Abandon
Hearts Aflame
Flesh and Bone
The Seeker
Chasing Love
Conquest
Wholehearted
The Midnight Room
Snow Angel
The Practitioner
Freedom to Love
Under Her Wing
Private Passion
Dark Euphoria
The Last Seduction
Olivia's Awakening
A Love That Leads to Home
Passion's Sweet Surrender
A Turn of Fate
Watching Over Her
The Business of Pleasure
Something to Talk About
Decadence "Passionate Pursuance"
The Murders at Sugar Mill Farm
The Curse writing as Alexandra Riley
The Breakdown
Stranded
Behold My Heart

Behold My Heart

by

Ronica Black

Bold Strokes Books

2025

BEHOLD MY HEART

ISBN 13: 978-1-63679-810-3

This Trade Paperback Original Is Published By
Bold Strokes Books, Inc.
P.O. Box 249
Valley Falls, NY 12185

First Edition: July 2025

Credits
Editor: Cindy Cresap
Production Design: Susan Ramundo
Cover Design By Tammy Seidick

Acknowledgments

Many thanks to BSB. I absolutely could not do this without your continued support. You guys are truly the best!

I don't say it enough, but a huge thank you to my editor, Cindy Cresap!

And always, a warm thank you to the readers, for continuing to take a chance on me. Your kindness and support mean more than you know.

CHAPTER ONE

Alora Anders slowed her Maserati to pull into the parting gate of her neighborhood subdivision. She smiled up at the rearview mirror and eyed the Toyota Corolla following her, carrying one fine specimen of a beautiful woman, if she did say so herself.

The sherbert colors of another beautiful sunset burst forth from the ridges of Camelback Mountain ahead of her as she drove slowly through the gate. What a sight. God, how she loved the desert and a good sunset. But the view was short-lived as the ridges of the mountain blurred and grew wavy. She rubbed her eyes, blinked, and turned onto her street. The waviness dissipated and she breathed a sigh of relief. Though the vision trouble was happening more and more frequently, it always eventually went away.

She'd considered seeing an eye doctor, but she'd put it off, hoping the trouble would right itself for good. But the blurriness kept returning, and this was the third time today it had happened. A new record. Maybe she really should see someone. She'd set a reminder to call first thing on Monday. She couldn't have anything interfering with her work, and the impaired vision was starting to. She'd had to stop painting twice already just this past week because she'd had trouble seeing and that was just unacceptable.

She pulled onto her circular drive and eased to a stop across from her front door. Normally, she'd pull into one of her three garages, but she knew from experience that her guest might get caught up in the presence of her other luxury cars. So to keep things simple, and the ball rolling, she made it a point to just go through the front door when she had someone over.

The Corolla stopped behind her and Alora killed her engine and crawled from her car. She smiled as she watched her nightly guest emerge from her vehicle.

"Nice place," the woman said. Her name was Diane. Or Denise. One of the two. They'd only just met at a coffee shop in Paradise Valley, thanks to a popular hookup app. "You rich or something?" She flicked her auburn locks and slinked toward her, the tight black dress she had on hugging her curves like the Maserati did the road.

"Something," Alora said, lightly gripping her waist to tug her close.

"Really? Does that mean I can go for a ride in your car?"

"Wouldn't you rather see the house first?"

Her green irises, which looked even more brilliant in the light of the sunset, shifted beyond Alora to the house. "Sure."

Alora took her hand and led her to the rustic Tuscan-style door where she quickly inserted her key and turned the lock. She pushed her way inside, pulling Diane or Denise along behind her. Spanish music blared from the house speakers, nearly drowning out the door chime announcing their entry, causing Alora to sigh. "Shit, it's Fatima's night to clean."

"What?" Diane or Denise said. "Who's Fatima?"

"My—housekeeper." Truthfully, she was a lot more than that. But Alora didn't want to explain. They hurried farther into the house, to the kitchen, where Fatima was singing and wiping down the counters.

"Fatima!" Alora shouted.

Fatima jerked and covered her heart with her hand. "Aye, dios mio. You scared me."

"Sorry." Alora released Diane or Denise's hand to cross to the panel where the volume of the music was controlled. She quickly lowered the sound and changed the setting to soft, vocal jazz. "There, that's better." She turned to face Fatima, who was giving Diane or Denise a close once-over.

"Fatima, this is, er, Diane?"

"Denise."

"Ah, right. Denise, this is Fatima. My right-hand woman around here. And she was just finishing up."

Fatima hung the dishcloth over the arched faucet and quickly gathered her water bottle and purse. "Yes, I finished." She knew the routine. When Alora had an evening guest, Fatima made herself scarce. "I made some enchiladas, mija. They're in the oven."

"Sour cream and chicken?"

"Sí. Your favorite."

"Thanks, Fatima." Alora planted a kiss on her cheek and inhaled her deep lavender scent.

"De nada. I see you later, no?"

"Yes, later."

Fatima gave Denise one last quick look and headed for the door. Alora listened as she closed it behind her.

"Now, we're all alone," Alora said, rounding the counter to once again grab Denise's hand. But Denise's gaze was on her surroundings.

"You really are rich."

Alora dropped her hand. "Can we move on from that, please?" Why, oh why, did she keep bringing women to her home when it was always the same thing? *Because I like to wake up in my own bed, that's why.*

"What do you do?" Denise asked.

"I paint."

"Seriously?" She finally focused on her.

"I'm an artist."

"Damn, maybe I should pick up a brush."

"Yeah, well, it's not that easy." If she only knew the hours she put into each piece, she'd think differently. Alora plopped down onto the couch, deciding to give up on the immediate seduction of Denise. The woman was going to have to get over the allure of her home first. With its high-end finishings, ten-foot ceilings, and accordion-style doors leading out to her elaborate patio with a panoramic view of that sunset, she could see how her home was a bit awe-inspiring to some. Nevertheless, she wished, for once, that her overnight guests weren't so overly impressed. It only detracted from the sport of lovemaking. Her sport of choice.

"Is that a spa?" Denise asked, standing at the threshold to the open travertine patio. Filipa always loved to open the patio doors when she was there. Especially since it was March and the weather was more than accommodating with mild, sunny temperatures and a lovely evening blooming desert breeze.

"Would you like to go for a soak? It's already heated." Alora had turned that feature on before she'd left, hoping for a dip with her date.

"I don't have a suit."

Alora laughed. "Who needs one?" She stood and slipped out of her silk shirt, tossing it aside. She stood unabashedly in front of Denise in her bra and slacks. "Well, what do you say?"

A smile came across Denise's lips. "I say, you're on."

"Excellent." Alora unfastened her pants, kicked off her leather loafers and slid out of her pants. She led the way to the bubbling hot tub.

"Won't people see?" Denise asked as she slowly peeled out of her tight-fitting dress.

"Do you care?"

The patio was virtually exposed with see-through barriers, but she'd never had any trouble with onlookers before. Most of the golfers on the surrounding golf course were too focused on their handicap to squint at her and her guests in the spa.

Denise allowed the dress to drop around her feet, exposing her delectable curves covered in black lacy lingerie.

"Very nice," Alora said as she eased into the hot water. "Come here." She held out her hand and helped her step into the tub.

"Oh, this feels good." She settled in next to Alora and closed her eyes.

"You like?"

"Mm, do I ever."

"Then you'll really like this." Alora leaned back and opened the cooler to pull out a chilled bottle of champagne along with two glass flutes.

"Champagne? You're kidding." She eagerly took a glass and held it for Alora to fill. "You're spoiling me," she said before taking a sip. "And I could get used to this."

Alora laughed softly and sipped from her own glass. She didn't mention the fact that it was highly unlikely that Denise would ever set foot in her place again. Alora liked keeping one-night stands to just that. One night. The few times she'd tried it any other way had ended in disaster. Women just wanted more than she did and she couldn't offer them anything more than just one brilliant evening. But what was so wrong with that?

"Just relax and enjoy," Alora said, setting her glass aside to move closer to her guest. She took Denise's flute and lightly kissed her lips. "Mm, you taste better than I imagined."

"Do I?" She reached up and grazed her fingers through Alora's scalp. "I love your haircut. The way you have it shaved close on this side. It makes you look so stylish, so modern and hip."

"Thank you." Alora grinned. "I don't think I've ever been called hip before."

"No?" Denise cocked her head. "You are though. I mean for your age."

"For my age?" She slowly backed away.

"You know, what are you, like fifty?"

Alora had had many overnight guests at her place over the years and yet none of them, not one, had brought up her age. Most were too caught up in her wealthy lifestyle and the pampering to even ponder the fact that she was older than them.

"No," Alora spat, suddenly very turned off. "I'm not fifty." She was pushing fifty-four to be exact, but she wasn't about to share that.

Denise shrugged like the whole conversation was no big deal and gulped down the rest of her champagne. "Whatever. I mean you look great. However old you are."

Alora stared beyond her at the disappearing sun. The sherbert colors of the sunset were giving way to deeper hues like magenta and purple. It was breathtaking, but the beauty was lost on her as a dark spot entered her vision, ruining the mood worse than Denise already had. She tried to blink it away, but unlike the blurriness, it wasn't vanishing.

"Something wrong?" Denise asked. Alora rubbed her eye, trying desperately to erase the darkness.

"Just my eye. It's nothing." She blinked some more, but the spot remained, right in the center of her vision. Then floaters drifted into view and she panicked. "I need to get out." She found her way to the steps. She slipped as she tried to emerge.

"Whoa," Denise said, grabbing her sides. "Careful."

"I'm fine." She managed to climb out to lean against the spa in her bra and panties, dripping wet in the cool evening breeze. But she ignored the chill and spread her eyelids apart with her fingers, hoping that would help, but it didn't.

"Did you get something in your eye?" Denise was peeking over at her with her arms resting on the rim of the tub. "I hate it when that happens."

"No. Yes. Just—it's nothing." But it wasn't nothing. It was definitely something, and now she could no longer ignore her vision problems like she had been doing the past couple of weeks. "I think you'd better go."

"Aw, really? We were just getting started."

"I'm not—feeling well." She started to head back into the house but stubbed her toe on a lounge chair. She yelped and cursed and hopped on one leg only to slip and fall. "Damn it!" She lay flat on her back, looking up into the darkening sky, her tailbone on fire. Denise came into view above her.

"You okay?" She held out her hand and pulled her up.

"Thanks." Alora gripped her lower back and eased down onto the lounge. She winced from the growing pain in her backside and clenched her eyes closed, still trying to rid herself of the black hole in her vision.

"You sure you're okay? I mean I don't want to leave you here alone if you're not."

"I'm fine," Alora said, a little harsher sounding than she'd intended. She opened her eyes. "Look, I'm sorry. I just don't feel well."

"Do you need anything? Should I call someone?"

"No. Yes." She pointed. "My phone is in my slacks. Can you get it?"

Denise went inside the house where she dug the phone out of the back pocket of her pants. She brought it to her and Alora held it up to her face to unlock it. She pressed a button and dialed Tabby, her best friend. She held the phone to her ear as she watched Denise slink back into her dress, after first slipping out of her wet lingerie. *That's a beautiful body I won't be feeling beneath me tonight. Not that I can even see it properly. Christ, what is wrong with my fucking eyes?*

Tabby answered on the third ring. "Heya, hot stuff, what's up? I thought you had a date tonight?"

"I do. I did. Look, can you come over?"

"Right now?"

"Yeah."

"Has something happened?"

"You could say that."

"You okay?"

"Mm, not really."

"You hurt?"

"I'm not dying, but yeah, something's definitely wrong."

"Okay. Give me a half hour to get the kids settled with David and I'll be right over."

"Thanks."

Alora ended the call and Denise stood awkwardly before her, holding her wadded up underwear in her hand.

"Can we do this again sometime?"

Alora dropped her head into her hands. "Sure. I'll call you."

Denise was silent. Then Alora heard her walking away. She looked up to see her enter the house to pick up her heels and head to the front door. A moment later, she heard the distant chime alerting her that the door had opened and closed, despite the soft jazz still playing over the speakers.

Alora sighed, stood carefully, and made her way inside. After switching off the music, she fumbled down the hallway to her bedroom where she stripped out of her bra and panties to slide into her soft pajamas. Then she made her way into the master bath to look into the mirror. She leaned forward and peeled her eye open, searching desperately for the cause of her distorted vision, but she saw nothing abnormal. "What the fuck is going on?"

She took a step back and ran her hand through her hair, pushing it over to one side, like she preferred to wear it. Denise's words about her age replayed in her mind.

"I am not old," she said to her reflection. "Am I?"

She blinked again and when the dark spot still lingered, she turned and walked away.

Chapter Two

There was an abnormal hush to the house that Bodie Banks found unsettling. So when her young nieces and nephews came tearing through all shrieks and giggles from the backyard, she couldn't help but breathe a sigh of relief.

"There's nothing quite like children to lighten a mood."

Bodie glanced over at the older woman sitting across the kitchen table. She had a pleasant face, a sweet smile, and a huge cross hanging from her neck. Bodie had seen her before but she couldn't place her.

"Grace McGwire," the woman said. "I live two streets over. Worked with your mom at the plant for some years."

"Right," Bodie said. "Mom spoke very fondly of you."

"Did she now?" She chuckled. "We had fun, we did. At the plant. Teasing that supervisor of ours. Old man Lucious. He was a holy terror, he was."

"I remember Lucious. He was the one who never let Mom have any time off when one of us was sick." She remembered because she'd had to pick up the slack and miss school to stay home to tend to whichever younger sibling was ill. Not that she was complaining. She would've gladly stayed home from school for any reason at all. Even if that meant having to play mom to her brother and sisters.

"That was him alright." She shook her head and played with her cross. "Bastard finally passed away a couple of years back. Can't say he's going to be missed none."

Bodie stared at the marred Formica tabletop. She hadn't expected such language to come from Mrs. McGwire and she wasn't sure what to say or think. Though she had to agree with her assessment on old man Lucious. He'd made her mother's life hell while she'd worked at the plant, forcing overtime and holding her and the others to ridiculous quotas. And of course, being overly stingy with the needed time off. Which was why her mother had eventually lost that job. She'd left without permission when Jimmy had fallen off the tree in the backyard and broken his arm. Bodie had been too young to handle the emergency so her mother had had to rush home to get him to the hospital quickly, prompting Lucious to fire her.

They'd gone three days with very little food because of that. Living off what little the local church had provided until that had run out.

"He wasn't a very good man," Bodie said, choosing her words carefully. She didn't like to speak ill of people, even if they deserved it. It just wasn't her way.

"No, he wasn't. Your mother though, she was good people."

Bodie smiled. "I appreciate you saying that." The kids rumbled into the kitchen again, chasing each other, one of them shooting a bubble gun, leaving a cascade of floating soap bubbles in their wake as they banged out the back door.

"She'll be missed," Mrs. McGwire said, sipping from her paper coffee cup.

"Can I get you a refill?" Bodie asked as she stood. It was time to get back to serving people and making sure everyone felt welcome and at home. She'd only sat down for a moment, at the behest of her sister, Kristy, who'd said she was running herself ragged and hadn't stopped since their mother had passed four days before. But Bodie had never done this, so she wasn't sure how to behave or how to grieve. Was there a guidebook on losing a family member? If so, she'd gladly read it. She needed all the help she could get.

Mrs. McGwire drained her cup and handed it over. "If you wouldn't mind, dear."

"Of course not." Bodie took the cup and poured her a refill at the kitchen counter. She returned it to her and excused herself to walk into the small but cozy living room where she found the couch and love seat overcrowded with people, most of whom, she did not know.

"Can I get anyone anything?"

They all looked at her but said nothing and Kristy once again appeared at her side. "Why don't you go lie down, Bodes?"

"Because I don't need to lie down."

"I beg to differ," she whispered, putting on a plastic smile for the others to see as she verbally chastised her. "You look like death warmed over."

"Nice choice of words, Kris, considering we just came from Mom's funeral."

"You know what I mean. You haven't taken a moment for yourself since Mom got sick over a year ago. And now she's gone and you're still going nonstop."

"There are things to do. Things that need tending to."

"Like what? The funeral is over and done with. The guests, well, they can serve themselves. God knows they've brought enough food to feed an army, and us, well, Bodes, we'll be okay. We aren't five years old anymore. We can take care of ourselves now. You don't have to worry."

"Jimmy's not okay. He's not handling this well at all."

"He's the baby. Give him time."

"He needs me."

"He has a girlfriend, Bodes. Let her care for him right now. If he needs you, he'll tell you."

Bodie sighed and sank her hands into her pockets. Everyone had someone but her. Maybe that was her problem and the reason why she couldn't let go and ease up on the control. She rubbed her temple, feeling a bitch of a headache coming on. She hadn't had any caffeine. That explained it. "I'm going to go get some coffee."

"Let me," Kristy said and she left for the kitchen.

Bodie offered a polite smile to the folks on the couches as she headed out the front door. She sat on a worn patio chair next to a dying agave and leaned back to extend her legs. The day was bright and sunny when it should be anything but. She squinted into the sunlight and inhaled the stale scent of cigarette smoke from the few smokers who were lingering just off the porch. She recognized some of them from the neighborhood, kids she used to play with growing up. It amazed her how time flew and how everyone she knew was now well into adulthood with real life problems of their own.

Like losing one's mother for instance.

"Hey."

Bodie's sister Monica settled into the chair next to her.

"Hey."

"Kristy asked me to bring you this." She handed over a mug of coffee. It was a Wonder Woman mug, one she'd bought for her mother years ago, because that had been her favorite superhero. And well, to Bodie, her mother had been like a Wonder Woman, taking care of them all as a single mother working two jobs. Bodie still didn't know how she did it.

"Thanks." She took the coffee and sipped. It was a dark roast and tepid at best. But somehow it tasted like heaven itself. Her stomach growled in greeting as the liquid invaded and Bodie couldn't remember the last time she ate. She knew it hadn't been that morning. Could it have been sometime yesterday?

She couldn't recall.

"I think I need to eat."

Monica stared at her. "Ya think?"

"Don't give me a hard time. I just forgot. I've been busy."

"Yeah. No shit, Bodie." She pulled out her phone and began texting. "I'm telling Kristy to bring you out a plate. And—don't even think about arguing with me."

"I wasn't."

"Good."

"Jesus, what crawled up your ass?"

Monica guffawed. "Come on, Bodie. You know we're worried about you and you know why. Don't play dumb."

"I wouldn't dream of it."

"You're pale as a ghost and you look like you're going to blow away in the wind. Not to mention your exhaustion and the black circles under your eyes."

"Gosh, thanks. And here I thought I was runway ready."

"Don't be a smart-ass. We're really worried here, Bodes. Truly."

"I'll be okay."

"You say that, but so far you haven't taken any steps to ensure that."

"I've been caring for Mom," Bodie said softly.

"Yes. But now she's gone. It's time to take care of you."

"What do you want me to do?"

"Go get some sleep for starters."

"I will. After everyone leaves."

Monica shook her head.

"I will. I promise," Bodie said.

"What about after that? What are you going to do next, now that she's gone? Have you thought about that?"

Bodie squinted up at the sky. "I haven't given it much thought to be honest. I still have my shift at the bakery, if I want it."

"Do you want it?"

"Not really. I only worked there because I needed the money. And Mom's care, well you know, it wasn't cheap."

"Which was why we all helped as much as we could."

"Yeah." They had. They'd given their time as well as their money. And they'd barely scraped by in caring for their mother, even with all that.

"Why don't you do something else?" Monica asked. "Something other than the bakery?"

The bakery had been perfect because it had allowed her to work nights while her mother slept and one of her siblings came to stay overnight with her. Bodie had watch during the day. It had saved them a lot of money in caregiver fees. But working at the bakery was getting old and there was no room for advancement. She was ready to move on.

"I want to, but I'm not sure what I'd do."

Monica shrugged. "Look around. I'm sure you'll find something. Maybe you can find some sort of job that's artistic. Since, you know, you like to dabble."

"Maybe." Though she doubted it. She taught sculpting to beginners at the rec center from time to time, but that wasn't lucrative. She did it simply because she loved it. And truth be told, she'd like to do way more than "dabble." The word offended her. Her art was important to her. Unfortunately, her family never seemed to grasp that.

Monica patted her knee. "You'll figure it out. You always do."

"Thanks, Mon."

The kids darted around the side of the house and spewed gravel as they slid to a stop in front of them.

"Mommy, Darren's not sharing the bubble gun," Bodie's niece Harper whined.

"Yeah, and he's had it for centuries," her nephew Wyatt added, tiny hands on his hips.

Bodie couldn't help but grin. "Centuries?"

"Yeah. Centuries," he said, exasperated.

Monica massaged her temples. "Go tell him I said he has to share."

"He says he doesn't have to because his daddy gave him the gun."

"Uncle Jimmy wants him to share. Tell him that."

"'Kay." They took off running again, their shoes leaving small mounds in the gravel.

"Jimmy's going to have to do something about Darren," Monica said. "He's too selfish."

Bodie linked her hands together in her lap. She didn't say anything. She left the parenting up to her siblings, unless she was alone and solely responsible for the kids.

"I think his mother spoils him when he spends time with her. And unfortunately, Jimmy's having to deal with it. Along with the rest of us."

"Jimmy's a good father. He'll handle it," Bodie said.

"Yeah, you're right." She patted her leg again and stood as Kristy emerged with a plate of finger food for Bodie. She handed it over.

"Here. And you better eat it all."

"Yes, ma'am."

Kristy followed Monica back inside, leaving Bodie alone to enjoy her food. Bodie picked at the small sandwiches and listened as the kids shouted from around the side of the house. The sounds of play soothed her, just as they always did, and she relaxed further into her chair as the sun massaged her face and arms. And very soon thereafter the plate of food was all but forgotten as she slowly drifted off to sleep.

CHAPTER THREE

It's going to be okay," Tabby said, popping a small piece of red Trident chewing gum into her mouth. "Whatever he says, it's going to be okay." She crossed her tanned legs and bobbed her foot, the bottom of her sandal slapping against her heel. She held out a piece of gum for Alora, but Alora shook her head. Tabby returned the gum to her purse and set the leather Sak bag beside her on the floor.

Alora sat waiting anxiously, clenching her hands in her lap. The doctor had yet to come in and it was going on twenty minutes now since they'd been shown into the room. She rubbed at her eye, still disturbed by the dark spot, but she quickly lowered her hand, recalling that the first eye doctor she'd seen, had told her to refrain from messing with her eye. Now she was at the Mayo Clinic in Scottsdale, seeing a retina specialist who'd run more tests and she was on pins and needles waiting for the results.

"Haven't we waited long enough?" Alora asked, standing to pace.

There was a knock at the door, however, and she eased back down onto her chair as the doctor entered with a resolute smile. "Ms. Anders." He gently took her hand in his warm one and did the same with Tabby. Then he settled on a stool and crossed his legs, just like Tabby. He stroked his salt-and-pepper goatee as he silently appraised her and Alora didn't understand how either the doctor or Tabby could be so calm.

"Well?" Alora asked, looking from him to Tabby and back again. "Am I going blind or what?" She snorted, joking. But the doctor's smile gave way to solemness and she felt her heart drop to her stomach.

"Doc?"

"Ms. Anders, I'm afraid you have something called wet macular degeneration."

"Wet what?" She tried but struggled to focus on him. "Look, don't bullshit me, here. Just—tell me. Am I going blind?" Surely not. Surely this was something that could be fixed. This day and age? Of course it could be fixed.

"You're going to continue to progressively lose your vision, yes."

"Whoa." She leaned back, feeling sick. "What the fuck?"

Tabby spoke. "I don't understand. She's only fifty-four. How can she be losing her sight?"

"This condition rarely occurs in people Ms. Anders's age, but it can happen." He looked at Alora. "Do you have anyone in your family history with vision loss?"

Alora could hardly hear him over the thrumming of her heart. She forced down some saliva. "I don't know my family history. I was adopted."

He nodded.

"Well, what the hell are we going to do about it?" Alora asked. "There is *something* we can do to treat this, right? I'm an artist, for Christ's sake. I can't go blind."

"There are treatments, yes. And we'll try them all. But your condition is already rapidly progressing."

"Because I ignored it? I should've come in sooner. Fuckin' A."

"Starting treatment earlier would have helped some. But, Ms. Anders, your condition would've continued to progress eventually. Now what I would like to do is start you on some monthly injections of anti-VEGF in addition to photodynamic therapy…"

Alora stared beyond him at the wall and blocked out what he was saying. Her mind couldn't take any more. Her system was in shock. Her whole life upended. She was losing her vision. She was going blind. Nothing and no one could help her now. What was she going to do? A lava-like panic began to ooze through her body and the rest of the visit went by without her comprehending any of it. She was given information, quite a bit of it in brochures and pamphlets, but she simply tucked them in the binder the clinic had given her and allowed Tabby to lead her out through the lobby, past the black baby grand piano, across the shiny floor, and into the impossibly bright desert sunshine.

Tabby guided her to a bench at the arc of the circular drive. "We could take a walk along the nature trail," Tabby said, motioning off toward the trail in the near distance. "It's a beautiful day."

Alora didn't even bother to look up at her. "I'm not in the mood for a walk."

"It might cheer you up."

"Nothing's going to cheer me up. I'm going blind, Tabby. Do you get that?"

"I'm having a hard time accepting it at the moment. As I'm sure you are." She placed a hand on her shoulder. "Which is why a short walk might do us good. There's nothing like the desert in the spring."

"Just go get the car, Tabby. Please."

Tabby left her and headed across the drive to go get the car. A few minutes later, she pulled up in Alora's white BMW 4 series M440i convertible with the top down. She quickly climbed out and steered Alora into the passenger seat and closed the door.

Alora settled in, slid on her sunglasses, and fastened her seat belt. Her throat felt raw with emotion, but she refused to cry. She'd rarely cried before over hard times and she wasn't about to start now. She'd just have to suck it up. "Will you close the top? I don't feel like dealing with the wind."

Tabby pushed the button to raise the top and drove along the drive out to the main road. She signaled to turn toward home and spoke. "It'll be fine. You'll do the treatments and wear the glasses and they'll help. You'll see."

"Glasses? And I assume you didn't intend the pun."

"It wasn't intentional, no. And yes, he wants you to wear glasses. Said they might help. Didn't you hear him?"

"What I heard is that I'm going blind. It's inevitable."

"But the treatments should help. They'll slow it down at least."

"That's not good enough. And what if they don't help? What then?"

"We'll find someone else. Go somewhere else."

"That was the Mayo Clinic, Tabby. That *is* the best."

"I'm just saying—"

"Don't. Just don't, okay? My life is fucked and I don't want to hear how it's all going to be okay, or how we'll go to someplace different like Mexico to get experimental treatments. It's all bullshit."

"I'm just trying to stay positive. Make you feel better."

Alora pushed out a breath. "I know and I'm sorry. I just—I can't deal with this. And unfortunately, there isn't anything you can do to make me feel better."

"Not even a fresh horchata from Filiberto's?"

"No."

"You really are down if you're refusing that."

Alora settled further into her seat and crossed her arms. She felt cold even though the day was warm and the car cozy. Her head swam with dizziness and the dark spot clouded her vision of the surrounding desert and tall saguaro cacti standing guard. So she did the only thing she could do. She closed her eyes and tried to pretend that her life was just as it was a few weeks before.

❖

"Alora? Alora, we're home."

Alora blinked herself awake and glanced over at Tabby in the driver's seat. She was looking at her expectantly as they sat in the shade of the garage. "Wake up, sleepyhead."

Alora groaned and unfastened her restraint to open the door. She'd only just closed her eyes a second ago and now they were home. Had she slept that long? Tabby rounded the car to help her out, but Alora refused.

"I can get out. And I know my way into the house."

"Okay. Suit yourself."

Alora crawled from the car and shuffled slowly to the interior door of the house. She paused for a moment at the threshold to get her bearings, and then entered. The alarm system sounded and she cursed, having completely forgotten about it. She hurried as best she could to the nearby panel and tried to type in her code, but she couldn't see well enough to do it.

"Fuck!"

Seconds ticked by. She yelled for Tabby. Where was she? She tried two more times and failed and the beeping morphed into a loud, ear-busting siren. She cuffed her ears and turned to find Tabby rushing at her, her ears covered as well.

"I couldn't see to type in my code," Alora shouted over the noise.

Tabby cupped her elbow and tried to lead her back out through the garage, but Alora pulled away, and rushed for the landline, which she knew would be ringing soon with the alarm company. She was halfway to the kitchen when she hit something, an end table, a piece of furniture, she wasn't sure what, but she went down. Hard.

"Oh, my, God!" Tabby was at her side in an instant, helping her to turn over. "You're bleeding."

"What?" The siren was deafening, filling her head with a painful fog.

"You're bleeding!"

Alora sat up and felt hot liquid pouring down over her eye. Her vision worsened as the blood glazed over it. She wiped at the mess and stared at the dark red on her hand.

"You've got a cut on your brow!"

Alora swiped away more ooze and grew weak. She wasn't used to seeing blood, especially this much. What was happening? Why was everything spinning out of control? And why did Tabby look so terrified?

She watched as Tabby scrambled into the kitchen to return with a tea towel. She pressed it against the wound and then fumbled with her phone to call 911.

"I'm fine," Alora said, holding the towel to her brow. But she felt far from fine. She was dizzy and nauseous and the fucking alarm was maddening. She drew the tea towel away and examined it. Blood had nearly soaked it through. The weakness increased and seemed to melt her bones. The last thing she remembered was Tabby's face just before the darkness overtook her.

❖

"Hey."

Alora opened her eyes against a bright overhead light. "Tabby?" She turned and focused on Tabby's face. "What's—going on?"

Tabby tried to smile but Alora could tell, even with her poorer vision, that it was forced. "You're in the emergency room. You fell and cut your brow. Then you passed out."

Alora thought back and recalled the fall and then seeing all the blood. She also briefly recalled snippets of being strapped to a gurney inside an ambulance. "Did I bleed too much? Is that why I…"

"No. They think you just got overwhelmed in seeing the blood."

"It was so much." An image of the blood-soaked towel came to mind and she felt woozy all over again.

"They said head wounds bleed a lot. Yours definitely did."

"But…I'm okay?"

"You just need a few stitches."

Alora raised her hand to her head, but Tabby stopped her.

"You shouldn't touch it. It might start bleeding again."

"Why did I have to wake up before they stitched me?"

Tabby smiled, this time a full, genuine smile. "You would've woken up when they started. I'm pretty sure."

Alora furrowed her brow and winced from the pain it caused. "I missed all the hoopla with the paramedics?"

"And the police and the firefighters."

"Police? Firefighters?"

"The alarm went off, remember? So the police responded. And the firefighters responded to my call before the paramedics arrived.

There was a cute firefighter too. You would've drooled over her for sure."

"Damn. Not that I would've been able to see her all that well. But yeah, I'd have liked to have tried."

"She looked pretty good. Even to me. And you know, I like—"

"Dick. Yeah, I'm well aware."

Tabby fanned herself. "Whoo, the whole lot of those firefighters got me going. Her included."

Alora couldn't help but smile.

"Hey, that's what I like to see," Tabby said, touching her face.

Alora kissed her hand. "Thank you, Tabby. For everything. I know I'm being a bear, but I'm…"

"Scared?"

"Shitless."

"I know, hot stuff. But we're going to get through this. We really are."

"We?"

"Well, yeah. I'm right here with you, girl. Always."

"Thanks."

"But that doesn't mean it's going to be easy. You're going to have to do some things you're not fond of. Like, talk with me about getting you some help for starters."

"Help?"

"Alora, you need someone with you full-time right now and I can't do it."

"Why not? I'll pay you. Handsomely."

"I know you would. But I can't do it. I have the kids and David and all their activities. I'm just too busy with those responsibilities to be able to help you full time."

Alora swallowed as she began to panic. She and Tabby had been best friends since they were fourteen and she trusted no one else like she did her. Except for maybe Fatima, but Fatima had her own family to care for. Including grandkids that lived with her now, so she wasn't an option either.

"Can't you all just move in with me?" She knew the notion was crazy, but she was desperate. She didn't want help in the first place, and she certainly didn't want it from a stranger.

Tabby teared up, obviously sensing her desperation. She touched her cheek again. "You know that would never work. The kids, they'd drive you nuts."

"I love the kids."

"Yes, but loving them and having them around you all the time, are two different things, Alora. Trust me on that. Why do you think I'm always ready to pull my hair out?" She kissed her forehead. "We'll find you someone great. Don't you worry."

"Funny. You know I'll do nothing but. First I'm going blind and now I'll have to have a complete stranger helping me about in my own home."

"It won't be so bad."

"Don't even say, 'you'll see' or I'll smack ya."

Tabby laughed and the physician came in to suture her up.

Things couldn't possibly get much worse. Could they?

CHAPTER FOUR

"Does anyone else need more aluminum foil? If so, there's some on my desk," Bodie said as she strolled along the aisles to observe her students' work. "Remember, you're beginning sculptors here, so take your time and play around with the flexibility of the armature. Keep in mind what you've learned about anatomy, contours, and balance. And most importantly, relax and have fun."

She glanced up at the clock as she neared the front of the classroom. It was nearing five o'clock. Time to close up shop. "Okay, everyone, that's about all we have time for today." She rounded her desk and folded her arms as her students began to clean up. "And don't forget your homework assignment."

"Drawing!" a young woman, whose name was Peyton, called out with a smile.

"Yes. Draw as much as you can. It will help you with your sculpting and vice versa."

"Did you see what I drew this week?" Peyton asked. She brought her sketch pad up to Bodie and proudly showed off several still life sketches.

"These are really good, Peyton. You're really coming along."

"You think so?"

"I do."

She beamed. "Thanks, Bodie."

"Have you ever thought about studying art in school?"

She shrugged. "Not until recently. I'm not sure I can afford it."

"With your talent, you might want to look into it. Talk to an admissions advisor at some of the local art schools and see what they can offer you as far as scholarships."

"You really think I stand a chance?"

"I wouldn't mention it otherwise."

"Wow. Imagine getting to do art for a living. I'll look into that, thanks. But I'm still going to come to your class here at the rec center. It's fun and I learn so much."

"We love having you."

After another lingering smile, Peyton returned to her table and finished putting away her supplies.

"Your students sure do love you," a voice said. Fellow instructor Simone Richards was standing just inside the doorway, wearing her trademark chenille shawl, this one a maroon in color. She clutched the ends together and came closer, nudging Bodie with her shoulder. "That one especially. I think she's got a little crush."

She was referring to Peyton and the suggestion unnerved Bodie. "Noo."

"Yees. She definitely does."

"She's just young. And she's very talented. I think I just talked her into trying art school."

"Good for you." She nudged her again. "And what about you? You given any thought to finishing up your bachelor's so you can teach full time, like me?"

"I just don't have the time or money right now."

"You only have one semester left, yes? Could it be that you just don't have the will?"

"I don't know, Simone, going back to school sounds so… tedious. When what I really need to do is find a new job to make some money."

"You know what?" She wagged a finger. "I might have something for you, Bodie. You're obviously a great caregiver with the way you took care of your mother and all, and I have a friend who needs some help. Live-in help."

Bodie sighed, unsure. "My time with Mom was pretty heart-wrenching there at the end. I'm not sure I could go through that a second time."

"She's not sick. She's just, well, losing her vision."

"She's going blind?"

She nodded. "She's a former student of mine and she's done quite well for herself in the art world. Maybe you've heard of her. Alora Anders? She's a painter."

Bodie felt her eyes widen. "Alora Anders? Of course I've heard of her. You've even got a couple of her pieces in your home."

"Her early works, yes. She gave them to me. They'd cost a fortune now."

"She's going blind?"

"It's very sad and rather traumatic for her, I'm afraid. She's not doing well. Having trouble adjusting. But you might be the perfect fit for her. With your patience and the fact that you're also an artist…"

"She lives in Phoenix?"

"Scottsdale. She's got quite the pad. Plenty of room for a live-in guest."

Bodie's mind reeled as she considered all that Simone was saying. She had been looking for a new adventure. And it would do her some good to get out of her childhood home for a while. The memories of troubling times when she was younger still lingered, along with the recent memories of her mother and how she struggled with her illness. "How soon does she need someone?"

"As soon as possible I believe. You got a pen?"

Bodie plucked one off the desk and handed it to her. Simone scribbled a name and phone number on a piece of paper. "Tabby is who you should call. She'll give you all the details. But you should call soon if you're interested. She's already interviewing. Now I'm off to wish my students another good weekend of painting at home." Simone leaned in and whispered, "I wish half of them had the talent that Alora Anders does. But I suppose someone like her only comes along once in a teacher's lifetime." She winked and breezed away to walk through the open entryway, leaving Bodie to stare at the name and number in her hand.

She gave the piece of paper a quick flick with the backs of her fingers and folded it to place neatly into her pocket.

"Did she just give you her number?" Peyton asked as she gathered her things to stop in front of Bodie's desk. "That's kind of unprofessional don't you think?"

Heat rushed to Bodie's cheeks. She didn't like the prying question, or the suggestion that Simone was being anything other than professional. "Not that it's any of your business, Peyton, but no, she did not. And Simone is the utmost professional."

The answer obviously stunned Peyton because she seemed to stutter over her words.

"I just—I mean—I thought she did."

Bodie let her struggle, refusing to comfort her or to assure her that her prying and assumption was okay. She didn't appreciate nosiness and she certainly didn't like people making assumptions. What was the old saying? When one assumes they make an ass out of you and me? Something like that.

"Have a nice weekend, Peyton. Practice those drawing skills."

"I will. And I didn't mean to offend."

"Understood."

She headed out the door without saying anything further and Bodie bid her remaining students farewell and locked up after checking to make sure everything was cleaned up and in its place. She moseyed down the hall, carrying her large tote, and took the elevator down to the ground floor. Normally, her mind would be roaming free, thinking about nothing in particular now that her mother had passed, but at the moment she couldn't get that job out of her head. So when she slid into her black 1998 Honda Accord, she closed the door and dug her phone out of her book bag. She pulled the paper with the number from her pocket and dialed.

It rang five times before a woman answered, breathless and seemingly flustered.

"He—llo?" The sounds of children echoed in the background.

"Is this Tabby? Simone Richards gave me your number. I'm calling about the live-in job? For Alora Anders?"

There was a pause and the quick snapping of fingers as she shushed her children. "Simone? She gave you my number?"

"She said I might be a good fit. My name is Bodie Banks and I'm a friend of Simone's."

"Yes, of course. Simone is great. Gosh, if she thinks you'll be a good fit—when can you come by for an interview?"

"Tomorrow?"

"Can you come, say around eleven?"

"Sure."

Tabby relayed the address and Bodie entered it into her notes on her phone. They once again confirmed the time and ended the call with the kids shrieking in the background. Bodie chuckled as she fastened her seat belt and returned her phone to her bag. Tabby seemed to have her hands full. She knew the feeling. When her brother and sisters were over, along with all their kids, things could get crazy and loud. Even at her mother's funeral. She recalled having to break up several petty arguments over the soap bubble gun, despite the solemn mood of the house and their guests. Kids just lived in their own world often times, oblivious to everything else. She supposed that that's the way it should be though. She had paid too much mind to things in the adult world, and she'd paid the price. Her young mind had worried about things no child should have to worry over, much less think about. But she was the eldest and her mother had needed help and had no one else to depend on. So Bodie had had to step up and become a second mother at a very young age. She was still fulfilling that role, even if her siblings claimed they no longer needed her to. She just couldn't seem to let it go. After a lifetime of caring for them, it seemed that the path had been permanently engraved in her brain and there was no way around it. She was just a natural caregiver.

"Is that why I want this job? Because it comes so easily to me?" Could be. But there was also the fact that it was Alora Anders, a very well-known artist. "Maybe she'll inspire me." She had to admit her own work as of late in her tiny studio in her mother's garage was anything but great. She'd fallen into a bit of a lull, and she suspected it was because she'd had so much on her plate with her mother's illness. She hadn't been sculpting as much as she normally did and when she did happen to go into her studio, she just felt null and void of creativity, even though her mother had been gone a couple of weeks now. It didn't make sense. She should be feeling more relaxed now, the ideas flowing easier. But it just wasn't happening. So if working for Alora Anders and maybe discussing art and the process could help, then yes, she was very much looking forward to the job. Besides, she'd always been rather curious about her. She'd admired her and her work from afar for years. She'd known she was from the Phoenix area, she just hadn't realized she still lived here.

Bodie drove the rest of the way home in silence, thinking about Alora Anders and her vision loss. She couldn't imagine how she must be feeling and Simone had said she wasn't handling the news well. Bodie wondered who *would* handle that kind of news well. And an artist to boot? No, it didn't surprise her to learn of Alora's struggling to accept her situation. After all, how would she paint?

She smiled as she thought about maybe showing her how to sculpt. Imagine, teaching something creative to someone like Alora Anders. What a treat. She continued to smile as she finished the drive home, more than excited to meet the famous Alora Anders and have a positive impact on her life. Tomorrow couldn't come soon enough.

CHAPTER FIVE

Alora stopped at the edge of the hallway and groaned. She felt like hell.

"Morning, sleepyhead," Tabby greeted her, rising from the couch to come to her. "You really crashed hard last night."

"Good tequila will do that to you," Alora said.

"Too much good tequila will do that to you. You shouldn't have had that many margaritas."

"Give me a break. I needed a drink." They ambled slowly together to the kitchen counter where Alora slid onto a barstool.

"You could've fooled me. You were wobbling all over the place at that restaurant."

"I can't freakin' see."

"And you were fall down drunk."

"Let's just drop it, okay?"

"Fine by me."

"Will you pour me a cup of that wonderful-smelling coffee?"

Tabby retrieved a mug from the cabinet and filled it with the steaming dark liquid. She placed it in front of Alora and poured in her cream and sugar. "Mm, extra sugar this morning, please," Alora said.

Tabby gave her an extra spoonful and set about gathering a pan and a spatula. "You want some eggs?"

"And bacon, please."

"We don't have time. The woman I told you about will be here soon and we still have to get you presentable."

"What woman?" She racked her brain but could come up with nothing.

"Bodie? I think that's what she said her name is. She knows Simone. She's coming to interview for the live-in job."

Alora shook her head. "No." She rubbed her aching temples. "I told you, I don't want some stranger living with me."

"And I told you that I can't keep doing this, Alora. You need someone. And you're going to have to open your mind a little bit as far as choosing. You've turned your nose up at everyone so far. Run them off with your poor manners and bad attitude."

"Because I don't want them here."

"Well, that's tough. You're just going to have to choose and get used to them being around. Unless you want to keep tripping over things and cracking open your head?"

Alora lightly fingered the staples along her brow. They were a harsh reminder of her new and worsening disability. She sighed and stretched her upper body along the countertop, resting her cheek on the cool speckled granite surface. "Ugh, I hate this. And I don't like you very much right now."

"The feeling's mutual, sunshine." Tabby cracked open two eggs, dumped them in a bowl, and stirred them, along with some milk, adding some salt and pepper to finish it off.

"Why would you be upset with me?" Alora asked, oblivious.

"You really have to ask?" She poured the egg mixture into a pan and Alora heard the sizzling. "You're being a stubborn, cranky ass."

"So?"

"So? So, knock it off. It's not going to make your situation any easier to be that way, Alora."

"Maybe not, but I just can't seem to perk up and wear a permanent smile like you want me to."

"Not permanent. But every once in a while would be nice."

"Can't." She pushed herself up. "I don't have the strength."

"Well, maybe after you eat this egg sandwich you will." She finished scrambling the eggs, toasted some bread, and placed the goods in front of Alora after cutting the sandwich in half.

"You're hilarious by the way," Alora said. "As if an egg sandwich can make everything all better."

"You never know. I am a pretty good cook."

Alora grinned, unable not to, and Tabby playfully slugged her on the shoulder. "Hurry and eat, we've got to get you ready. I shouldn't have let you sleep so late."

"I'm glad you did. I needed it." Her nights had been restless since her diagnosis, with her tossing and turning with worry. She'd been walking around zombie-like for days now and it was finally getting to her. So Tabby had taken her out for dinner the night before and she'd had one too many margaritas, convinced that people could tell she was nearly blind and were staring at her. But according to Tabby, they'd been staring because she'd gotten drunk and was stumbling around. Not because of her poor vision.

Alora took a big bite of the sandwich and chewed. It was rather good. But she didn't say anything. She didn't want it to go to Tabby's head. "What's wrong with the way I look right now?"

Tabby began cleaning up the dishes. "You look like you have a raging hangover, for starters."

"That's because I do."

"Right. But we don't want her to know that, do we?"

Alora shrugged and took another bite. "Why not? If she's going to live with me, she'll be seeing me at my worst."

"It's about first impressions. You don't want to give off the wrong vibe."

Alora laughed. "If she really wants the job she won't care what I look like."

"You're really not going to at least change clothes? Get out of those pajamas you've been sleeping in for days on end?"

"Nope."

Tabby tossed down a wet dish cloth but said nothing. Alora knew she was pissed. She could see it in her pinched face and sense it in her clipped movements. But she really didn't care. In fact, she cared very little about anything anymore. And that included getting all glammed up for some stranger. She finished half her sandwich and pushed the plate away. Tabby scooped it up, threw away the scraps, and washed the plate. Alora sipped her coffee and watched her.

"Thank you for breakfast."

Tabby didn't respond. She must be really frustrated with her. Alora tried again.

"It was very good." There, she'd told her. That should do it. But Tabby said nothing.

Then, "Jasmine called again this morning."

Alora raised her brow. "Oh?"

"She really wants to talk to you. She's…concerned."

"Yeah, right. Concerned about her pocketbook."

"She's your sister, Alora. Family. Don't you think it's time to give her a chance?"

"She's just like my mother. Always has been always will be. And why is she so concerned? She couldn't possibly know about my condition. Unless…"

Tabby lifted her shoulders.

"Tabby, you didn't." Alora slammed her hand down onto the counter. "Please, tell me you didn't."

"I thought maybe she could help. She's family."

"So, you keep saying. Yet they certainly didn't act like family, did they? My mother kicking me out of the house at fourteen for kissing a girl. And Jasmine? Where has she been all these years? Absent. That's where. Thank God I was adopted. I wouldn't want to be related to those two."

"She's trying, Alora. And I think it's unfair for you to assume she only wants money. She may be nothing at all like your mother."

The doorbell chimed, startling them both.

Tabby glanced at the clock. "She's early."

"Great."

"I think that's a good sign. Means she's mindful and responsible."

"Great."

"Hey, you need someone like that. You don't want someone who will flake out on you."

"Whatever."

Tabby waved her arm at her. "Fix your hair. It's all mussed on the right side."

Alora tried to half-heartedly tame her hair while Tabby hurried to the door. Alora heard the door open and then polite voices in greeting. She let out an exasperated breath and tried to prepare herself for yet another boring interview. She'd been through four already, and none of the applicants had been even remotely interesting. Three had been older than her and had the personality of a rock. She'd put a stop to those interviews by outright voicing her disapproval and the women had up and left, much to Tabby's chagrin, who'd then lambasted her for her behavior. But Alora hadn't wanted to waste her time on such people. She'd known they wouldn't have been a good fit, so she'd taken care of it, before things had gone further. She figured she'd saved everyone some trouble. Why couldn't Tabby see that?

Alora smoothed her hands down her flannel-clad thighs and fought for a practiced smile as Tabby led the new applicant into the house. But as soon as Alora could make out her form, she was in complete awe. Though she couldn't see her completely, thanks to the dark spot in her eye, she was able to see enough. The woman was stunning with short, thick black hair, a classically structured face, with full, tantalizing lips, and a curvaceous body. Alora had to clear her throat and inhale deeply again to try to control her rising heart rate.

"Alora Anders, this is Bodie. Bodie Banks," Tabby said, standing to the side as if presenting royalty.

Alora hastily stood from the barstool and extended her hand. "Hi." She caught Tabby's surprised look but ignored it.

Bodie shook her hand. "Ms. Anders, I'm—honored. I love your work."

"You know my work?"

"Oh, yes. I've been following you for some time now."

Alora smiled. "Thank you. That's always nice to hear." Beautiful and an admirer. Maybe this one wouldn't be so bad after all.

"Please, have a seat," Tabby said. She came to Alora's side and tried to steer her toward the sofa, but Alora shooed her away and made her way carefully to the couch on her own. She sat across from Bodie, crossed her legs, and then, as she ran a hand through her hair, she recalled her dreadful appearance. She quickly tried to tame her hair, but soon gave up, knowing it was useless. She flushed, hating that she looked her worst and hating more that she'd ignored Tabby's suggestion to make herself presentable.

Why don't I ever listen?

"So, Bodie, tell us a little about yourself," Tabby said.

Bodie shifted and rested her hands in her lap. The sunlight coming in through the open patio doors glinted off the numerous piercings in her ears and when she angled her head ever so slightly, the sun gleamed against a piercing in her aquiline nose. Her large, dark, almond-shaped eyes seemed to flash as she readied to speak. As if what she were about to share was of the utmost importance to her.

"First and foremost, I'm an artist."

Alora's spine straightened. "An artist?"

"Yes."

Alora tensed some more. She'd had run-ins with dozens of amateur artists, all of them wanting a piece of her, hoping she could help them make it big. It had soured her on intermingling with them, so much so that she tried to avoid them at all costs.

"That's interesting," Tabby said, smiling over at Alora. Tabby had obviously forgotten how Alora felt about these wannabe artists. "Isn't it, Alora?"

"Mm. It is indeed. Tell me, Bodie, what's your medium of choice?"

"Clay."

"So you sculpt?"

"For many years now."

"Are you any good?" Alora pinned her with a look. Obviously, she wasn't very successful in selling her work, otherwise she wouldn't need this job. Therefore, it was safe for Alora to assume that she wasn't successful in her craft either.

"I'm pretty good. Or so I've been told."

"Have you now?"

"Yes."

Tabby seemed to be catching on and she laughed nervously. "Tell us what brings you to apply for this job. Have you had any caregiving experience?"

"My mother was very ill for some time here recently. And before that, she was disabled. So I cared for her for a few years until she passed."

"Oh, I'm sorry to hear that," Tabby said.

"Thank you. She's definitely missed, but I'm glad she's no longer suffering."

"I'm not sick," Alora let out. "I just need help getting around."

"And with cooking, driving, and doing a lot of different things," Tabby clarified.

"I can help you with all that," Bodie said.

"Are you willing to live here, with Alora?" Tabby asked.

"Sure. That wouldn't be a problem."

Alora cleared her throat. *It will be if you're trying to use me to further your sculpting career.* "I don't have any connections in the sculpting world," she said, though she was fibbing. She did know a few people who sold sculptures and several sculptors themselves who did very well. But she didn't want Bodie to be aware of that.

Bodie blinked at her. "Pardon me?"

"I can't help you," Alora said. "With your career."

Bodie looked at her in confusion. "I didn't expect you to."

"Really? It never even crossed your mind?"

"No. I mean—I thought we might discuss our process and that I might get some inspiration but—"

"You want me to inspire you?"

Tabby stood. "Alora, can I speak with you in the other room please?"

She cupped Alora's elbow and led her rather forcibly into the hallway, out of Bodie's earshot. "What the hell are you doing?"

"She's here for one reason only. To use me to further her career."

"Are you out of your mind?"

"No. Funnily enough, I'm not. I still have brain cells. And this woman, this Bodie, is here for herself. Can't you see it?"

"I see a nice young woman who just cared for and lost her mother, who's willing to move in here and help you out. She just happens to be an artist, Alora. Probably because she's a friend of Simone's. You know how many artists she knows."

"She's an amateur artist." Alora tapped her temple. "Get it? She's going to want me to help her advance her career."

"So what if she does, Alora? Would that be the end of the world, if she wants to talk to you about her art? Or about your art? How is that so awful?"

"She's just here to use me."

Tabby sighed and ran a hand through her hair. "You're not even giving her a chance."

"I don't need to. I can see right through her."

"No pun intended?"

"Ha. Ha."

"This is it, Alora. I'm done. You can find, or don't find, someone on your own. I give up." She stalked back into the living room where she offered Bodie a drink. Alora joined them, treading carefully and stood near the couch. Tabby brought Bodie a bottle of water and Bodie opened it to sip slowly, as if she just needed enough to wet a dry mouth.

"So, if that's why you're here, for some sort of inspiration, I can assure you that I'm not interested," Alora said, trying to lead the way to the front door. Tabby, meanwhile, sank onto the accompanying sofa and rested her head in her hands. She didn't look up.

"Actually," Bodie said, standing herself. "That's not why I'm here. Yes, I thought that both of us being artists, would be something we could discuss, but I'm here to help you. I'm a damn good caregiver, ask anyone. And I don't appreciate the assumption or the accusation of otherwise."

Tabby finally raised her head. She was smiling.

Alora wasn't sure what to say.

"But if you don't want my help, then, yes, I'll show myself out. I wish you nothing but the best, Ms. Anders. And for what's it worth…I'm sorry for what you're going through." She nodded at Tabby. "It was nice to meet you."

"You as well, Bodie. Thank you for coming."

She turned and headed for the door. Alora wanted to call out to her, to at least apologize, but her lips felt glued together.

If she wants to go, let her. You don't need her. You don't need anyone.

She thought again of her sister Jasmine and the sting of betrayal crept up her spine. What could she possibly want? Why couldn't she just leave her alone? Leave her alone like this Bodie person was doing?

Alora watched in silence as Bodie walked out the front door and disappeared into the daylight. But surprisingly, the sight did not make her feel any better.

CHAPTER SIX

Bodie pulled into the parking lot at Rio Vista park and gathered her tote before exiting the car. She treaded slowly past the fenced baseball fields and crossed to the shaded picnic tables, looking for her sister. She found her on a bench facing the pond, and beyond that, the hiking and bike paths that ran along the waterless canal. When they were younger, before Kristy had kids, they used to meet there to ride bikes, cruising for miles in the mild winter sun, inhaling the fragrant desert blooms. Those had been good times, and she wondered if they'd ever get back to them.

"Hey, how did it go?" Kristy asked as she stood to greet Bodie with a quick embrace.

"A complete waste of time," Bodie breathed, graciously taking the offered cup of coffee Kristy had brought for her. She eased onto the bench and took a tentative sip. The liquid was still hot and she wished she could melt right along with it as it traveled down her throat.

Kristy held out her hand expectantly and Bodie handed over the tote. Kristy sat alongside her to dig out the bag of cracked corn. "You were really looking forward to working with her."

"Was, yes. But she's—rude. Arrogant. And she's got it in her head that I only want the job so I can further my art career."

"Seriously?" She scooped a handful of corn, dumped it carefully into Bodie's palm, and tossed some into the water for the lingering ducks. Bodie did the same, always amused at how the ducks called out, as if alerting their friends to food as they swam toward them.

"Like I said, a complete waste of time. And suffice it to say, I'm no longer a big fan of Alora Anders."

"Alora Anders? The painter? Jesus, I didn't realize you were interviewing with her. Wow."

"No, not wow."

"I hear she's an eccentric loner. Filthy rich and goes through women like underwear."

Bodie raised her brow. "She does?"

"According to the rumors."

"And where have you heard those?"

"Around." She reclined and sipped her Frappuccino. "You know how Gayle talks. Well, apparently, she knows someone who dated her. And she did not have good things to say. I guess she just uses women for one-night stands and then cuts them loose."

"*She* uses people? How interesting. She accused me of wanting to do the same. What a joke." Bodie shook her head and squinted into the sunlight. They were mostly in the shade, but the rays were still powerful, penetrating through her sunglasses. Around the pond, a few people mingled, walking the cemented path, some headed toward the rec center, others just out for a leisurely stroll.

Bodie allowed the warmth from the sun to massage an exposed patch on her left arm. It felt nice, as did the small breeze toying with her hair. It was a beautiful March day and she knew she should try to enjoy it, before the looming heat of April and May came storming in, but she just couldn't shake that interview. She'd really been looking forward to getting that job and to say she was disappointed was an understatement.

"So, what now?" Kristy asked, sprinkling more food, this time on the ground in front of them. The ducks eagerly waddled ashore, seemingly fearless, and fed at their feet.

"You mean today? I don't know. I guess it's another night shift at the bakery."

"It's not so bad, is it?"

"It's not. Not really. I just wanted something different."

"Well, caregiving isn't all that different from what you did with Mom. If you really want something different, why not try for a totally different job? Or even go back to school?"

"This was just so perfect for me, Kris. It really was." She played with the cardboard wrap of her cup, tearing it off, preferring to feel the full heat of the coffee against her skin. "But I guess I'm stuck for the time being."

"You'll figure out something."

"It's not going to be school. I'm just not motivated, nor do I want the debt."

"I understand." She pulled another sip off her Frap. "You know Steve said they're hiring at his company."

"What, drivers?"

"You got something against driving a truck?"

"No, it just sounds nerve-wracking. I can't see myself driving a rig like that. Even if it is local."

"The pay is good and you get to work nights and deal very little with people."

"God, do I really come off that way?"

Kristy laughed. "Well…"

"I'm an introvert, not antisocial."

"Okay, okay." Her laughter subsided. "It's there if you change your mind. Steve can put in a good word for you."

"I appreciate that."

"So, how are you doing otherwise? You're looking a little more rested."

"Sleep has been better, thankfully. But I still wake up and expect her to be there." She welcomed more corn from Kristy and leaned down to allow the ducks to feed from her palm. They hesitated, but one, a beautiful mallard, waddled up to her and attacked the kernels. She tried to hold in her laughter, but it tickled and the duck backed away, frightened. She dumped the rest of the food on the ground and reclined to watch them poke at the grass.

"It's going to take a while. You were with her for a long time, longer than any of us."

"I really miss her." Bodie stared off into the glassy reflection of the sky in the pond, thinking of her mother and the last real conversation they'd had. It had been two weeks before she'd passed and she'd been concerned about Bodie's future. She'd wanted to know her plans, wanted to know where she was going to go, if anywhere. She'd said she wished that she'd had enough life insurance for her to use to travel, or to get her own place. She'd voiced regrets for the past, for the way Bodie had had to grow up too soon. And then she'd cried.

Bodie lifted her shades to wipe a tear from her eye. "She blamed everything on herself."

"She felt responsible," Kristy said. "I tried to tell her that we all understood that she did the best she could."

"But she wouldn't listen."

"No."

"It wasn't her fault, though. Circumstances, well, they sucked. She couldn't help that. Dad, if we can even call him that, up and left her with four kids and no money. She had to do what she had to do."

"Yes, but I think her biggest regret was how it all affected you, Bodes."

"I'm fine."

"Are you?"

Bodie glanced away from her penetrating stare. She swore she could feel her eyes boring into her through the shiny lenses of her sunglasses. "Sure. I'm okay."

"Because you haven't done a thing for yourself in years. You've always been so focused on everyone else."

"I tried to do something for myself today. Didn't exactly turn out the way I wanted."

Bodie's phone vibrated in her pocket. She fished it out and stared at the number.

"Who is it?"

"I don't know. It's a Scottsdale area code."

"You going to answer it?"

"Should I?"

"Yes, take it."

Bodie swiped the screen to answer the call. "Hello?"

"Hi, is this Bodie?"

Bodie straightened. "Yes, speaking."

"Bodie, this is Alora Anders."

Alora? What the hell? Had she left something behind at her house?

"Alora, hi." She forced down a swallow, unable to speak. The pause extended, until Alora spoke once again.

"Right. Okay."

Next to her, Kristy began mouthing words and waving her hands. Bodie had to wave her off in return so she'd stop.

"I was wondering if you'd still consider taking the job?"

Bodie felt her mouth drop open. "Sorry?"

"The job. It's yours if you still want it."

"Really? Uh, yes, of course. I mean, sure. If it's still available."

"Great. I'll see you tomorrow. Say seven?"

"A.M.?"

"Bright and early."

"Should I—bring my things?"

"I think that would be wise, seeing as how you're going to live here, don't you?"

"Sure. Yes. I'll be there."

The call ended and Bodie drew the phone from her ear and stared at it in disbelief.

"You got the job, didn't you?"

"I think I did, yes."

"Well, why aren't you more excited?"

Bodie lowered the phone. "Because the whole thing is just so strange."

"Like I said, she's eccentric. You'll get used to her."

"I'm not so sure. We haven't even discussed anything yet and she just told me to bring my things so I can move in. And that's after she accused me of wanting to use her."

"So, she changed her mind. Probably didn't have many other choices as good as you."

"Thanks. I think."

"Oh, come on. This is cause to celebrate." She lifted her Frap and toasted Bodie's coffee cup. "To you, Bodes. May your future be bright and your pockets full."

"I just want happiness."

"That too."

They sipped their drinks and Bodie sighed, long and deep. Though she was momentarily happy and somewhat relieved, she knew somewhere in the deep recesses of her mind that everything was far from hunky-dory. Alora Anders was not going to be a walk in the park.

❖

Bodie looked out into the pale pink sky as the sun fell behind the jagged-toothed mountains. She slowly lowered the blinds and turned the lock on the front door, ready to settle in for the evening before she had to report to the bakery. She'd thought about giving her notice, but decided that maybe it was best to keep her shift, at least until she knew for sure if things were going to work out with Alora. After all, her mother had always said it's better to be safe than sorry, and she couldn't afford to be without an income right now. What little her mother had in life insurance went to cover funeral expenses and some lingering medical bills, leaving very little else behind. Thankfully, she wouldn't have to buy groceries for a while, so that was one less expense, thanks to all the food the neighbors and friends brought over.

She sank onto the couch and folded more fresh laundry to place in her duffle bag. She was only going to bring the minimum, until she knew for certain she was going to stay on permanently. She set the last T-shirt into the bag and lifted the framed photo of her mother from the scarred coffee table. She reclined and stared at it, running her thumbs gently across the glass. The photo had been taken years before, before the cancer, before her disability from the rheumatoid arthritis. Before things went to total shit.

"You were so beautiful, Mom." She kissed the photo and placed it, too, inside the duffel. Then she zipped it closed and set it aside to sip her beer. The house was quiet, save for the distant sound of barking dogs and a kid or two outside at play. It was odd sitting in such silence. She wasn't sure if the small, two-bedroom house had ever been so quiet. There had always been someone else at home, whether it be her siblings, her nieces and nephews, or her mother. Someone had always been there. But now she was alone. Totally alone. And she didn't like it.

"It's a good damn thing Alora's offering me the job." She took another pull off her bottle of beer. It was warm and pretty much tasteless, but what did she expect from cheap beer? She grabbed the remote and turned on the television. But after flipping through the channels for a moment, she switched it off. Nothing interested her. And Netflix and chill might as well be meaningless as far as she was concerned. It just wouldn't be the same streaming a movie or a series without her mother by her side.

She rose to wander into the kitchen, carrying her beer along the way. She dumped the remainder in the sink, not wanting to be too buzzed for work later. She cracked open the fridge and stood staring inside. She searched through some casserole dishes, eyed a dish of what appeared to be seven-layer dip, and closed the fridge, deciding against eating. She just couldn't get settled. Not with a movie, not with a meal, not within herself. She crossed to the windows in the nook and stared out again at the sunset. The sky was scarlet now and breathtaking with puffy cotton candy-like clouds. She got lost in it for a long moment and lowered the blinds before turning to grab her keys off the coffee table.

She had no idea where she was going, she just knew she couldn't be there. She gave the living room one last long look before she pulled the door closed behind her, whispering, "I wish you were here, Mom."

CHAPTER SEVEN

Alora stood staring at herself in the bathroom mirror, trying to finger comb her hair. She'd showered and used the hair dryer, wanting to look her best for her new guest, even if she wasn't exactly thrilled about her arrival. She reached for the hair spray and tried to add some volume to her salt-and-pepper mane, flipping it over from one side to the other. She'd insisted on going for a haircut the night before, wanting to tidy up the sides where she was closely shaved. Tabby had taken her and she'd been more than curious as to why she suddenly cared about her appearance again. But Alora had put her off, refusing to answer. She didn't owe her or anyone an explanation. She just wanted to look nice.

And it had nothing, absolutely nothing, to do with Bodie Banks, despite what Tabby thought. Okay, so Bodie was beautiful. So what? That didn't mean anything. It certainly didn't mean she was trying to impress her.

She finished messing with her hair and rolled on some lip gloss. Smacking her lips together, she turned to view herself as best she could at varying angles. Satisfied, she left the bathroom and maneuvered slowly, cautiously, into the living room where Tabby stood waiting. When she caught sight of Alora, she let out a long whistle.

"Someone's looking good," she said, coming over to kiss her cheek. "And smelling good, too. What is that? One of your expensive perfumes?"

"Not really. It's Clean Classic. The scent is called Rain."

"Damn, I'm ready to jump your bones."

"Hold off on that will you? We have a guest arriving." She toyed again with her hair, making sure it was still in place.

"Look at you, girl. Caring about yourself again. I love it." She squeezed her shoulder and gave her a wink.

"Yeah, well, don't read too much into it."

"Hey, I wouldn't dare."

Alora glanced up at the clock. "Is she late?"

"Not yet." Tabby cocked her head. "You nervous?"

"Don't be ridiculous. I was just curious."

Tabby led her gently over to the couch. "I'm really glad you decided to hire her. I think she's going to be a good fit and a big help."

"Let's hope you're right."

Tabby sank down next to her and offered her a mug of coffee from the end table. "I'm curious, though. What changed your mind?"

Alora took the cup and sipped the piping hot liquid. It was divine. "I thought about all the other candidates, and realized I didn't like any of them, not even a little, so it was just a no-brainer. Nor did I want to sit through any more interviews."

"For what's it worth, I think you made the right choice. She seems really nice, and Simone and her references had nothing but stellar things to say about her."

"You called her references?"

She shrugged and drank from her own mug. "I liked her and wanted to know more about her. So after I left here last night I called."

"You shit. You knew I was going to hire her."

"I was hoping you'd pull your head out of your ass. Especially after I laid down the gauntlet."

"Which had no effect on me whatsoever, by the way."

"Uh-huh. Right. Why are you such a stubborn ass?"

This time, Alora shrugged. She had no answer, not even a bullshit one. She knew she was difficult. Numerous people had told her so throughout the years. But Tabby, Tabby had always stuck with her. She reached for her hand and squeezed. Tabby smiled and returned it. They stared out the open patio doors into the morning light. The desert was awakening to another fresh, balmy day and the mourning doves were gently cooing their greetings. The pool glistened as the sound of the filter kicked on and Alora got lost in the dancing sparkles of the teal green water for a moment.

Tabby rested her head on Alora's shoulder. "I so love it here. You know I would move in and care for you if I could, right?"

"I do."

"Because Christ knows, I love you. And I'm worried sick about you."

"I love you too. And I'll be fine. Always am."

Tabby was silent and Alora wondered, not for the first time, if she really would be okay this time around.

"You're not still worried about Bodie trying to use you for her art, are you?"

"It seems to be all these amateur artists want from me."

"I don't think she's like that."

"And you know her well, do you?"

"Even if she did have something like that in mind, it doesn't mean you have to do anything for her. You made things pretty clear to her yesterday, so I don't think she'd dare ask or even suggest—"

The doorbell interrupted them, and Tabby set down her coffee and rose. She looked down at Alora. "You ready?"

"As I'll ever be."

Tabby crossed to the front door and pulled it open to welcome Bodie inside. They made small talk as they headed for the living room. Alora stood and forced a smile, smoothing down her shirt as she did so. Her breath shook as she took Bodie in. She was in black jeans and a crisp white shirt that hugged her body like a second skin. Dark leather bracelets adorned her wrists and a matching necklace fit snugly around her neck. And once again her piercings seemed to shimmer in the sunlight.

"Hi," Bodie said, giving a small wave.

Alora stepped forward and offered her hand. "Good morning. And welcome."

"Thank you."

She was carrying a duffel bag, which Tabby took and placed on the adjacent sofa, while offering her a seat at the same time. "Would you like a cup of coffee?"

"Yes, please. That would be great."

She went to pour her a mug and returned before Alora even had a chance to sit back down.

"Thanks. It smells wonderful." Bodie settled onto the couch and took a tentative sip. She seemed pleased with the rich flavor.

"It's Kopi Luwak," Alora said.

Bodie looked at her quizzically.

"It's the best money can buy," Alora explained as she too, settled once again.

Bodie nodded and took another sip, careful to inhale the aroma.

"You're probably wondering why we asked you to be here at seven," Tabby said, sitting next to Alora. "Alora likes to get started early. She rises at six and eats by seven. Then she heads into the studio to work."

"Oh."

"Yes, I'm still going to work," Alora said. "Did you think otherwise?"

Bodie lowered her cup. "No, I—"

"Because I can still do it. Make no mistake."

"I wasn't—I didn't—"

"I took a break. A little break. But I'm starting back up." She had no idea if she could still paint like she used to with the damn dark spot in her vision, but she was soon to find out. The mere thought of trying had her nerves all atwitter though. What if she couldn't do it? What if she couldn't see well enough?

"That's great," Bodie said.

"So, you'll have no problem rising early?" Tabby asked, giving Alora a stern glance. It was obvious that she was uneasy about Alora's sudden reaction to the conversation. She probably didn't want a repeat of the day before, nor did she want Alora to scare Bodie off.

"Not at all." Bodie said. "I'm actually used to being up early in the morning. I've been working nights at a bakery."

"Perfect," Tabby said. "Maybe you'll be able to make us fresh baked goods, eh?"

"I'd love to."

Alora smiled along with Bodie and Tabby, but she didn't feel it. She was still concerned over what Bodie thought of her and her ability to work. What would others think if she stopped producing? Her reputation would be ruined, if it wasn't already. The rumor mill had already started and artists and friends from all over the world had been calling in to check on her after hearing the news. She hadn't spoken to them of course, too upset to, but Tabby had. They'd all wished her well, but she wondered if they'd disappear if she could no longer paint. The possibility made her feel sick to her stomach. She'd always been a hard worker, a diligent perfectionist when it came to her painting, and that wasn't about to change now just because she had a little problem. People would see. She would prove them all wrong. Alora Anders was here to stay and she was determined to remain relevant in the art world.

"I could make you some bread, right now if you'd like," Bodie said.

"Oh, good heavens no. I was just teasing. Besides, we need to show you around, show you the ropes."

"Actually," Bodie stirred. "I was hoping to talk about salary first."

"You don't have to worry about that," Alora said. "I will pay you well. More than well."

"What's—more than well?"

Alora studied her and then looked over to Tabby who rose and lifted a folder off the coffee table. She passed it to Bodie.

"You'll find all the particulars in there," she said.

"It's a contract." Bodie sifted through the pages. "And—what's this? A nondisclosure clause?"

"It's for everyone's best interest," Tabby said. "Did you find your salary? Does it seem fair?"

Bodie scanned the documents in silence. Then she lowered the folder. "It does."

"Then what's the issue?" Alora asked, sensing there was something by the look on her face.

"I'm just a little unfamiliar with contracts and clauses."

Alora looked again to Tabby, and then spoke. "Please, feel free to take those to an attorney to look over before you sign."

"I don't really—have the money."

"We'll pay," Tabby said. "We'd be happy to."

Alora shot her a look. She was already going to pay the woman very well, she didn't want to have to fork out any more for an attorney to glance over some papers. And what was the problem anyway? It was pretty straightforward. Bodie would perform certain duties, get paid for them and not share any information. End of story. Maybe this was a mistake. Maybe Bodie wasn't the right fit after all.

"Of course, if you're not comfortable," Alora said.

Tabby laughed, her nerves showing. "Why don't I show you around, Bodie? So you can get a feel for things around here. We'll just forget about the paperwork for the time being."

Tabby stood and Bodie joined her, though hesitantly. She followed Tabby down the hallway, leaving Alora alone.

"Well, this is going just fantastic," Alora said to herself. She grabbed her cup of coffee and slurped, hoping for some energy and clarification. Bodie was obviously uncomfortable with the contracts, but what else was she supposed to do? She had to protect herself. She was a well-known artist and she had a reputation. She wasn't about to let that be tarnished because some hotshot young sculptor got upset and wanted to speak ill of her.

She sighed. Tabby would just say that she didn't think Bodie was like that. In fact, she had said that when Alora first proposed the nondisclosure clause. She thought it unnecessary and even feared that it might unnerve Bodie.

"Damn it, why does she always have to be right?" She heard them talking as they exited the family room to head farther down the hallway. Tabby was laughing, trying to keep things lighthearted. God bless her. She was always trying to keep the peace and keep things running smoothly. Alora just didn't always agree with her, and she didn't in this matter either.

No, Bodie would have to sign the agreement. Otherwise, they'd all be looking for a new arrangement.

CHAPTER EIGHT

"And this is the TV room," Tabby said with a dramatic sweep of her arm. Bodie took in the sunken room with the flat screen television mounted above an elaborate stone fireplace. The sofas were spacious and overstuffed and the room, even though very well lit with large arched windows, had a rather cozy feel to it. Bodie didn't know much about design or architecture, but she knew enough to know that this home must run in the millions of dollars. Everything seemed purposely chosen and placed, and yet it felt warm and comfortable. It didn't have the stark "museum" feel to it that she'd heard some expensive homes did.

"It's…very nice."

"You're welcome to watch TV in here," Tabby said.

"Are you sure Alora's okay with that?" She wasn't getting quite the welcoming feeling she'd been hoping for.

Tabby gave a wave, as if dismissing Alora's attitude. "Alora's fine. She just…she has trouble trusting people. But she'll get used to you."

"Maybe I'd better watch TV somewhere else until she does."

Tabby continued and they bypassed a large dining room area with a grand wide maple table and elegant high-backed chairs. The room was across from the sunken TV room, but it didn't look like it was used very much. Bodie didn't imagine that Alora had many dinner parties. Especially if she really was the eccentric loner Kristy claimed her to be. But then again, how did she wine and dine her one-night stands? Maybe she didn't need to. Maybe all it took was one foot stepping into this illustrious abode and they were overwhelmed and turned on.

"You can always watch TV in your room." She opened a darkly stained wooden door and ushered Bodie inside. The room was vast with a tall, thick-mattressed bed, decorative heavy-looking headboard with matching end tables, two chaise lounges, and a TV mounted above another stone fireplace.

"This is too much," Bodie said. "I couldn't possibly need something this nice."

"You aren't used to nice things?"

"No. Not like this." It even had an attached bathroom with a huge clawfoot tub and walk-in shower.

"I'm not either. But this is how Alora lives. And now you, if you accept the job, do as well."

"It's just all so much."

"It can be. But it's also wonderful, don't you think?"

Bodie continued to look around in awe. She'd never had a bedroom so big, so *fancy.* Could she really relax and sleep in there? "Is there a smaller room, perhaps?"

The house was massive, at least six thousand square feet, surely there were other rooms. Maybe ones that weren't so…extreme.

"You don't like it?"

"No, no, I do. I mean, it's beautiful. It's just that I'm not used to all this."

Tabby touched her arm. "Do you not feel deserving, Bodie?"

Bodie flushed at her accurate insight. "I do feel a bit like an imposter."

Tabby smiled. "It's okay. Really. You'll love it in here. And we chose it because it's close to Alora's room."

"Alora's room?"

"Yes, it's just right down here at the end of the hall." She stopped at the threshold of a pair of open double doors. The master bedroom was easily three times as big as Bodie's room and it was decorated in equally expensive taste, with a gabled, wood beam ceiling, a heavy-looking oak king-size bed with matching furniture, polished wood floors, a large marble fireplace, and what looked to be an adjoining bathroom and walk-in closet.

"Wow," Bodie said.

"I know, right? She lives like the queen she is. But you can see how close you are to her. I thought that important, considering her poor vision. If she happens to need something at night, you'd be close by."

"That sounds reasonable."

"So, you'll take the room?"

"I'll take the room."

"Wonderful, you won't regret it." They continued and Tabby showed her the laundry room, a couple of spare bathrooms, three more bedrooms, and finally, Alora's studio. But she didn't open the door. "This is her private space. She asked that you not go in here unless you're given permission. She's…very particular about her work space. I don't even go in there."

Bodie nodded. It made sense that at least one area of the house was off limits. Everyone had a right to their privacy. Especially an artist. Her studio was sacred. She understood. "I get it."

"I knew you would." They headed back into the great room where Alora sat sipping her coffee, staring out the patio doors.

"How do you like the place?" she asked.

"It's magnificent."

Alora smiled but it appeared forced. "Glad you like it. Now all you have to do is sign."

"I thought—"

"I think she needs some time to go over it," Tabby quickly said. "And maybe see a lawyer."

"What's the problem? It's very straightforward."

"I just don't feel comfortable signing something so formal without taking my time reading it over."

Alora stood. "How much time do you need? And why do you need time to decide if you're going to spread rumors about me or not?"

"Spread rumors?"

"Or whatever. That clause just simply states that you won't share my personal information or lifestyle."

"I have no intention of harming you in any way, Alora."

"Then sign."

"Alora," Tabby said. "Can I speak with you in the other room, please?"

Alora set down her coffee mug and allowed Tabby to lead her away. Bodie sat with her heart racing, unsure as to what had just transpired. Was Alora really that distrusting? If so, why? What had happened to her? Had someone betrayed her? Then she recalled what Kristy had said about her. Maybe that was it. Maybe the women she dated had spread negative things. If so, then why not have them sign the clause? Why did she have to? And what was with all the pressure? Jesus, couldn't she even be afforded the time to read it over?

They returned to the great room after having a whispered, obviously heated conversation. Alora looked flushed and Tabby flustered. Neither spoke until they were seated once again on the sofa. Tabby intertwined her hands in her lap and cleared her throat.

"Alora."

Alora gave Bodie a stern, hard look, and for a moment, Bodie was sure that she was going to ask her to leave. But then she spoke and completely shocked her.

"There's no need for you to sign the nondisclosure clause."

Bodie blinked. "No need?"

"If you don't want to, you don't have to sign it. But you really should sign the other contract. It protects us both. Ensures your salary, etc."

Bodie flipped through the pages again. What she was giving her was more than generous. And the terms all sounded very fair and basic. But she still wasn't sure. Alora seemed so volatile, so angry. What if it didn't work out?

"Can we give it a few days first? To see how we get along?"

"You're worried about getting along?" Alora asked.

"Well, we don't know each other and we're kind of being thrown together rather suddenly. Wouldn't you like to know for sure if you want me to remain here?"

Alora rubbed her thighs and sighed. She looked at Tabby. "She's making a lot of sense, isn't she?"

"I think it's a reasonable request."

"Okay then. We'll give it a week. That'll give us both some time."

"Thank you."

Alora stood. "Now, I haven't had breakfast yet, so if that's all, I'd like to eat."

Bodie stood hesitantly. "I can do that for you."

"That would be great." Alora stumbled over to the bar and maneuvered onto a stool.

Bodie looked to Tabby for reassurance. She didn't want to step on her toes if she'd been planning on staying and cooking.

"Go ahead," Tabby said. "I need to get going anyway." She carried the coffee cups over to the sink and gave Alora a quick embrace as she whispered something in her ear. Alora nodded and Tabby shook Bodie's hand. "Thank you again, Bodie. You have my number should you need anything. Oh, and, Fatima, the housekeeper, comes three days a week to cook and clean. She's wonderful, you'll love her."

"Got it."

Tabby gave her a warm smile, grabbed her purse, and walked out the front door.

Bodie remained still for a moment, in front of the sofa, unsure what to do. Should she try to make small talk as she cooked? How did Alora like her eggs? Scrambled or over easy? Maybe sunny-side up? Did she like her bacon soft or crispy? Oh, God, what if she was vegan?

Bodie coughed and forced herself to move. She rounded the counter and faced Alora in the overly white kitchen. "What would you like for breakfast?"

"What can you make?"

"Pretty much anything."

"Yeah?" She seemed curious. "Can you make me some fresh bread? You being a baker and all?"

"In a jiffy. If you have the right ingredients."

"Isn't it rather simple? Flour, etc?"

"Do you have yeast?"

"Oh. I don't think so. I don't think that's been on the grocery list."

"A lot of people don't have it on hand. Not anymore anyway. But I can run to the store real quick."

Alora shook her head. "I'm good with just bacon and eggs for the time being. You can make the bread later. Oh, and lots of orange juice, please. Vitamin C is good for the eyes."

"How do you like your eggs?" Bodie plucked the eggs, bacon, milk and juice from the fridge.

"Scrambled."

"And your bacon?"

"Cooked."

Bodie laughed. "Does that mean crispy?"

"Extra crispy."

"Would you like toast?"

"Not this morning, thanks. Not if I'm going to have fresh bread later."

"Ah, are you a carb watcher?" She poured her a tall glass of OJ and cracked a couple of eggs into a bowl to scramble them with some milk.

"Gotta keep this girly figure."

Bodie glanced up at her.

"What?"

"Nothing."

"You don't watch your carbs?" She sipped her juice.

"No."

"Well, you being a baker and all, I'm not surprised. So how do you stay in such great shape?"

Bodie felt herself flush again. "I just—I don't know. Stress?"

Alora cracked up. "I understand. Believe me I do."

Bodie turned away from her and began cooking the bacon. "I guess you have been under a lot of stress lately."

"You mean with my going blind?"

Bodie stiffened, afraid she'd said something wrong.

"It's okay, you can be honest. I'd actually prefer it if you were. I hate being nice just for nice sakes."

"I—yes. It must be very stressful."

"I don't think I can even adequately explain it. It's a real bitch."

"Has it gotten any easier? The adjustment?"

"I'm accepting it more and more, if that's what you mean. But then again, what choice do I have?"

Bodie flipped the bacon. "For what it's worth, I'm really sorry—"

"Please, don't apologize to me. I'm really sick and tired of everyone feeling so sorry."

"Sorry," Bodie said and stiffened again. But surprisingly Alora chuckled.

"You're funny, Bodie Banks."

"Am I?"

"You're like a nervous little bird. So afraid to say or do the wrong thing. How do you live like that?"

"I don't know…survival?"

"You've had a rough life?"

"No more than most, I guess. Raised by a single mother who had to work two jobs to support us. How about you?"

Alora grew quiet. "I had a rough time for a bit."

Bodie poured the eggs into the adjacent pan as she considered how to respond. "How—"

"But I don't like talking about that."

Bodie swallowed but didn't say anything in return. She gave her her space and cooked the eggs in silence. Was that why Alora had trouble trusting people? Because she'd had a rough life? More importantly, would Bodie ever know? Or would this whole thing be moot?

CHAPTER NINE

Alora took a bite of her eggs and added more pepper. Bodie had been right. She could cook. At least a simple breakfast anyway. "Thank you," she said as she took another bite, this one of the bacon. It was extra crispy, just how she preferred it to be. "It's good."

"You sound surprised." Bodie was across from her, washing the dishes and tidying up.

"Pleasantly so, yes. You're not going to eat?"

"Not right now."

"Not hungry?"

"I ate when I got home from work this morning."

Alora lowered her piece of bacon. "You went to work? At the bakery?"

"I wasn't sure how this was going to work out."

"You're not going to go to work there tonight, are you?"

Bodie was quiet. She began drying one of the pans. "I said I would give this a week and I intend to honor that."

Alora relaxed a little. "Good. Because—" she stopped short. She had been about to admit that she needed her, which would go against everything she stood for. Even though it was true. She feared falling in the middle of the night and needing help. Trips to the bathroom at two a.m. were tedious as it was. She didn't need to be falling while all alone in the house at night.

Alora took another bite of bacon and chewed on. Bodie seemed to let the matter drop. Alora spoke. "So, are you going to lose your job then?"

"Most likely."

"Does that worry you?"

"It does. But…I wanted and needed a change anyway. So even if it doesn't work out here, I'll just move on to something new."

"Sounds like you're pretty concerned about the way things will go here."

Bodie quickly met her gaze and held it. "I am."

"Why? Am I that scary?"

She glanced away and busied herself refilling the juice. "You don't seem to want me here. That unnerves me."

"Let me clarify that for you. I don't want *anyone* here. Period. But I have no choice in the matter, do I?"

"I guess not. But why choose me? You pretty much accused me of having an ulterior motive for wanting the job. So I thought for sure you'd turn me down."

"You were the best candidate. The one I thought I could at least tolerate."

"Ah, okay." She laughed. "Thanks for the honesty."

"Always." She finished her plate and pushed it toward Bodie who took it and washed it. When she was done drying it and putting it away, she stood looking awkwardly at Alora.

"You know," Alora said. "You don't always have to clean up. Fatima gets paid to do that."

"I don't mind."

"A neat freak, huh?"

"I just figure the less clutter around the less likely you are to hurt yourself on something."

"Looking out for me already?"

"It's my job."

"That it is." She stood and stretched. "Time to get to work." She took a few tentative steps toward the hallway and paused. "I work from eight until noon and then stop for lunch."

"Okay." Bodie rounded the counter. "Do you need help with getting to your studio?"

"No, I got it."

"Will you, you know, need help in your studio?"

"Absolutely not. I'll be just fine."

Bodie backed away. "Understood. What, uh, should I do?"

"Unpack. Get settled in. Watch TV. Whatever floats your boat. Just—keep the noise level down."

Bodie gave a nod and Alora continued slowly on down the hallway. She squinted when she opened the door to her studio as the bright light from the large arched windows shone into the room. She loved her studio for precisely that reason. There was plenty of natural light and plenty of open space with a sizable floorplan and the gabled ceilings. She inhaled the familiar scent of turpentine and paint and stepped inside to close the door behind her. She walked carefully to her shelves which lined the back wall and began sifting through her various brushes, tubes of paint, and her palettes and painting knives. She couldn't quite recall where she'd left off so she carried several different goods over to the paint-splattered table near her largest easel and deposited them. Then she grabbed her rags, her medium, and positioned her small Bluetooth speaker at an angle she liked. She retrieved her phone, and took a long moment to find the music she preferred on Pandora. Luckily, she pretty much had her stations already chosen. Tom Petty began to croon about an American girl and she breathed deeply and removed the cover off of the canvas in front of her. All the anxiety about whether or not she could paint came flooding back. The 60x80-inch piece wasn't quite finished, but her base layers were painted and dried. She'd already painted her figure, a lone woman sitting and looking out the window, and now she needed to finish the natural hues with more loose brushstrokes. She moved from left to right, trying to get a view of every part of the canvas. She turned her head, leaned down, and stood on her toes. Nothing worked. She just couldn't see the whole piece like she needed to.

"Fuck."

She sank onto a nearby stool and slouched. What was she going to do? Sure, she could ditch the piece and start over fresh on something else. But this piece was important. She'd had a vision for it and she intended to finish it. She also had several top collectors already bidding top dollar for it.

"Double fuck."

She stood again and readied a brush. Maybe once she started it would come to her, just as it always did, and maybe her good eye could guide her. She dipped the brush in her medium and then in her raw umber paint and a bit of white, and mixed the two on her plastic palette. She began making one loose stroke after another, taking the time to step back and observe after each one. This was the way she worked. Slow. Meticulous. Every placement had meaning, purpose. But damn it, she couldn't see like she needed to.

She cursed again as she stared. No, the new strokes didn't look quite right. They weren't cohesive with the flow of the painting. She'd fucked up. Six strokes in and she'd fucked up. Quickly, she grabbed a rag and wiped off the fresh paint, careful not to smear the residual layer beyond what she could paint over. She tossed the cloth onto the floor and hurried over to the north-facing wall and got another canvas, this one smaller in size, and carried it over to a different easel, which sat next to the other. She dragged her stool the short distance across the wood floor, then cleaned her brush to start anew. She had to figure out how to paint on something other than her important work. With great concentration, she inhaled through her nose, covered her brush in paint and medium, and once again began to make the careful strokes, ignoring the fact that she had not pretreated the canvas or painted a background. Right now she was just trying to work out her flow and practice her strokes. She didn't have a vision, she just wanted to see where the paint would lead her. One mark after the other, she began to build until it eventually became what looked to be a sky bursting forth in sunset. So she went with that down the canvas to where she stopped and changed colors, this time choosing a cerulean blue and an ultramarine, along with a little white. She mixed the paints on her palette and continued to paint. She worked quickly, too anxious not to, leaving her meticulous method behind. She had to know if she could do this.

The hues of the mixed colors looked like a turbulent sea and she smiled as she worked, feeling good about it. She couldn't wait to step back and get a good look, but she forced herself to keep working, to keep at it as she hummed along to Joan Jett and the Blackhearts not giving a damn about their reputation. The song seemed more than appropriate and soon she was belting out the lyrics as she moved along the canvas, making her marks, stopping only to clean her brush and begin with a new mix of colors, this time for a Mediterranean cottage along the shore.

She continued for an unknown amount of time, completely engrossed in her work. She often grew trancelike when she painted, time having no meaning to her. Some days she'd work for hours upon hours, lost to the outside world, oblivious to life beyond her studio. Fatima would sometimes knock at the door, letting her know there was a tray of food for her on the hall table. But most of the time she ignored the signal, too caught up in the zone to even comprehend hunger or thirst. Only when she was forced to stop and use the restroom did she leave the room, returning as soon as she could to finish her painting.

Tabby used to get onto her about working that way, but she soon gave up when Alora refused to change. It was her process, her way to make art. People just needed to understand, and eventually, most did. Fatima would leave the tray of food and drink, along with leftovers in the fridge. Tabby would text, but not even attempt to call, knowing she would get back to her when she stopped for the evening. Alora was good about that when she finally cleaned up her supplies and trudged down the hall into the kitchen to dig through the fridge for cold water and whatever Fatima had made for her to eat. She'd take a plate and her water and collapse on the couch and check her messages, and call Tabby back right away to see what was up. She'd eat while they talked and Tabby would fill her in on her day. After the phone call ended, and she set her plate aside, she'd fall asleep where she sat, right there on the couch, wake sometime in the early morning hours, and stumble off to bed.

That was the routine she was used to and had been for years now, working every day of the week. Though weekend hours were often cut short so she could relax some. Her muscles often felt strained and tight after a long week of standing and working over a canvas. So the spa felt wonderful, along with a nice bottle of wine. And of course, should she be in the mood for romance, a beautiful woman sitting across from her in the spa was always nice as well.

Speaking of, she paused mid stroke, paintbrush in hand. Would she be able to have anyone over with Bodie in the house? Or should she just give her the evening off when she had a date? Also, how would she handle herself without help? She couldn't depend on her date to help her around, or to understand. That would be awkward as hell and she wasn't ready to show that kind of vulnerability. So how would she go about dating?

A brief, fleeting thought came of Bodie sauntering toward her wearing a black bikini, and her skin instantly caught aflame. "No, I can't. She's here to help me, nothing more." She forced the image away and clenched her jaw as she finished the last of the strokes. The painting was complete, save for any adjusting strokes needed to tidy it up. But first, she needed to examine the work as a whole.

Wiping dampness from her brow, she began to back away to view the painting. But as she did, she felt her stomach knot. She backed up some more and tilted her head, left then right. She blinked. Tried to focus better. She stepped closer. Then back again. But regardless of where and how she looked at the painting, it just didn't look right. Not at all like she expected. Once again, the painting as a whole didn't feel cohesive. The strokes looked boxy and amateurish and was just downright terrible. Her breath quickened as panic and then anger set in. Her heart thudded in her ears and her throat went dry. It was shit. Total and complete shit.

Holy fuck, what was she going to do?

She eyed the paintbrush in her hand and threw it at the canvas where it hit with a thunk and clamored onto the floor. She rushed the painting, intent on destroying it with her bare hands, wanting to smear the paint everywhere and throw the piece off the easel and across the room. But just as she was about to reach it, she tripped over something, something soft, and fell directly onto the painting, stumbling to the floor in a heap of splintered wood and wet paint.

She was still for a moment before she opened her eyes.

And that's when the pain set in.

Chapter Ten

After watching Alora slowly make her way down the hall, Bodie quietly unpacked and tried to get settled. Her room was nice, beyond nice, but it just didn't feel like home. Everything was perfectly placed and each piece carefully chosen, probably by a designer who made more in a month than she made in a year at the bakery. It didn't feel cozy like the sunken TV room.

She wasn't sure how she'd be comfortable there. Even the bedding seemed brand new. The comforter and pillow shams felt rough and stiff, like they'd had just been pulled from the packaging. She supposed that was better than sleeping in bedding that wasn't clean. She was staying at one hell of a house after all and even though it was different for her, she was rather fortunate.

She put the last of her belongings in the empty dresser drawer and sifted through the three paperbacks she'd brought. She chose one, a new sci-fi she'd picked up at the local used book store she frequented and, seeking comfort that was more like home, headed for the TV room. She made herself comfy on the roomy couch and cracked open her book, grateful the spine had already been broken. Beyond her, down the hall, and behind the closed door of Alora's studio, she heard music playing. She also heard shuffling and items being moved about, and she considered knocking on the door to check on Alora, to make sure she didn't need any help getting set up. But she recalled the warning to stay out of the studio and Alora's refusal for most help in general and she decided to leave her be.

"If she needs help bad enough, she'll call for me."

But would she? She was rather stubborn.

Bodie glanced down the hall, listening keenly for any sounds of frustration or distress. When she heard none, she relaxed and began reading again. Her eyes threatened to fall closed after the second chapter and she had to fight to stay awake. Nights at the bakery were doing her in, though she usually would be asleep by now at home after such a long shift. She settled farther into the couch, sipped some cold water, and continued reading. She had just started in on chapter six when she heard a crash that made her freeze. At first, she thought she'd imagined it. But with ears perked, she listened closely for more, trying to discern sounds from the music. That's when she heard a voice. Distant, muffled, but definitely a voice. It was crying out for help.

Bodie tossed her book aside and sprinted down the hallway. Heart hammering, she skidded to a stop at the studio door and hesitated as again the warnings to stay out of the studio played across her mind. More music came from the room, but the cries had stopped. She raised a fist to knock on the door and heard the voice again. It was muffled and curse- and profanity-laced, but it wasn't calling for help. Bodie's fist connected with the door, rapping.

"Alora? You okay?"

"No, I'm not okay! I need help, goddammit!"

Bodie turned the knob and opened the door. She squinted against the bright sunlight shining in through the large arched windows as she scanned the room desperately for Alora.

"Over here."

Bodie followed the voice and found Alora on the left side of the room, in a tangled heap on the floor with paint smeared all over her. Bodie rushed to her, trying to make sense of the scene.

"Are you hurt?" Bodie asked, kneeling by her side. She searched her for signs of blood, but it was difficult to tell if she was bleeding with all the paint marking her skin and clothes.

"Yes, I'm hurt. Get me out of here." She tried to move, but she was caught in broken bits of what used to be an easel.

"Do I need to call an ambulance?"

"No, dammit. Just help me. And don't look at the painting."

Bodie saw the blood, oozing down her forehead and ignored whatever the hell she was referring to. She tried not to panic. "Okay, I'm going to move the easel first, so we can get you free." She gently extracted the broken pieces of wood, freeing them from around and beneath Alora, who groaned as she shifted her weight on the wet canvas beneath her. "Okay, here we go," Bodie said, gripping her arm. She lifted as best she could to get Alora started, and slid her free hand around her waist to help her the rest of the way up. Alora slipped on some paint but managed to right herself and stand. She brushed her hair back with her palm and stumbled over to what appeared to be a small speaker and threw it against the wall, killing the music.

"There, that's better," she said, swaying a little on her feet. She palmed her head again and brought her hand down for inspection. It was red.

"You're bleeding," Bodie said as her concern grew. It looked as though the staples on her forehead had opened up.

"Seems so."

"I should call someone."

"No. Don't. I'm fine."

"But you're injured. Bleeding."

"I said no."

Bodie wanted to say more but she decided against it.

"Just get me to the bathroom where I can get cleaned up," Alora said.

Bodie led her to the hall to head toward the master bedroom, but Alora stopped suddenly and glanced down at her feet. "Shit, we're tracking paint along the floor."

"I'll clean it up."

"It's Brazilian walnut, Bodie."

"It'll come up."

"Not without ruining the floor. Oh, my God." She kicked off her shoes and rubbed her temple as she studied Bodie. "Well? Take your shoes off. I don't want the paint tracked anywhere else."

"Right." Bodie knelt and untied her shoes and slipped them off. Then she guided Alora through her bedroom and into the bathroom where she began to strip.

Bodie turned away, unsure as to what to do.

"Now's not the time to be shy," Alora said. "Can you turn on the shower?"

Bodie switched on the multi-head shower and adjusted the water accordingly. When she faced Alora again, she was completely and unabashedly nude. Bodie stared at her in disbelief as her heart lodged in her throat. She was breathtakingly beautiful, slightly curved, and seriously toned in all the right places. Her olive skin nearly glowed in the bathroom light, and her small, taut breasts puckered in the cool air.

"If you blink you'll miss the show," Alora said as she bypassed her to step into the glass-walled shower.

Bodie did blink then, rapidly. She flushed fiercely and attempted to clear her throat.

"Do you—uh—need anything else?" she asked as she focused on the swirl in the marble of the bathroom counter.

"A towel. They're in the closet."

Bodie got her a towel, ignoring the rows and rows of color-coded clothes hanging in the closet, along with the vast array of shoes. She hung the towel on the rack next to the shower.

"You don't have a robe, or something?" Bodie asked, thinking of her nude form once again.

"Don't use it."

Of course not.

"Anything else? Or should I just wait for you in the bedroom?"

"No, you can stay. I'm almost finished. Damn, my head is still bleeding."

Bodie turned, concerned, and caught sight of her glistening body beneath the streams of water. She faced front again.

How can I help this woman if I'm so caught up in her looks?

"Are you sure I shouldn't call for help?"

"I'm done with hospitals."

"Yes, but if you have a head injury—"

"It's just the staples. I didn't hit my head that hard."

Bodie didn't like the sound of that and she quickly slid out her phone and texted Tabby. At the very least, her friend should know.

Tabby didn't respond and Bodie tucked her phone back into her pocket. The shower cut off and the door opened. Bodie saw Alora reach for the towel in the foggy mirror. She turned and handed it to her.

"Thanks." She dried herself and stepped from the shower uncovered and headed for her closet. Bodie waited while hangers scraped across rods and items sounded as if they were being tossed about. Shoes, thumping against carpet.

"Need any help?"

"Nope." Alora emerged, freshly scrubbed and freshly dressed in khaki shorts and a light pink T-shirt. She stood at the counter and carefully pressed a dry washcloth she'd brought with her from the closet against her forehead. She combed her hair before turning to head into the bedroom. "The first aid kit is beneath the sink on the right."

Bodie retrieved the first aid kit to follow Alora to the padded bench at the foot of the bed. Alora sat very straight, hands in her lap as if she were waiting patiently for a ride at a bus stop.

"There should be some latex gloves in there," Alora said.

Bodie checked herself for any wet paint before sitting next to her. Then she opened the kit and snapped on the gloves. She leaned in to inspect the staple line near her scalp and caught the fragrant, flowery scent of her shampoo. It stirred her insides and she clenched her jaw to fight against it. She had to focus. Alora was hurt and her charge. This was no time to be thinking about desire. "It's still bleeding a bit."

Bodie dabbed the wound with some gauze which caused Alora to wince. "Am I hurting you?" Bodie asked.

"I'll live."

Bodie held the gauze to her head and managed to stifle the bleeding. She set in on cleaning the wound. "Sorry," she said as she knew she was causing her pain. "But we've got to get it clean."

Alora gazed at her and wet her lips before speaking. "It's okay," she breathed. "I'm rather enjoying the view."

Bodie paused. "Pardon me?"

"You're a very beautiful woman, Bodie Banks." When Bodie did nothing but blush profusely, she cocked her head. "What's the matter? Not used to hearing such compliments?"

"No."

"What a shame." She eyed the butterfly bandage in Bodie's hand. "You about done?"

Bodie swallowed against a dry throat and applied the bandage over the staples. Alora lightly touched it and ran her hands down her arms. "Damn it, I'm scraped up here too."

Bodie noticed the faint red scratches and tended to those wounds as well. When she finished, Alora stood. "I'm assuming by the way you reacted to my nudity that you're a lesbian."

Bodie was speechless.

"No need to worry. I am as well. So you're in good company." She padded toward the hallway, still touching her head wound. "But we should probably have a rule." She stopped at the doorway. "No sex." She turned and pinned Bodie with a hard stare. "We can both have sex of course. Just not with each other."

Bodie peeled off the gloves, trying to ignore how sweaty her palms were. "Agreed." Did Alora really think she would have sex with her? Had she reacted that obviously in the bathroom? *Get control of yourself, Bodie. For God's sake.*

"Good. Glad we got that settled. Oh, and…don't bring women to the house. If you want to date, do it elsewhere on your time off."

"Time off?" They hadn't discussed her getting any time off.

"I assume you'll be wanting some time to decompress, won't you? Get out and about, see your people, etc? You do have people, don't you? Most folks do."

"Yes. Do you?"

She frowned but recovered quickly to speak. "I'll have Fatima clean up the studio."

"Are you sure? Because I don't mind, and you said the flooring was—"

"The flooring in there is different. Cheaper. Obviously, with it being where I paint and all. And you don't need to be in there. It's private. My workspace. You didn't…see anything did you?"

"Like what?" Bodie had no idea what she could possibly mean.

"Like the painting."

"The one you fell on?"

"No, the one next to it. On the easel."

"I didn't even get a chance to look." Why did that matter?

Alora seemed satisfied with that answer and the matter seemed closed.

"What about the paint in the hallway?" Bodie asked.

Alora sighed. She turned as a chime sounded letting them know the front door was opened. Tabby's voice resounded through, asking if everyone was okay.

Alora faced Bodie once again. "You called Tabby?"

"I texted her. I thought she should know."

"Damn it. She didn't need to know." She pressed a finger to her forehead. "Next time, ask me, okay? Before you do that?"

Bodie nodded and Alora left the room, answering Tabby with a light, carefree voice, letting her know that she was just fine.

Bodie stood and deposited the gauze and the gloves in the bathroom garbage. She stared at herself in the mirror.

What in the hell have you gotten yourself into?

CHAPTER ELEVEN

I'm fine, Tabby, honestly," Alora said swatting her searching hand away.

"You should be seen. Have a CAT scan."

"No."

"Alora, you could have a brain bleed."

"I didn't hit my head that hard. Good God."

Tabby thumbed the screen on her phone. "I'm calling the paramedics. At least have it looked at."

Alora reached out and gently covered her phone. "Tabby. Stop. I'm fine."

Tabby finally relented and lowered her phone. "You're going to be the death of me, woman."

Alora squeezed her arm. "Stop worrying so much. Bodie was here. She helped and everything is good. Everything except my floor."

"Your floor?"

"There's paint in the hallway. On the Brazilian walnut."

"Oh, no."

"I can clean it," Bodie said from her position against the kitchen counter.

"You don't know how."

Bodie held up her phone. "Actually, I just looked it up. You just need a little water and some dish detergent."

"It's paint. And it's already dried on."

"It says to use a credit card or something similar to scrape it off with after you try cleaning it with the soap and water."

Alora studied her, surprised. "Well, aren't you resourceful?"

Bodie smiled. "Should I give it a shot?"

"I suppose. But be careful. Don't ruin my floor."

Bodie began gathering supplies, asking for a bucket and a soft cloth which Tabby helped her to locate. Then she disappeared down the hall.

"She's wonderful." Tabby said, lightly brushing Alora's hair away from her bandaged wound. "I'm glad we found her."

"She's gay," Alora said, dodging her touch.

"So?"

"So, it could be a problem."

"How so?"

Alora checked the hallway to make sure Bodie was still out of earshot. "Have you seen her? She's gorgeous. And…I think she thinks the same about me."

"How could you possibly know that?"

"She saw me naked and she about passed out from blushing alone."

"So, cover yourself up. Not everyone is as comfortable with nudity as you are."

"Obviously. Especially not my young lesbian friend down there."

"You don't know for sure she's gay, Alora. She was probably just shocked at seeing her new boss naked."

"I told her that I assumed by her reaction that she was gay and she didn't disagree."

"Maybe she's scared to. You are very intimidating. And even if she is a lesbian, so what? Just keep your paws to yourself and everything will be fine."

"You make me sound like some sort of sex-crazed older woman."

"You are, aren't you?"

Alora rolled her eyes. "She agreed to give it a week. So we'll see how things go." She headed toward the hallway.

"Where are you going?" Tabby asked.

"To see how she's doing with the flooring."

Tabby hurried along after her.

"How's it going?" Alora asked as she glanced down at Bodie who was gently wiping the floor with the damp cloth.

Bodie smiled up at her. "It's coming up. See?" She moved her hand to show off the spotless wood.

"No kidding?" Alora knelt next to her and ran her finger over the floor. "Well, how about that?"

"You should have more faith," Tabby said. "Bodie knows what she's doing."

"I guess so." Alora returned the smile, so relieved that her flooring wasn't ruined. "Thank you."

"You're welcome. I can start on the studio next."

"No," Alora said quickly. "I don't want you going in there."

"Why?"

How could she tell her that she didn't want her to see her unfinished painting? The one that was supposed to already be completed. The one she couldn't seem to paint any longer. The one she'd fucked up.

"It's private."

"But you'll let Fatima in?" Bodie said.

Alora straightened. "Fatima's different. She's…like family."

For a brief second, Bodie appeared hurt, but she refocused on the floor, wiping up what was left of the track marks. Alora let her be and pushed open the door to the studio. She felt Tabby at her back. "Give me a minute?" She went to where she'd fallen. The broken easel lay in pieces and the canvas was crushed and smeared with paint, which had gotten onto the floor. She recalled the way she'd tripped and saw the small rag she'd likely stumbled over.

I was so mad I was careless.

She pushed out a breath and looked to the unfinished canvas on her left. She couldn't bear for anyone to see it. It was a huge beacon of her current failings. She carefully stepped around the mess on the floor and covered the painting once again. Then she angled the easel the opposite direction, not even wanting it facing her. Maybe she should just toss it once and for all. But then where would she be? She needed to figure out how to finish it and quickly.

"Lor?" Tabby was at the doorway. "You okay?"

"Yeah. Just tidying up a bit."

"Need some help?"

"No, I'm good." She walked toward her, saw Bodie standing with the bucket and cleaning supplies, and called out to her.

"You can leave that bucket and soap for me, thanks."

Bodie, who had a flash of confusion, lowered the bucket and handed over the wet cloth. Alora took both and turned to go back into the studio. "I'll be out in a few minutes. Just going to clean up in here."

"Alora, you shouldn't do that," Tabby said. "Wait for Fatima if you don't want me or Bodie doing it."

"It's okay," Alora said over her shoulder. "It's my mess. I can do it."

Serves me right for my temper tantrum.

She set the bucket and cloth on the table and grabbed a black garbage bag from the roll on one of her shelves. She plucked out the pieces of broken easel and slid them inside the bag, one at a time. When she had the bag nearly full with wood and the wet canvas, she set it aside and started in on the flooring. She worked slowly, wiping up the paint gently and taking the time to rinse her rag in the warm water in the bucket. She made her way back to the door, cleaning up more track marks along the way. The paint was coming up nicely, but it was thicker there on the studio floor so it took longer before she had it clean. Finally satisfied, she rinsed and wrung out the rag and stood at the door. She pulled it closed behind her and went into the laundry room where she emptied the bucket, tossed the rag in the bag, and set the bag at the rear door to be taken out to the trash. She headed for the kitchen to wash her hands.

"Did it come up?" Tabby asked from her position on the barstool. She was watching Bodie, who was kneading what appeared to be dough on the kitchen counter.

"It did. What's going on here?"

"Bodie's baking."

"I thought we needed yeast?"

"I found some in the pantry," Bodie said.

Alora grinned. "Good old Fatima. She never lets me down."

"Yeah," Tabby said. "So Bodie is showing me how to make a quick loaf of fresh bread."

"Excellent." Alora slid onto the stool next to Tabby to watch. Bodie worked the dough expertly, like she'd been doing it for years. She had such strong, yet gracefully beautiful hands. Alora had always been fond of hands, even sketching some from time to time. And the hands of a beautiful woman? They made her weak in the knees more often than not. That however, could not happen with Bodie.

Her phone rang and she grimaced as she recognized the number.

"Who is it?" Tabby asked, looking concerned.

"Peter."

"Oh, no."

Alora pressed the phone to her ear and took the call, leaving for the TV room.

"Peter, how's it going?" Her heart beat in her throat, creating a strain to her voice. She knew the reason for the call and she'd considered not even answering, but she'd avoided him for a while now and his messages were sounding more and more desperate. It was time to bite the bullet.

"Alora, what the hell? Where have you been? I've been calling and calling. Leaving you messages."

"I know, Peter, and I apologize. I'm just—dealing with a lot here."

He sighed. "I know and I feel for you, I really do, but I need an update on that painting. Any ETA? The clients are getting antsy."

She perched on the edge of her favorite chair and pinched the bridge of her nose.

"It's coming along." But she knew she didn't sound convincing and she just couldn't bring herself to speak with a more positive tone to her voice. She was failing and it was difficult to hide. She wasn't used to imperfection. She didn't know how to handle it, much less admit it. Especially not when people were depending on her.

"And?"

"You'll have it soon."

"How soon?"

"You know I can't tell you that. It'll be finished when it's finished."

"You've always been able to give me an accurate estimate before."

"Things have changed, Peter. I'm having to…adjust."

"And how is that going? You said you could still paint, right? And that you still want to work."

She hesitated. "It's taking some time. But I'm figuring it out."

"Well, make sure you do. This is an important piece and your buyers are chomping at the bit to see it."

"I'm on it."

"Great. And, Alora, sweetheart? Answer my calls."

She hung up and sat rubbing her forehead. What was she going to do? Admit defeat? Crawl under a rock and die?

Fuck.

This was not good. Not good at all.

She returned to the kitchen where she slid back onto the barstool next to Tabby. She offered a smile, and hoped it would pass as genuine. But Tabby saw right through it.

"Tough call?"

"I don't want to talk about it." The last thing she wanted to do was discuss it in front of Bodie. Her new employee did not need to hear about her failings. It was bad enough she knew about her deteriorating vision and had had to help her after an embarrassing fall. She didn't want to add anything else to the pile of embarrassments.

"That bad, eh?" Tabby touched her shoulder and looked at her with great empathy. She knew Peter wanted the painting and she assumed Alora was having trouble in finishing it, though Alora hadn't said as much. She'd just been putting off working on it. But Tabby knew her well and she was wicked intuitive. Alora wouldn't put it past her discerning the reason why she'd put off working on it.

Tabby lowered her hand and presumably gave up trying to get Alora to talk. Instead they both watched as Bodie placed the dough in a bowl and covered it with cling wrap.

"Just need to let that rise," she said. "It'll take about an hour." She looked to Alora. "How about some lunch?"

"I'm not very hungry." The phone call had distressed her considerably and she had nothing on her mind other than the painting and how she was going to finish it.

"Let's order in," Tabby said. "And eat on the patio." She touched Alora's shoulder again. "You have to eat, Alora. Please. For me?"

Alora shrugged. She was in no mood to argue. "Fine."

Tabby whipped out her phone. "How's Wildflower sound?"

"It's fine," Alora said. They frequented the establishment at least once a week and Tabby knew what to order.

"Bodie, you want to look over the menu?" Tabby asked.

Bodie took the phone and scanned the screen, scrolling with her finger. Finally, she chose and Tabby placed the order. Alora wandered out to the patio without them and sat beneath the umbrella at the table near the pool. The sun was high and bright and it hurt her eyes, but she welcomed the slight discomfort, at the moment unable to care.

Her phone pinged from her pocket and she withdrew it to view the screen. One of her colleagues was texting her, asking how the painting was going since her diagnosis. She slammed the phone face down on the glass tabletop and reclined in her chair. She just wanted to be left alone to figure this shit out. But she knew that wouldn't happen. People were people. Some were genuinely concerned, and others…well, curious. And some, no doubt, wanted to see her fail.

But what could she do? Ignore them all?

Yes. That's what she'd been doing and it was what she'd continue to do. Besides, she didn't know what she'd say even if she did have the desire to talk to them.

"You need these?" Bodie said from behind as she approached holding out Alora's Prada sunglasses.

"Thanks." She slid them on and continued to stare out at the craggy mountains.

Bodie eased into the chair next to her and sat in silence, as if sensing her need for quiet reflection. She appreciated that and thought about saying so, but she refrained. Bodie really was turning out to be a good choice. She seemed to be as kind and as intuitive with her as Tabby. And Alora knew that that was something money could not buy.

After a few long moments, Alora spoke. "I'm sorry about the nondisclosure clause. I guess I'm just not someone who trusts very easily."

Bodie glanced over at her, squinting in the sunlight. Her dark eyes had lightened to an amber molasses in the sun, making her all the more breathtaking.

"I can understand that."

Alora chuckled. "I know you think you can, but you really can't. I've been—hurt by someone before."

"I'm sorry to hear that."

Alora said nothing.

Bodie spoke. "I have no ill will toward you, Alora. None at all. If something should happen to where this isn't working out, well, I'll just leave. I won't cause trouble for you."

Alora stared up at the light blue sky. "I appreciate that."

In the distance, Alora heard the doorbell, followed by the chime of the front door opening. A few moments later, Tabby emerged carrying a large paper tote.

"One southwest superfood salad for you," she said, placing the bag on the table to dig out the contents. She set Alora's salad in front of her, along with a fork and some napkins. She dug in the bag again. "And one almond tuna for you," she said as she handed Bodie her container with her sandwich.

"What did you get?" Bodie asked her.

"I got…" She pulled out another container. "My favorite. The chipotle chicken melt." She placed hers on the table and then held up a finger. "Drinks."

Bodie stood. "I'll get them. What does everyone want?"

"Water's fine," Tabby said.

Alora nodded in agreement.

Bodie left them to head inside to the fridge for the bottled water.

Tabby sat and smiled. "I'm telling you, she was a good choice."

Alora glanced back toward the open patio doors. She looked back at Tabby.

"I think you're right."

"What? You agree with me?"

Alora almost grinned. "Don't push it."

"Oh, like I always say, I wouldn't dream of it."

Alora opened her salad and smiled fully. At least one thing was working out for her.

And her name was Bodie Banks.

Chapter Twelve

The bedroom was too dark and Bodie couldn't sleep. She tossed and turned on the overly thick mattress, disliking the way it contoured to her body. The damn thing was too nice, too fancy. She was used to her plain old hard mattress, along with the light from the moon and street lamps shining in through her blinds, creating shadows on the wall. Shadows she could stare at, form shapes with in her mind until she fell asleep. But there was nothing like that here. Just the pitch-black of night.

The house was also freezing. Alora kept her temperature set way below Bodie's comfort zone. She was used to sleeping with the windows open in the mild Arizona spring, and the air set at eighty degrees during the summer. Utility bills ran high in the Phoenix area, so she and her mother had had to get used to keeping the house warmer, and after years of living that way, she was now acclimated. She burritoed herself into the covers and forced her eyes closed. She had to sleep. She was dead tired after working all night the previous evening and then being awake with Alora all day.

She listened keenly for her, hoping she was settling in nicely and was already asleep. She thought she'd heard something earlier, but a quick check of the hallway had revealed nothing. The house seemed quiet, peaceful. No dogs barking, no sounds of the neighbor's clanging wind chimes. Just the occasional sound of the AC kicking on to further cool the house. And once, a distant coyote howling to its compadres.

She opened her eyes, nearly frozen solid beneath the stiff comforter and starched sheets. She unwound and sat up, swinging her feet off the tall bed to dangle in the darkness. She wondered briefly if Alora's room was this dark. Surely not. Surely she left on a light or two.

She glanced back at the windows and noted the blackout drapes. After reaching for her phone, on the night table, she awakened the screen and turned on the flashlight. She crept to the windows and drew the curtains apart to open the blinds behind them. Some light filtered in from the patio light that burned above the wide glass doors, but it wasn't much. Not enough to appease her. So she headed for the bathroom and switched on the light there and pulled the door almost completely closed.

It was better, but she was still cold. She searched the closet for extra blankets but found none. She padded across the floor and gently opened the door to the bedroom. Again, she listened for Alora. Quietly, and still using her phone as a flashlight, she headed out into the hall searching for the laundry room where there was a sizable linen closet. She inched along the shiny wood floors, which were frigid on her bare feet. When she reached the TV room a voice called to her and she froze in her tracks.

"Bad dream?"

Bodie grabbed her heart and shone the light into the sunken room. Alora was sitting in the oversized chair, looking right at her, a small table lamp glowing next to her.

"No, I'm—a little cold."

"Cold?"

Bodie lowered the phone and dropped her hand from her chest. "My house is much warmer."

"Oh. I like it cool, like this."

"Yes. As you should. It's your house."

"But if you're uncomfortable…"

"I'll be fine. I just need to get used to it. And…maybe grab an extra blanket or two?"

"Of course." She rose. "Let me show you where they are."

"You don't need to. I know where they are."

But Alora was already on the move, walking toward her in the dimly lit room. And that's when she stubbed her toe on the back end of the chair, yowled in pain, and dropped to the floor, holding her foot.

Bodie rushed to her, panicked.

"What's wrong? Is it your foot?"

"My—bloody toe." She gripped it and rocked back and forth. "Holy fuck, it hurts." Her face was contorted in pain and Bodie struggled to get her to still so she could see what, if any, damage was done.

"Let me see," she said calmly, feeling anything but.

"No. It hurts too badly. I think I broke it."

"There's no way we'll know unless you let me see it." Bodie placed her hand on top of Alora's and carefully stopped her movement. Alora opened her clenched eyes and breathed through her clamped teeth.

"Be careful. It's literally throbbing."

Bodie gently pushed Alora's hand aside and shone the flashlight on her toes. She saw the culprit immediately. "It's your pinky?"

"Yes."

"It's already swelling. Can you move it?"

"I don't know."

"Try wiggling your toes."

Alora grimaced as she attempted to wiggle her toes. She couldn't move her pinky without crying out in pain.

"You may have broken it."

"Great."

"Come on, let's get you up." Bodie helped her stand and hobble over to the couch. "Lie down, I'll get you some ice." She switched on two more lamps.

"There are cold packs in the top freezer drawer."

Bodie got them, along with a tea towel, and returned to the couch where she mindfully placed them on her toes.

"It's already turning black and blue," Bodie said.

Alora made a face. "Wonderful. God, why do I keep doing this? Am I going to trip and fall every single day?"

"If you keep trying to do everything yourself you might."

"That was rather blunt."

"You asked me to be honest."

"Right. I suppose I did." She palmed her forehead and exhaled.

"What were you doing in here anyway?" Bodie asked, settling into the chair across from her.

"I can't sleep."

"Why not?"

She laughed as if that was the stupidest question on the planet. "Do I really need to explain?"

Bodie was more than curious. Just what all ailed Alora Anders enough to keep her awake late at night?

"I don't want to get into it," Alora added before Bodie could question her more.

"Ah, so it's work then?"

Her brow crinkled. "What makes you say that?"

"That's how you responded when Tabby asked you about that phone call. You said you didn't want to talk about it."

Alora grew quiet. Bodie waited her out.

She finally spoke. "You're very perceptive, aren't you?"

"I try to be."

"Why is that?"

Bodie shrugged. "I guess I had to be growing up. I had siblings to care for while our mother was away at work. So, I had to become adept at reading people and situations well in order to function and keep us all safe."

"That's a lot to ask of a child."

She shrugged again. "It was, but I managed. How about you? You said you had it rough."

"Do you always ask this many questions?"

"I'm just trying to get to know you better." *And figure out why you're so distrusting.*

She covered her eyes. "Switch off some of those lights, will you?"

Bodie complied, leaving the small lamp on next to her. That seemed to comfort her and she removed her hand from her brow.

"I think I can sleep now."

Bodie hesitated. "You sure? I can stay up with you if you need me to."

"No, I'm okay. I'm just going to fall asleep right here."

"You want me to bring you that throw over there?"

"If you don't mind."

Bodie brought her the soft throw and spread it over her.

Alora thanked her and said, "You know where to find the extra blankets then?"

"I do. Would you like one in addition to the throw?"

"No, I'm good. Like I said, I like it cool."

Bodie moved toward the side table. "Light on or off?"

"On."

Bodie nodded, wished her a good night, and left her to head for the laundry room where she got herself two thick blankets before returning to her bedroom. Once there, she snuggled into bed, beneath several layers of covers, and forced her eyes closed once again. This time, thankfully, she didn't have to wait long for sleep to find her.

❖

Bodie woke to her phone alarm at five thirty. Dawn had yet to break and the house was cold and quiet. She showered quickly, though she was tempted to remain beneath the hot stream for hours on end, dressed, and emerged into the hallway. She paused at the TV room and stared at Alora, who was sleeping soundly on the couch right where she'd left her. She looked so peaceful in her sleep. Like she didn't have a care in the world. Bodie again wondered what had happened to her to make her so distrusting. A bad breakup perhaps? Did Alora ever even have a serious relationship before? Bodie tried to imagine what that woman would've been like. Just what was it that Alora Anders was attracted to?

Why am I even going there?

Bodie tucked the throw more securely around her and made her way into the kitchen where she started the coffee and busied herself making another loaf of fresh bread.

Alora had loved the first loaf, along with Tabby, who'd taken more than half of it home to her family. Bodie had reassured her she could, promising to make another loaf for Alora this morning. Alora woke as she was kneading the dough.

"Morning," Bodie called as she wiped her hands to go assist Alora in the dimly lit room.

Alora stood and started to wave her off, but then tried to step with her sore foot and seemed to change her mind. She readily offered her arm to Bodie.

"Ugh, it is so not a good morning," she croaked as they ambled into the kitchen.

"Foot hurt?"

"Like a bitch."

Bodie gave it a look. The bruising had spread down from the toe to the middle of her foot.

"Looks pretty painful."

"It is."

"Think you should go in somewhere, have it x-rayed?"

"No, I'm sure it's just my toe. I've broken it before. It just takes some time to heal."

"You really don't like the doctor's office, do you?"

She laughed as she slid onto the barstool. "Not in the least."

"I can understand that."

Bodie poured her a cup of coffee and a glass of orange juice and returned to her dough.

"Oh, more bread. You're an angel." Alora sipped her coffee and ran her hand through her mussed hair. Her voice was deep and raspy and Bodie thought it sounded rather sexy and wondered if she sounded like that every morning. "Tabby, the thief, took most of mine."

"She liked it," Bodie said with a smile. "And I can always make more. I'll keep you in fresh bread."

Alora smiled back at her. "Christ, I think I have a doctor's appointment today anyway."

"You do?"

"Yeah, Tabby's taking me. She wanted to be there for my first treatment. You should probably come too, of course."

"Of course."

"I'm a little nervous about it. They're going to stick a needle in my eyes."

Bodie glanced up at her. "Really? That doesn't sound like fun."

Alora dropped her gaze to the countertop and traced an imaginary pattern with her fingertip. "None of this is fun."

Bodie stopped kneading and looked at her for a long moment. She felt for her, could see the stark sadness on her face and in her gaze. "I'm so sorry, Alora."

"Don't be. Just—" She looked up and plastered on a smile. "Don't feel sorry for me, okay? I'm fine and I will be fine."

Bodie lifted the wad of dough and set it in the mixing bowl to cover with cling wrap. "You ready for some breakfast?"

But Alora shook her head. "I'm not hungry this morning."

"You sure?"

"Maybe later."

Bodie checked the time. "When is your appointment?"

"Early. I should probably start getting ready."

Bodie felt heat rush to her face. "Do you—need help?"

Alora pinned her with a stare. "More than likely."

Bodie forced a swallow, once again recalling her nude, wet body. "Okay."

Alora grinned, as if she could read her thoughts. "Don't worry, I think I can manage the shower on my own. But you can get everything else ready for me and wait in the bedroom while I bathe."

Bodie nodded.

Alora slid off the stool and winced as she put weight on her foot. "Come to think of it, I might need help with the shower after all. My damn foot is killing me."

Bodie hurried to her side, all thoughts of anything else vanishing in an instant. She carefully cupped her elbow to help her walk. "Whatever you need, I'm right here."

"Thanks, Bodie. I'm…glad you're here."

Bodie led her down the hallway, hoping that she would continue to feel that way by the end of the week.

CHAPTER THIRTEEN

"It will be okay," Tabby said, squeezing Alora's hand as they sat in the waiting area at the Mayo Clinic.

"I'm getting deja vu," Alora said. "So, please, stop."

"Sorry. Just trying to comfort you."

Alora rubbed her temple and eyed Bodie, who sat quietly across from them. She wished she could be that calm. But something about having a needle stuck in your damn eye prevented that. Funny how that worked.

"I don't want to do this," she whispered, mostly to herself. Tabby heard her.

"It's going to help. You'll see." She clamped her mouth shut. "Sorry."

"You've got to stop saying that."

"I know. My bad."

A medical assistant opened the door, holding a file. "Alora Anders?"

Alora stood and Tabby and Bodie did so along with her, Tabby leading her by the arm. Her foot hurt like hell to walk on, but she was managing. Still, the help was nice.

"I'm sorry, but she needs to come back on her own," the assistant said.

"But she can't see very well and her foot is injured."

"We'll take good care of her and I'll call you back when the treatment is finished."

Tabby released her and she and Bodie fell back as Alora was led through the doorway and down a long hallway. She was brought into a room where they first dilated her eyes and gave her a quick examination. She was taken into another room, this one with a reclining chair where she sat and gripped the armrests. Her heart pounded uncontrollably and by the time her doctor breezed in with a smile, her hands were sweating so badly she had trouble keeping her hold on the chair.

"Ms. Anders, good morning. How are you today?"

"Nervous as hell."

"That's to be expected," he said, sliding onto a stool and snapping on a pair of latex gloves. He rolled closer to her and positioned a tray next to him. The medical assistant from before entered the room and she too snapped on some gloves and moved to stand beside the doctor.

"Just try and relax," the doctor said. "You won't feel any pain and your examination went well."

"How is it possible to not feel any pain? You're going to stick a needle in my eyes."

"I'm going to numb you."

"With what? Another needle?" She imagined the Novocain injection at the dentist's office and cringed.

He chuckled. "No, with eye drops. But first, I'm going to put in these drops to sterilize your eyes. And we're going to wipe around the eyes a little bit, okay?"

She swallowed. "Yeah."

He cleaned her eyes and put in the drops and then placed a device on both her eyes that kept them open. Her heart pounded harder. "This is so you won't blink," he said.

"So I gathered. I feel like I'm in a horror movie."

"It'll all be over before you know it. And by the way, your eyeglasses came in. You can pick those up on your way out."

"My eyeglasses? Right. Forgot about those."

"I think the bifocals and the yellow tinting will really help you to see better."

"I'm sure to be on the cover of magazines with those."

He laughed again. "They're not the most attractive, but they serve their purpose." He moved some things around and asked the assistant for the next container of drops. "Now, these are to numb you."

"Great. Give me plenty." She gripped the armrests tighter.

He put the drops in and made small talk as they readied the syringes. Then, it was time.

"Here we go. Again, you won't feel any pain and I'm going to place the needle down and toward your ear, in the whites of your eyes, okay?"

She swallowed again. "Sure."

She wanted so badly to clench her eyes closed but the devices prevented it. She saw the doctor lean in closer, saw him hovering above her. And then she saw the syringe, coming down toward her. She bit her lip and held her breath. She felt a slight pressure in her eye as he hovered there for a moment and then drew away.

"There. All done with that one."

"That's it?"

"Mm-hm. Didn't hurt, did it?"

"Not at all."

"You ready for the next one?"

"If you must."

He went around to the other eye and did the same there. Again, there was no pain.

"All finished," he said as he handed the syringe to the assistant and tugged off his gloves. "I'll see you in four weeks, Ms. Anders, for your next round."

"What about…the other treatment you suggested?"

"We'll decide that in four weeks. I want to see what this does for you first."

He smiled, shook her limp, sweaty hand, and left the room. The assistant got her cleaned up, provided some oversized plastic sunglasses for her, and went to the door to go call Tabby and Bodie back.

"What about my eyeglasses?" Alora asked. She wasn't exactly thrilled about wearing them, but if they would at all help her see better, she wanted them. After all, she had an important painting to finish.

"I'll grab those for you too."

She left her alone and Alora took in a big breath and exhaled. It was over. She had done it. And it hadn't been so bad. She wondered if the other treatment he'd mentioned was this painless. She decided not to think about it. Maybe she wouldn't need it. *Hopefully,* she wouldn't need it.

Tabby and Bodie led her slowly from the building and out to the front circle drive where she and Bodie waited quietly on the bench for Tabby to bring the car around.

"Are you in pain?" Bodie eventually asked.

"I wasn't at first. But now it's starting to hurt a little."

"Can you notice a difference yet? In your vision?"

"Maybe a little."

"That's good."

"Right now I see floaters, but they said those should disappear in a few days."

"I really hope this helps you."

Alora glanced over at her. "Thanks, I do too."

Tabby pulled the BMW around and Bodie assisted Alora into the front seat. The drive home was mostly quiet, with Alora too tired to say much. She, of course, told Tabby how it went and that she wasn't hurting too badly and Tabby took her at face value and allowed her to rest. When they arrived home, Alora went to her bedroom, stripped out of her shoes and reclined on the bed. The stress and anticipation of the morning had worn her out and she was exhausted. She closed her sore eyes and thought back to earlier in the morning when Bodie had helped her get ready.

Alora had once again disrobed in front of her and Bodie had averted her gaze, helping her as best she could, while being sure not to stare. She'd blushed profusely again too, which Alora found endearing, but mainly the focus had been on getting her safely in and out of the shower with her aching foot. And Bodie had been great, honestly, laying out her clothes and assisting her with dressing when she needed it. All in all, it had been a successful start to the day and she was glad. Now she could finally relax and get a little more sleep. Work, for the time being, would have to wait, as her eyes were still dilated and the floaters still present. Not to mention, the increasing pain.

A knock came from her door just as she was about to drift off and Tabby poked her head in, holding out her cell phone.

"You have a call."

"Tell them I'll call them back."

"I told him you were indisposed but he insisted."

"Who's he?"

"Peter."

"Peter?" She sat up and motioned for the phone. Tabby brought it to her and sank down onto the foot of the bed. She appeared worried and obviously wanted to see what the urgent phone call was about.

Alora pressed the phone to her ear. "Peter, to what do I owe the pleasure?"

"Alora, good morning." His voice sounded clipped and tight. He was obviously distressed.

"Is it? Why don't you tell me what's going on so I can decide for myself?"

He exhaled. "There's no easy way to say this. Alora, the clients you had showing interest in your latest painting have bailed. They're no longer willing to wait and they've moved on."

"What?"

"They've moved on."

"Jesus, we just discussed this yesterday."

"Word is, is that you won't be able to paint any longer."

"Says who?"

"Alora, your diagnosis is getting around and people have done their research. They know the odds that you'll be able to paint again are slim to none. And unfortunately, the buyers caught wind of this after we hung up yesterday."

"Well, fuck them, then. They don't know me." Her voice cracked with emotion. How dare they? How dare they make such an assumption.

"How is it coming along? Any progress?"

"You mean since I last spoke to you *yesterday*?"

He sighed. "People are going to need proof that you're still able to work and produce. Finishing that piece would really go a long way to secure your buyers."

"Well, I—they're just going to have to wait." Tears gnawed at her throat, but she forced them back down. She was not going to cry. She was not. Fuck them and fuck Peter.

"Don't let them wait too long, or I'm afraid you'll find that you have very little interest left at all."

Alora ended the call, unwilling to say goodbye properly.

"What's going on?" Tabby rested her hand on her leg.

Alora closed her eyes, upset and disoriented at the floaters slugging through her vision. "He said I've lost buyers for that painting I'm working on. Said people are aware of my diagnosis and that they fear I won't be able to continue to work."

"What? Well, that's shitty of them." She shook her head. "They don't know you. You'll prove them wrong."

"They don't know me, do they?"

"No, they don't."

"But what if—they're right?" Her voice caved and she covered her face with her hands.

Tabby drew her in for a hug. "Alora, they're not right. They don't know how determined you are, how ambitious."

"But none of that matters if I can't freaking see." She swallowed back more tears and pulled away, searching Tabby's face, wanting, needing her to be correct. But she saw only concern and the determined reassurance of her best friend. "I can't see, Tabby. Not well enough to paint. I mean—I tried with this dark spot and it didn't go well. Like not at all."

"But the treatment. It might help. It's going to help."

"I think it might save what vision I have remaining, but as far as improving my eyesight…I'm not holding my breath."

Tabby held her hand. "Try to have faith, Alora. And think positive."

"Easier said than done when I can't even see to walk."

"What can I do? Anything?"

"You've done plenty. More than enough."

Tabby squeezed her hand. "You want to go back to sleep for a while?"

"I can't sleep now." She swung her legs over the side of the bed to stand.

"What are you going to do?"

"I'm going to try to paint."

"Now?"

"I have to try. I don't have time to wait around anymore."

"Alora—"

"Don't try to stop me, Tabby. I'm determined and I'm going to do it. So just help get me into the studio."

"Okay," she breathed. "But be careful and don't be so hard on yourself."

Alora scoffed and said yet again, "Easier said than done."

CHAPTER FOURTEEN

"Come on," Tabby said, picking up her glass of iced tea with lemon. "Let's go sit on the back patio."

Bodie grabbed her own glass of tea and followed her outside. They sat in the padded lounge chairs and took in the looming presence of Camelback Mountain, while a handful of golfers teed off just below that in the distance.

"Alora asleep?" Bodie asked. She'd seen Alora retreat to her bedroom for a nap, but since then she'd also seen Tabby go to her with her phone to report an urgent call. She wasn't sure what happened after that, but Tabby came back looking upset.

"She's working."

"Working? How is she managing that?"

"Not very easily. But she's determined."

"I hope she doesn't fall again."

"Me too."

Why was she trying to work now of all times? Was it the phone call?

"Is there something going on I should know about?" Bodie asked.

Tabby sipped her tea and lowered her glass. "Alora is having trouble painting. She's been struggling for a while, a few weeks actually, she just didn't tell anyone. And now people are bailing on her, convinced she can no longer produce."

"Oh, no."

"It has her seriously stressed, and Alora, she's not one to admit defeat."

"But…you think she might have to?"

Tabby glanced over at her. "She can't see. And unless this treatment gets rid of that black spot, I don't see how she can continue like she was."

Bodie sipped from her glass and squinted into the sunlight. "She must really be stressed then."

"She's beyond stressed."

"So what will she do if she can't paint?"

Tabby's gaze drifted to the sparkling teal water of the pool. "She's going to have to make some big changes."

"Such as?"

"This house for starters. It's too big and too costly. And there are the cars. She has too many and it's unnecessary. She also has a beach house in Mexico and a cabin up north in Payson. Those will probably have to go."

"And me? Should I go? It would save her quite a bit of money to not have to pay my salary." She didn't want to cause Alora any more trouble than she was already having to deal with. So if she needed to pack up and go, she would, without an argument.

"She needs you, Bodie. Your presence is nonnegotiable."

"But—"

She met her gaze again. "She can't function without someone here. So please don't worry about your job."

Bodie nodded. "Okay."

"But I'm going to have to have a serious talk with her about all of this. And I'm worried that's not going to go well. She's used to a certain lifestyle and she's earned it. But more than that, I think not being able to paint is hurting her the most. It's a shock to her ego. Painting is her whole identity."

A loud thump came from inside the house followed by a strangled scream. They sat up, poised.

Tabby took off into the house and Bodie quickly followed suit. She could hear Alora screaming, wailing. Tabby burst through the door, leaving Bodie at the threshold. She hurried to Alora and threw her arms around her, stopping her mid-motion as she was about to throw a glass jar full of brushes against the wall. She was crying, tears streaming down her face. Canvases were strewn across the room, along with wooden easels and bits of art supplies like brushes and tubes of paint.

"Alora," Tabby whispered, holding her tight. "Shh, I've got you, babe. I've got you."

"I can't do it," she cried. "I can't paint, Tabby." She sank to the floor and Tabby went down with her, still embracing her. "What am I gonna do?"

Bodie swallowed the ball of emotion in her throat as she watched the painful encounter. She knew she was witnessing an extremely vulnerable moment for Alora, so very quietly, she turned and walked away, knowing it would embarrass Alora if she knew she'd seen her at her weakest. She'd only known Alora a very short time, but she knew enough to know how proud she was and she wanted to respect her and her privacy.

She and Tabby had a lot of talking to do, and Bodie wanted to respect that as well. So, she headed into the kitchen and scribbled out a note and grabbed her car keys to leave, giving Tabby and Alora the alone time they desperately needed.

❖

Bodie drove home, telling herself she was checking on the house. But really, what she needed was the safe familiarity of home for a while. So she entered and took a can of off-brand cola from the fridge and headed out to her studio, which was actually just the garage. She lifted the big door and allowed the sunlight to spill in, grateful that there was a nice spring breeze blowing through. It wouldn't be long before the heat was too great to work in the garage and she'd have to work indoors, which meant, she'd do very little work until summer was over. The house, with just two bedrooms, was too small for her to move all her equipment inside, so she usually worked on smaller sculptures during the warmer months, sitting at the worn desk in her bedroom in front of her window. Her mother was gone now of course, leaving her bedroom available as a studio, but Bodie wasn't there yet. She couldn't bring herself to do it.

She stood at the metal storage shelves against the cement blocked wall and ran her hands over some of her previous works. Works she hadn't tried to sell or had yet to give away. She lifted the sculpture of a full-bodied woman, nude and smooth and posed with her arms reaching for the heavens. The figure was wrapped in metal cords, twining their way up and around her body. Bodie had made the piece with her mother in mind, imagining her as the woman, reaching upward, desperate to be free of the metal encasing her, holding her captive. The casing being the cancer and arthritis that had held her back and literally trapped her in her own body. Bodie wiped away an errant tear and carried the figure to her workbench. She sat and reached for her pair of steel cutters. Carefully, and with tears coming that she had to keep wiping away, she snapped the metal cords and pried them loose from the sculpture.

"You're free now, Mom." She smiled, kissed the sculpture, and ran her hands over the clay which was now nicked and rough where the metal had been attached in some places. She took some sandpaper and worked quietly, smoothing over those patches. When she was finished, she took the sculpture into her mother's bedroom, where she set it on the dresser, next to other pieces she'd made her over the years.

She opened the blinds so the sun could shine on the statue and warm her as she reached for the heavens. "Fly high, Mom," she said, gently closing the door behind her.

She trekked back to the garage and began packing up a few supplies to take to Alora's. She knew she didn't have a place to work like she preferred, but she could sit and play around with some clay, forming tiny figurines with her fingers. It was something she'd been doing since childhood and she found great solace in it.

After closing the garage, she went back inside, deposited the bag of supplies on the coffee table, and went to clean out the fridge. She'd given most of the food to her siblings and some friends, knowing she'd never eat it all, but there was still quite a bit left. So she put it down the disposal and washed the remaining dishes. When she was done, she took her bag of clay and sculpting instruments and locked up.

Tabby texted her, asking if she was returning soon, and Bodie answered and drove to the grocery store for more flour, eggs and yeast for baking. She arrived back at Alora's shortly thereafter and found them sitting on the couch with red-rimmed eyes.

"Everything okay?" Bodie asked as she deposited the goods on the kitchen counter and placed the eggs in the fridge.

"Come sit with us," Tabby said.

Bodie sat opposite them and waited. They'd obviously had a heartfelt talk, and she felt so badly for Alora, who appeared heartbroken and defeated. She wouldn't meet Bodie's gaze.

Tabby started. "Alora and I have had a long talk and she's decided on some things." She looked over at her. "Alora?"

Alora cleared her throat and spoke with difficulty. "I've decided to sell the house."

Bodie raised her brow.

Alora continued. "Since I can no longer—paint, I'm going to need to downsize and tighten my purse strings where I can until I figure something else out. And it's better if I start that process now rather than later when I'm in a bind."

"I'm going to help her put the house on the market," Tabby said. "As well as start looking for a new place for her."

"How can I help?" Bodie asked softly. Alora still wouldn't look at her.

"Just do what you can to help Alora around here." Tabby placed a hand on Alora's shoulder. "She needs all the support she can get right now."

"Of course."

"We cleaned up the mess in the studio as well as we could. Fatima will do the rest."

"I'm more than happy to do it," Bodie said.

"Alora still considers her studio to be a private place," Tabby said. "So she prefers that Fatima do it."

Bodie nodded.

Tabby stood. "I've got to run. I've got errands to tend to and kids to pick up from school. You have my number if you need me." She planted a kiss on Alora's cheek and slung her purse over her shoulder. "Try to have a better afternoon," she said to Alora and then strode toward the front door. The chime sounded, letting them know she left.

Alora reclined onto the couch and massaged her brow. "I know what you're thinking, and I can't handle it right now."

"What am I thinking?" Bodie said.

"What a loser I am now that I can't paint."

Bodie felt her eyes widen. "Alora, I'd never, ever, think that."

"Yeah, well, everyone else does, so you might as well think it too."

"No one thinks that, Alora—"

"They do," she snapped. "They're calling me, wanting more work and because I'm—a bit behind—and they now know about my eyes, they're all bailing on me. So it's pretty obvious." She swiped at a tear. "I just want to be left alone."

Alora was devastated and feeling a lot of anger and shame. Her entire world was crumbling and Bodie struggled to find a way to help her. An idea came to her. It was a long shot, but she brought it up just the same.

"Tabby mentioned that you have a beach house in Mexico," she said.

"Yeah, so? I'll be selling that as well."

"Well, what if you didn't? Not right away."

"What are you getting at?"

"What if we took a trip and went to your beach house? You know, to get away for a while? Escape the phone calls, escape all of this?" She motioned at their environment. "I think you need a break, Alora, and putting some distance between you and all of this might really help. You can always sell it when we get back."

"You'd really go with me?"

"Of course."

"But it hasn't even been a week yet. You might want to bail on me too."

"Alora, I'm not going to bail on you. Besides, if you get to be too much, I'll just take a walk on the beach." She smiled.

"It is nice," Alora said. "Really nice."

"Why don't you think it over and talk to Tabby about it?" She stood. "And in the meantime, why don't I heat you up a slice of homemade bread?"

Alora slowly nodded. "Okay."

Bodie headed for the kitchen, praying for all it was worth that she'd managed to give Alora some sort of hope for the near future.

CHAPTER FIFTEEN

"God, I wish I could go with you guys," Tabby said as she helped Bodie finish loading the metallic plum-colored BMW X7 SUV. "I'd give anything for a short vacation trip to the beach."

"So come with," Alora said, tossing a small piece of luggage into the back seat. "David can watch the kids."

"David is helpless without me, you know that."

"Well, David needs to man up. Moms deserve a break every now and again. And you haven't been to the beach house in ages."

"Don't remind me." She lifted the last piece of luggage and closed the hatchback to embrace Alora in a tight hug. "You have a wonderful time, Lor, okay? Don't think about anything back here. I've got it all covered."

"Even Peter?"

"Even Peter."

Alora felt the tension leave her body. "I don't know what I'd do without you, Tabby. You're the greatest friend a girl could ever have."

"Aww, don't get all mushy on me now, you'll make me cry." She kissed her cheek. "Go. Go and have loads of fun and relaxation."

"Call me if you need to. I have the satellite phone." She opened the passenger side door to climb inside.

"I know, but I'm not going to bother you. You're leaving all this behind for a reason, remember?"

Alora gave her a soft smile, blew her a kiss, and pulled the door closed. Bodie climbed in next to her behind the wheel.

"Ready?" She pushed the button to start the car.

"More than ready."

Bodie backed up out of the garage and down the drive, with Tabby waving goodbye.

"I really wish she could come," Alora said, returning the wave.

"I do too. It sounds like she needs to get away."

"She does. But she's totally devoted to her family. Wouldn't leave them for anything in the world."

"Ever?"

"Nope. The couple of times she's been to the beach house, her whole family came as well. Even her mother."

"Wow."

"I asked her if she wanted to bring everyone this time around, just so she'd come with, but she declined, said I needed peace and quiet."

"I hate to say it, but she's right. The peace and quiet will do you a lot of good."

"Let's hope."

"So how far is this drive?"

"Five and a half hours."

"That's not too bad."

"And we have to stop in Ajo to get some ice cream at Dairy Queen. It's a tradition."

Bodie laughed. "I won't object to that."

Alora reclined in her seat. "You okay if I sleep some?"

"Yep."

"Okay then, wake me in Ajo."

❖

After Alora awoke in Ajo and had ice cream with Bodie at a picnic table at the old Dairy Queen, the rest of the drive to the outskirts of Puerto Peñasco went quickly. Bodie was rather talkative, asking all kinds of questions about Mexico and the culture, and

Alora was surprised to learn that she'd never ventured out of the US. It seemed that Bodie had lived a rather quiet and sheltered life, caring for her siblings and her mother, while working full-time to help out since she was sixteen. She only had her passport because she and her sister had planned on taking a short trip to Mexico, to visit a friend near Nogales, but the excursion had to be canceled and they hadn't had a chance to try again.

Alora was glad she got to accompany her on her first quest into Mexico. She reveled at her expressions as they traveled through the main part of Puerto Peñasco, dodging traffic and pulling over to buy trinkets from numerous vendors. They also stopped at a panaderia where they purchased some bread and Mexican pastries and continued toward the beach.

"It's right up here at this gate," Alora said a little over an hour later after she chewed and swallowed a bite of a magdalena.

Bodie slowed at the entrance to the private neighborhood, which was called Playa Blanca, and Alora used a remote to open the gate. They drove through and Bodie took in the beach-side homes. Though it wasn't the most luxurious of areas in the region, the Spanish-style homes were quaint and beautifully painted in varying colors, surrounded in lush vegetation with red-tiled roofs. It was truly a Mexican paradise and Alora had forgotten how much she adored her home there.

"This is incredible," Bodie said.

"Turn right up here. Mine is the last house on the left."

Bodie slowed and pulled into the drive. Alora opened the garage door with the remote and Bodie eased the SUV inside. She climbed out and rounded the vehicle to assist Alora.

At first Alora hesitated, thinking that perhaps she could manage on her own. But then she remembered how long it had been since she'd been to the beach house and she decided to accept the help.

"Thanks," she said as she took Bodie's offered hand. They walked the short distance to the interior door where Bodie used a key to open it, allowing them to step inside. The house was warm as they entered the kitchen, and Alora breathed deep and soaked up her environment. She took in the calico oak flooring and coffee-colored marble countertops. The walls were painted a deep yellow, showing off some of her collectible Mexican art. Bodie was looking around in awe, already having made her way into the open living room where the oak flooring continued and the walls turned to a beautiful mauve, accented with copper antiquities. The furniture was handcrafted and purchased at a local shop just inside town. Alora knew the owner and admired his work greatly.

"That fireplace is just—gorgeous." Bodie was admiring the careful stone work and the rustic oak mantel.

"It is, isn't it? The artist who did that is very talented. She makes all sorts of things out of rock and stone. Wait till you see the back patio and what she did with the grilling area."

"This is just so amazing. I mean, it's not huge like I thought it would be, but it's so beautiful."

"I thought a beach home should be more on the cozy side. Although there are four bedrooms and three baths. But still, I wanted it to feel homey and comfortable and the interior traditionally Mexican."

"Well, you did a fantastic job. And whoa, look at that." She took a step back as she came to the double French doors and saw the view of the ocean.

Alora joined her and unlocked and opened the doors, allowing the cool sea breeze to blow into the room.

"Oh, my gosh, I've never smelled the ocean before," Bodie said, as her eyes drifted closed and she inhaled deeply.

"Never?"

She shook her head.

"Bodie, are you kidding me?"

She opened her eyes. "We never got to go. We were always too busy working and trying to pay the bills."

Alora placed a hand on her shoulder. "I'm so sorry."

Bodie offered a sad smile. "It's okay. We did what we had to do."

Alora saw the sadness overcome her as she stared out at the ocean. She'd missed out on so much and Alora wished she could go back in time and give her all the experiences she missed during her childhood. She'd do anything to help ease that sadness on her face.

"Well, you're here now," Alora said, a little surprised at the powerful empathy she felt for her.

"Yes. And it's wonderful. Thank you for allowing me to come along." She gave her a resolute smile.

"Bodie, I need—I'm happy you're here." Despite the intensity of the feelings she was having for her, she couldn't quite admit that she needed her.

They stood staring out at the sea for a few moments, breathing in the salty air before Alora crossed to the big picture window to draw back the curtains, showing off that view as well.

"You really do have an amazing life, Alora."

Alora hesitated as a sadness came over her as well. "I *did* have an amazing life. But it's disappearing one piece at a time. And soon, this piece too, will be gone."

Bodie looked as though she'd said something wrong. "I'm sorry, I didn't mean—"

"Don't worry about it. You didn't do anything wrong." Alora headed for the hallway, but waited for Bodie to help guide her so she could show her the bedrooms. Alora moved slowly, still limping on her injured foot, careful not to trip. "Bedrooms are back here." Bodie gently cupped her elbow and allowed Alora to show her three of the four bedrooms so she could choose which one she wanted. She showed her the master which also had a pair of French doors and was adorned in more Mexican art, wrought iron fixtures, and an intricate and colorful stained glass window. After Bodie openly appraised the room, she decided to sleep in the one directly across the hall.

"Just in case you need me," she said.

Alora agreed and Bodie brought in the luggage. She led Alora around and they continued to open up the house. They also ran the taps, ensuring they worked, and checked on the electricity.

"Everything good?" Bodie asked as she carried Alora's luggage into the master bedroom.

"Mm-hm. Seems so." Alora was lost in the billowing curtains as the sea breeze toyed with them. But she finally tore her gaze away and went to the bed to begin unpacking.

"Would you like some help?"

"I think I've got it." She wanted to do as much as she could herself. She hoped Bodie understood that without her having to explain.

Bodie watched her, hesitating. "Um, what about food?"

"Oh, that reminds me. I order it. Someone does the shopping for me and delivers it."

"Wow, that's nice."

"I never thought I'd be so grateful to have it," Alora said. "Now that I'm—unable to see very well."

"I could always go back into town and do it if you prefer," Bodie said.

"It's okay, it's easier this way. Why don't you make a list of what you'd like though? And I'll call it in."

"Sure."

Bodie left her and Alora continued to unpack and put her things away in the bureau drawers. She started in on her toiletries and gathered fresh sheets from the linen closet to make her bed. She also set some out for Bodie and her bed.

It took her longer than she'd expected to make her bed. It was more difficult with her impaired vision, but she managed to do it all the same and she was more than proud of herself. She walked back into the kitchen with a smile, feeling more confident in moving around on her own now, and found Bodie sitting at the table, making the grocery list. She read off what she had so far and Alora added to it. Alora placed the call to the caregiver of the house, who went by the name Tia, who provided the delivery service. She sounded thrilled to hear from Alora and said she'd have the groceries to her in a couple of hours.

Alora grabbed two bottles of Coke out of the box with the baked goods and handed one to Bodie. "Want to sit outside?"

"Absolutely."

They wandered out onto the vast back patio which was accented in more lush vegetation, as well as furniture, and Alora told Bodie where to retrieve the cushions for the chairs. They'd been wrapped in plastic and placed in a small shed. Bodie got them, shook them out, and arranged them on the wrought iron lounges where she and Alora sat to look out at the sea.

"What a gorgeous sight," Bodie said. "The sand is so white, it looks like powder."

"Mm, that's why they called it Playa Blanca. It means white beach."

"Really? Gosh, I can believe it. And the water. It's so blue. But that word doesn't really do it justice, does it? It just looks so massive and cool and refreshing. Is it cold?"

"Yes."

"I can't wait to feel it."

"Go ahead," Alora said. "It feels wonderful. Especially on a hot day in the middle of summer. Although the sand gets so hot it burns your feet."

"No kidding?"

"Mm-hm."

"Glad it's not summer."

"You and me both."

"You really don't mind if I head down to the water?"

"Of course not."

"Do you not want to go?"

"I need to rest my foot for a while." While her foot was getting better, she still needed to rest it from time to time after walking on it.

Bodie swung her legs off the lounge and stood. She looked toward the ocean and grinned like an excited child. Then she took off at a trot and Alora watched her go, increasing her speed the closer she got to the water. When she reached it, she waded right in up to her knees and shouted with glee as she raised her arms in the air.

Alora laughed, truly moved at the sight. Bodie was adorable in her excitement and Alora was so happy for her. So thrilled to be able to witness her joy in this moment. But as she was watching her experience the ocean for the first time, her heart suddenly skipped a beat as Bodie's incredible beauty overtook her once again. She looked like a goddess in the water with her curvy, glistening body and rich, dark hair. Alora had to close her eyes for a second to calm herself.

She forced herself to think of the first time she'd been in the sea. It had been when she'd first come to Mexico to vacation after one of her first paintings sold. She'd fallen in love with the ocean and with Mexico and had decided, a few years later, after she'd made considerably more money, to purchase a house there.

Bodie turned and waved to her as she continued to splash and push through the water, soaking her shorts. Alora waved and smiled, trying to keep her attraction at bay. She hoped Bodie could make some good memories there. She sounded like she deserved it. Because, Bodie, like her, had seemed to have had a bit of a rough time in life.

Alora, for many years now, had thought that her rough times were behind her, but it seemed that they weren't. Now a new storm was brewing on the horizon and so far the initial rainfall had been damn near catastrophic. She wondered though, just what kind of weather still lay ahead.

CHAPTER SIXTEEN

"Do you want your glasses?" Bodie asked as she stood hugging herself, dripping with sea water. Her shorts and the lower half of her T-shirt were soaked through, and as much fun as she'd had frolicking in the ocean, she was sure paying the price now with the cool March breeze chilling her to the bone. At the moment, she was somewhat grateful however, because seeing Alora lounging in the sun with her shapely exposed legs in her short shorts was stirring things in her she long thought dormant.

"No thanks," Alora said from her position in the lounge. She was squinting up at Bodie while shading her brow. Her staples had been removed before they'd left and she had a thin pink scar near her hairline. "You got really wet, didn't you?"

Bodie looked down at herself. "Yeah. But it felt good."

Alora was studying her closely. Then she cleared her throat and glanced away as if embarrassed. "You—uh, should probably dry off and change."

"I will. You sure you don't want your eyeglasses? You at least need your sunglasses, don't you? To protect you from the UV rays? I can get them and bring them back out after I change."

"I'm sure."

Bodie frowned, concerned that Alora had yet to wear either of her new pairs of glasses. She'd seemed eager to try them out when she'd first received them, but once she saw herself in them, she'd promptly taken them off and put them away in her purse, where, to

Bodie's knowledge, they had remained. She hadn't even tried the tinted bifocal pair when she'd been struggling to read the grocery list.

"Can I get you anything else?" *Can I do anything to help take my mind off how tantalizing you look in the sunshine with the sea breeze running its fingers through your hair?*

Alora shook her head and positioned herself to stand. "Tia should be here soon. I might as well come inside." Bodie helped her to her feet and they made the walk back through the open French doors. Bodie went to change, leaving Alora in the living room. When she returned, she found Alora on the couch, rubbing her temple and grimacing. For a split second, Bodie's heart lurched.

"Headache?" She couldn't stand to see her in pain. Regardless of how slight.

"Mm."

"Want some Advil?"

"If you don't mind. There's a bottle in my purse."

Bodie got the Advil and while she was at it, grabbed her tinted bifocal eyeglass case as well. She presented both to Alora, who just stared up at her. "What's this?"

"What you requested."

"I don't recall asking for my glasses. In fact, I specifically remember declining them."

"I thought, seeing as how you now have a headache, that you might've changed your mind."

"Well, I haven't." She took the bottle of painkillers but refused the glasses.

Bodie remained where she was, offering the case to her. "Alora, I think you should try them. I think it will help with the headaches. Maybe even prevent them."

"Oh, I see. You're suddenly an expert."

"No, it's just common sense."

"Oh, so now I don't have common sense?"

"That's not what I'm saying." She pushed out a breath. "What is wrong? Has something happened since I went down to the water?" Her mood had drastically changed.

"Yes, I have a headache."

"Probably because you struggled to read the grocery list and then you sat in the sun without any protection for your eyes."

Alora again rubbed her temple. "Can you just stop? Please? My head is killing me and I'm not in the mood to argue with you."

Bodie set the glasses case on the table next to her. "Just please try them." She started to walk away. "And if it's any consolation, I think you look great in them." Bodie believed she'd look good in anything. If only she'd believe it too.

Alora glanced up at her. "I look ridiculous."

"You don't actually. You look studious. Distinguished." She wanted to add sexy, but she refrained. "But hey, what do I know?" She returned to the kitchen to grab them some more Coke, which she'd placed in the fridge. But outside, through the kitchen window above the sink, she saw a faded teal Ford Fiesta pull up and park. A plump, dark-haired woman emerged, along with a lanky teenaged boy. They opened the hatch and began unloading bags of groceries.

"Tia is here," Bodie said as she opened the door to let them inside.

Alora made her way to the door. She reached it just as Tia and the boy did.

"Tia," Alora said with a grand smile. "So good to see you."

"Alora, mi amiga. Look at you!" She shifted the bags to her left hand and embraced Alora with the right. "Aye, I missed you."

"I've missed you too," Alora said, holding her tight. They drew apart and Alora looked at the boy. "And, Miguel, you've gotten so tall!" She touched his face causing the boy to blush.

"Hola, miss. How are you?"

"I'm okay," Alora said, with a wistful smile. "I'm okay."

"Yeah?" Tia grazed her arm. "You are sad, no?"

Alora forced a bigger smile. "No, don't be silly. Come in, come in." She ushered them inside and Bodie closed the door. Alora stood next to her as Tia and Miguel placed the groceries on the countertop.

"Tia, Miguel, this is, Bodie. She's, er, my assistant."

"Oh," Tia said, offering her hand. "Tia."

"Nice to meet you," Bodie said, shaking it.

Tia slugged Miguel in the arm. "And this is Miguel. My son."

Miguel winced but promptly offered his hand in greeting as well. Bodie took it and the four of them stood awkwardly for a moment before Tia spoke.

"There are more groceries in the car." She and Miguel moved toward the door. Bodie went with them.

"No, no," Tia said. "We can get them." She held her hand out, as if to stop Bodie's progression. She smiled. "It is our pleasure."

Bodie remained where she was and watched as they brought in the rest of the groceries. She felt like a heel allowing them to do all the work when she was perfectly capable of helping. But Tia and Miguel seemed happy to do it.

Alora limped to her purse and Tia rushed to her, concern etched on her face. "Aye, Alora, what is wrong? You hurt?"

"I broke my toe. No big deal." She unzipped her purse and pulled out her wallet.

Tia wasn't convinced, kneeling to examine her bare foot.

She hissed. "It looks painful, no?"

"It's not too bad. Not now anyway."

Bodie watched the exchange quietly. It was obvious that Tia was unaware of Alora's vision problem, and she wondered why she hadn't told her. They were in Mexico now, away from much of civilization. Wouldn't it be smart to let Tia know in case something happened and, God forbid, they needed help?

"You look skinny," Tia said as she rose and gripped her upper arm. "Too skinny."

"Oh, I'm fine," Alora said, counting out some cash. She handed it over with, Bodie noticed, a considerable tip included.

Tia took the money slowly, holding her gaze. "Gracias, mi amiga. You sure you okay?"

"Just fine."

Tia shoved the money in her pocket and shrugged. "Okay. You need anything else?"

"Mama, the water," Miguel said. "I'll get it."

"Ah, sí."

Miguel went outside and carried in three big cases of bottled water.

"You call if you need anything else," Tia said, still looking overly concerned.

"I will."

Tia embraced her again. Then she embraced Bodie, much to her surprise. "Welcome," she said with a smile.

"Thank you." Bodie returned the hug, moved by her generous show of affection.

"Adios," she said as she walked out the door, followed by Miguel who waved.

"Adios," Alora said. She and Bodie stood at the door and waved as they drove away.

"They sure are nice," Bodie said as they closed the door behind them to unpack the groceries.

"They're very nice."

"So she's the one who looks after the house when you're not here?"

"Mm-hm. She looks after several of the homes here. She's very dependable."

"Where does she live?"

"In a small village not far from here."

"You ever been there?"

"Once." Alora said, holding a carton of eggs. "What would you like for dinner?"

Bodie stared at her, confused as to why she'd changed the subject. "I don't know, I haven't really given it much thought. How about you?"

"I think I'd like some tacos."

"Sure. I can whip that up."

"With the fresh fish?" She pointed to one of the bags.

Bodie nodded. "Sure."

"Can you make a good sauce for them as well?"

Bodie smiled. "Yes." She cocked her head. "But only if you help me."

Alora's face fell. "Help you? But I—"

"I know you can't help like you'd like to. But I can give you a few small things to do." She wanted to help build her confidence any way she could. Alora needed that and Bodie was intent on making that happen.

"But what if I can't do them?" She seemed almost panicked, her confidence completely shot. She really was in a bad way and it pained Bodie to witness it.

Bodie retrieved the glasses case from the end table. She brought it to her. "These might make things a lot easier."

Alora stared at the case for a long moment, and then slowly, she took it. She opened it and plucked out the vintage-style yellow tinted glasses.

"Try them," Bodie gently prompted her.

Alora closed her eyes and slid them on. When she opened her eyes, she looked at Bodie like a scared little rabbit.

"You look great," Bodie said, meaning it. The retro turtle shell frames only seemed to amplify her beautiful eyes and accentuate the lines of her cheek bones.

"You sure?"

"Absolutely."

"I don't look—funny?"

"Not at all."

Bodie held out the grocery list. "Can you read this better now?"

Alora took the list and briefly scanned it. She lowered it. "Yes."

Bodie grinned. "That's fantastic, Alora."

Alora smiled, though it appeared bashful. Like she was embarrassed at how she'd refused to even try the glasses to begin with. Bodie kept smiling at her, but dropped the subject and moved on, wanting to remain positive.

"How about we get started on those fish tacos?"

"Yes, please. I'm getting hungry."

She and Bodie put away the rest of the groceries and began making the fish, which Bodie first cleaned, rinsed and chopped into two-inch fingers. Then she measured out the sour cream, siracha, lime juice, and garlic powder for the sauce and had Alora whisk it all together. When she finished, Bodie set it in the freezer to chill and got started on a pan searing the fish with lime juice, olive oil, and taco seasoning. Bodie made a quick pico de gallo while Alora heated the tortillas in a pan. They set the table next and brought everything over. Bodie sat down, watching as Alora grabbed a couple of cool beers along with the remaining half of a lime.

"It wouldn't be right to have fish tacos without lime and beer," she said as she settled in across from Bodie.

"You couldn't be more right if you tried."

Bodie opened the beers and they both began making their own tacos. Bodie was amazed at how much better Alora was doing with the glasses. She was moving quicker and more confidently, and making fewer errors in judgment. The lenses really seemed to be helping a lot.

Alora caught her staring. "What?"

Bodie smiled. *You're really breathtaking.* "Nothing."

"Liar."

"I'm just impressed at how well you're doing."

"And you're dying to say 'I told you so,' aren't you?"

"I would never."

"Liar."

Bodie laughed and sipped her beer. "Since I promised to always be honest, I'll just say that they seem to be helping you out quite a bit."

"Maybe." She forked some fish into her tortilla.

"Won't admit it, eh?"

"I said maybe." She smirked.

Bodie tipped her beer at her. "Good enough." She waited as Alora finished making her taco to take a bite. She chewed slowly, briefly closing her eyes.

"Well?" Bodie asked. "How is it?"

"Mm. Magnifico," she said, opening her eyes.

"Really?" Bodie began constructing her own taco, then took a small bite. "It is pretty damn good."

"The sauce is killer. Great job, Bodie."

"Thanks. And thanks for your help. You're an excellent sous chef."

Alora smiled and tipped her beer back at her. "Thank you."

"Think you might want to help out some more?"

"Anytime."

"Wonderful, I'll wake you at dawn to get started on breakfast."

Alora froze, mid drink. "Dawn?"

Bodie grinned. "You like to rise early, yes?"

"Er, sure, I guess."

"Then dawn it is. We'll make pancakes."

"About the whole early morning thing."

"Yes?"

"I don't usually rise so early here at the beach."

"No?"

"No."

"Well, when do you want to get up then?"

"I don't know. Nine?"

Bodie raised an eyebrow. "Nine? Okay. We cook at nine."

"Why are you grinning again?"

"I just like hearing that you plan on relaxing some while you're here." *Because you deserve to.* "I thought for sure you'd insist on sticking to your schedule."

"What's the point? I can't work." She tilted her head. "Unless… maybe the glasses could help me." Hope filled her eyes. "Yes. They just might." Alora pushed away from the table.

"Where are you going?"

"I need to see if I have the right supplies. I want to try to paint."

"What, now?"

"No time like the present."

"What about dinner?"

"Save it. I'll eat later."

"Alora—"

But she'd already headed off toward the bedrooms, leaving Bodie alone at the table, worried about what might happen if the glasses didn't help.

CHAPTER SEVENTEEN

She was sleeping peacefully, finally. Someplace quiet and nearly black with night. She wished she could say it was a safe place, but she wasn't sure. Not yet. But she had locked the door to help ensure that it would be. Now back to the sleep. Yes. Sleep. Beautiful peaceful sleep. It had been so long since she'd slept well. Too long. She was so exhausted. But now she could sleep. Sleep, sleep, sleep.

A knock came from the door. She didn't open her eyes. She'd probably just imagined it. But it came again. This time louder. Her name was called. She opened her eyes as her heart began to pound. More knocks. Aggressive and obtrusive. Her name being shouted. The door knob twists. She sat straight up.

Alora awoke and blinked into the bright light. She focused and realized she was on the floor. The hard, uncomfortable floor with a drop cloth as a covering. She pushed herself up as knocking sounded from the door. It caused her to jerk as she recalled her dream.

"Alora?"

It was Bodie.

"Just a second."

She stood, got her bearings, and went to the door. She opened it and rubbed the sleep from her eyes.

"I just wanted to make sure you were okay. It's after midnight."

"Is it?"

"Yes, and you never came back to finish your dinner."

Alora opened the door further and motioned with her hand toward the easel standing in the center of the room on top of the drop cloth. "I've been working."

Bodie glanced at the painting but quickly averted her gaze. Alora reached for her hand. "Well, what do you think?" She tugged on her and encouraged her to step into the room.

Bodie hesitated. "You want me to look?"

"Yes."

"Are you sure?"

"Yes, Bodie. I need you to look at this one. Give me your honest opinion."

Bodie stepped carefully up to the painting which was lit with two standing, angled lights. It was a smaller canvas, one Alora had lying around, and it wasn't like her usual work, but it was something. The glasses, which she grabbed off the table and slid back onto her head, had helped, along with the magnifying pair, though she still had the dark spot she'd had to work around. Nevertheless she'd painted. And she was anxious to know if it was any good.

Bodie stood before the artwork quietly. "Alora, it's beautiful."

"Forget beautiful, is it any good?"

Bodie stammered. "I don't know anything about painting, but yes, I think it's wonderful."

Alora's heart lifted. It was what she'd been hoping to hear. "I'll send it off to Peter."

"Peter? Really? I thought you'd wanted to take a break from all of that?"

"If this painting is good, then it's important he see it."

A look of uncertainty and panic came over Bodie. "Alora—I don't know paintings—you shouldn't take my word for it."

"There's only one way to find out and that's to send it off." She began cleaning her supplies. "All I need is one buyer to be interested and hopefully more will follow. But…" She paused and looked at the painting. She still couldn't see the painting in its entirety, but she did think it was better than the last painting she'd completed.

Bodie came to stand next to her at the table where she kept her supplies. "Would you like some help?"

Alora almost declined, but realizing just how tired she was, agreed. "Thank you, yes." They worked quietly together until the task was complete. Then they headed for the kitchen.

"Would you like a sandwich or something?" Bodie asked.

"No, I just want some juice, then I'm off to bed."

Bodie poured her a glass of orange juice and watched quietly as she downed it. Her thirst was stronger than she'd originally thought. She had a second glass and sighed. "You're not going to wake me at dawn, right?"

Bodie laughed. "No."

"Thank God." She turned to walk away. "Night, Bodie."

"Good night, Alora."

She moved slowly toward her bedroom with a smile. She'd painted. Dipped her line back into the water. Now she just had to wait and see if anyone would bite.

❖

The next morning Alora awoke feeling groggy but positive. She glanced at the clock, saw it was just past nine, and rose to walk into the bathroom. After she relieved herself and brushed her teeth, she dressed and made her way toward the kitchen where she could already smell the coffee. Bodie was standing at the island, steaming mug in hand. She appeared to have already showered, her dark hair slicked back and wet. Alora wondered if she smelled like shampoo and soap and she stood next to her to find out.

"You smell nice," Alora heard herself saying.

Bodie seemed as surprised as she was at the statement. "Thanks."

Alora decided to change the subject before her mind ran amok with newly awakening desire. "Did you sleep well?"

"I did."

"There's something about the sound of the ocean at night that just lulls you right to sleep."

"It's rhythmic," Bodie said. "And peaceful."

"Mm." But Alora's dream from the night before came to mind and she grew quiet. Bodie seemed to notice.

"You okay?"

"Hm? Yes. Just haven't completely woken up yet."

"Well, how about some breakfast? You up for those pancakes? You've got to be hungry."

But Alora wasn't feeling it. Her mind was still on her dream. Why had she dreamt about that place after so long?

"I think I just want some eggs," she eventually said. "And a cup of coffee."

"Sure." Bodie poured her a mug full and got started on the eggs. Alora sat and watched, knowing she had the ability to help, but she was too caught up in the sludgy swamp of the dream to offer. She sipped her coffee, hoping it would wake her and she could shake the dreary feeling.

"I'm going to paint some more today," she said. "So that means we need to run into town."

Bodie stood stirring the eggs in the pan, her back to her. "You sure?"

"About what? The painting or the trip to town?"

"The painting."

"Yes, why?"

"I thought you might want to relax a bit after last night. And maybe…"

"Maybe…?"

"Wait to hear from Peter."

"Ah, I see." She pushed away her coffee. "You think the painting sucks."

Bodie stiffened and removed the pan from the burner to dump the eggs onto a plate. "No, of course not. I told you, it's beautiful. I just don't know what he's looking for. And I'm no art critic."

"But you're afraid he's not going to like it."

"No, Alora. But it sounds like maybe you are." She slid her the plate, but Alora ignored it, suddenly feeling sick.

She met Bodie's gaze, considered arguing, but knew it was pointless. Bodie was seeing right through her. "I am," she finally breathed.

"So, wait until we're back home to even show him," Bodie said, leaning on her elbows across from her.

"I can't. If there's even a chance that someone might be interested, I need to know now, so I can continue working."

Bodie said nothing, just sipped her coffee. But there was obviously something on her mind.

"What?" Alora asked.

"Nothing."

"No, tell me. Please."

"If I were you, I'd just try to relax until I heard from Peter."

Alora laughed softly. "If only I could, Bodie, if only I could."

"You're worried about your finances."

"That's the understatement of the year."

"I get it."

"So you'll go into town with me? I'd really like to get some supplies."

"Of course."

Alora gave her a smile. Bodie really was very supportive. And so very kind. It was nice to have her around, especially right now when she was feeling so anxious about the painting. Alora took a bite of her eggs. Though she'd felt sick to her stomach, the eggs were good, and they stimulated her dormant appetite. She ate the rest in silence and went off to shower and dress. Bodie helped her while keeping her gaze averted as much as she could, and by setting out her clothes and towels.

When she was ready, they locked up to head into town. Bodie drove and Alora sat quietly, wearing her wraparound sunglasses.

"You don't want to have the supplies delivered?" Bodie asked.

"I need to see what all they have."

"Oh. You've never been?"

"I've always brought my own supplies." She adjusted the air vent, needing more of the cool air. "They may not even have what I need. It's just a craft store, but I'm betting most of it is just Mexican crafts and artifacts rather than actual supplies."

"What are you going to do if that's the case?"

"I'm not sure. I guess I could have Tabby send me some stuff, but I know that will be a big argument, seeing as how she wants me to relax. Plus, it will take a while to get here. I might just have to wait."

They continued into town and Bodie followed her directions. She seemed to know her way around rather well and she knew exactly where to find the craft store. They parked in front of the low one-story building adorned by hanging sombreros, T-shirts, and painted multicolored statues of owls and seahorses.

"I've always wanted to go in here, but never really got the chance." Tabby's kids always wanted to go to the more kid friendly shops where they could get their various trinkets. And her mother, well, she always wanted the leather goods.

They entered the open shop which was crammed full of homemade goods. The shopkeep welcomed them with a toothy smile and tugged on his straw cowboy hat in greeting. Alora spoke to him in Spanish and he led them to the back of the store where three shelves held some tubes of paint, paintbrushes, and a small stack of canvases.

Alora thanked him and sighed. "Well, it's not much. But at least they have canvases. And…" she said as she picked up a few tubes of paint after sliding on her magnifying glasses. "They have some colors I don't have."

She selected the ones she wanted, inspected the brushes briefly but put them back, and then looked to Bodie. "Would you mind grabbing the canvases?"

"Sure. Which ones?"

"All of them."

Bodie opened her mouth to speak but seemed to change her mind. She merely gave a nod and hoisted up the canvases to carry to the front of the store where Alora promptly paid and gave the man a nice tip. She spoke to him some more in Spanish, asking him if he planned on ordering anything more in the way of supplies. He said he could and said they should arrive in a week. Alora thanked him and they left the store.

"Do you want to look around at anything else?" Alora asked Bodie after they had loaded the supplies into the car. "While we're here?"

Bodie glanced up and down the row of shops, her eyes lighting up at all the diverse and colorful merchandise. "But what about your foot?"

"It's not hurting."

"And your eyes?"

Alora slipped on her sunglasses. "I'll manage."

Bodie smiled. "Sure, if you're really okay with it. I'd love to look around."

Alora slid her hand into Bodie's arm, happy to join her as she did a little exploring. Besides, if she was going to continue to paint, a little time spent doing something else might do her some good. "Lead the way then, Captain."

CHAPTER EIGHTEEN

Bodie sat in the lounge chair overlooking the churning sea while playing with some clay, forming a small wizard with a long, pointed hat and a long, hanging beard. She paused as she studied that beard and dipped her fingertips in the bowl of water sitting next to her to wet and smooth out the clay so she could continue working it. She lifted a potter's needle and once again etched in the details of the hair on the beard.

She turned her head as she heard someone approach from behind.

"Whatcha doing?" It was Alora and she was standing with her arms crossed, gazing down at Bodie and her tiny figurine.

"Just playing around with some clay."

"Can I see?"

Bodie held it up for her inspection. "It's still wet and it's not finished."

"What is that, a little gnome?"

"A wizard."

"Can I…hold it?"

"You can't, not yet. But…" Bodie reached over for the one she'd finished earlier. This wizard had a scepter and a sweeping robe. She'd decided to make a series of them, each one a little different than the last. "You can hold this one." Bodie handed it to her and Alora took it gently and began lightly running her fingertips over it.

“This is incredible, Bodie.” She removed her tinted bifocals and slid on her magnifiers, which she wore around her neck. “Look at all those little details. You even put in the tiny stars on the hat. And his hair. You’re very good at this.”

“Thanks. I enjoy doing it. Helps me decompress.”

“Is this what you do, when you say you sculpt? Make these little statues?”

“I mostly work on larger pieces. This I just do for fun, to kill time and, like I said, to decompress.”

She met Bodie’s gaze and lowered the glasses to hang on her chest. “Do you think I could try?”

Bodie straightened, surprised. “Of course. But I thought you were painting.” She’d been in her makeshift studio since well after breakfast, door closed and radio tuned to a Mexican pop station. Bodie hadn’t heard a peep out of her for hours and it had been like that the last few days, with Alora painting for long stretches only to join her for lunch and dinner, anxious to talk about her work.

She’d sent the first painting off a few days before and, as far as Bodie knew, she still hadn’t heard anything back from Peter. Bodie wasn’t sure how he was going to contact her, but she’d assumed she’d included the number to her satellite phone in with the painting. Bodie had her cell phone, of course, but service was tricky this far out from town.

“I’m done for the day,” Alora said. “I’m out of a color I need to continue and, well, my eyes hurt.”

She sat down next to Bodie and gazed at the ocean. Bodie wanted to say that what she should be doing was spending time enjoying that view, but she refrained. Alora knew what she was doing with the painting. Bodie just hoped it ended up being worthwhile.

Bodie sat up and reopened the package of clay. She tore off a good-sized chunk for Alora. “Here you go. Create away.” She pointed at the bowl of water. “Dip your fingers in the water to keep the clay moist as you work.”

Alora immediately began to play with the hunk of clay, leaning forward, magnifying lenses on. She even stuck her tongue out in concentration. "I like the way it feels, but I don't know what to make."

"It's supposed to be relaxing," Bodie said. "So it might help if you recline and take some deep breaths and then just let your mind go and let your hands lead the way."

Alora looked at her like she was crazy. "I don't know if I can do that. I really need to concentrate if I'm going to make something as good as what you did."

Bodie eased back and continued working on her wizard. "It's not a competition."

"Maybe not, but I always need to do my best."

Was this why she was always so intense with everything? Because she couldn't just relax and enjoy the process?

"Then maybe this isn't for you."

Alora grew quiet. She pushed out a long breath and reclined. "Okay, I'll try it your way." She worked her clay into a ball and then began to create something that looked like a face. "I still feel like I don't know what I'm doing."

"You're relaxing and creating. Just let it flow." Bodie paused in her own creating to follow her own advice. She inhaled the salty air and focused on the breeze toying with her hair. The day was cool and slightly overcast, with the sun peeking out to say hello only every once in a while. As if it too were trying to relax.

But next to her, Alora continued to struggle, groaning in frustration as she worked. Bodie glanced at her hunk of clay, which was now resembling more of a detailed face. It really wasn't bad considering her limited vision and the fact that it was her first time playing with the clay. But she didn't seem to be enjoying herself.

"How do I detail the eyes and make the hair like you did?"

"Use the tools next to you."

Alora ran her fingers across the tools and paused. "Are those toothpicks?"

"They work better than you'd expect."

Alora reached for one. With her tongue once again touching her upper lip, she began to etch in the eyes and hair. She worked quietly for a while and Bodie almost forgot she was even sitting next to her, save for the occasional grunts and groans of frustration. At last, she stopped, slid off her magnifiers, and put on her tinted bifocals. She held the piece at arm's length to examine it.

"What do you think?"

Bodie lowered her wizard and examined the face. The brow, nose, and jaw appeared well-crafted and proportionate, and the mouth had a wicked, toothy grin. The hair was long and detailed, along with a goatee and a pair of bushy eyebrows. Bodie smiled. "I think you just found yourself a new pastime. It's terrific, Alora. Very nicely done."

But Alora scrunched up her face. "I don't know. I think it's… mediocre at best. It's not nearly as good as your wizards."

"Like I said, it's not a competition. Just look at it for what it is. It's a face. A very ornate and finely detailed face. It's great."

"Meh." She set it on the table and leaned back to watch the waves once again, slipping on her sunglasses. "I don't even know why I tried. My eyes are killing me and I really don't know what I'm doing. Sculpting is your thing, not mine."

"Sculpting isn't biased. Anyone can do it. And, again, this type of work, just sitting here playing with some clay, it's supposed to be relaxing. Fun even."

"Well, I certainly wouldn't call that fun."

"Because you were too worried about everything being perfect."

"Excuse me?"

Bodie set her own wizard on the table and finished off her now lukewarm bottle of water. "You're a perfectionist."

Alora started to argue but seemed to change her mind. She crossed her arms over her chest. "I pride myself on my work. What's wrong with that?"

"Nothing. Unless you're trying to relax and let the creative juices flow, like we're doing here."

"Yeah, well, maybe you're right. Maybe this isn't for me."

Bodie dug in the small cooler sitting in the sand and plucked out a chilled bottle of water. She handed it to Alora who unscrewed the lid and took a hearty sip after thanking her.

Bodie opened a cold one for herself. "You ever try to just relax and paint? You know, without concentrating so hard?"

Alora laughed. "Are you kidding?"

Bodie said nothing, just sipped her water.

"You're serious?" She shook her head in disbelief. "No, I haven't."

"Why not?"

"Because it's my work, that's why. I take it very, very seriously."

Again, Bodie said nothing, allowing that information to process.

"Why do you ask?"

"Just curious."

Alora faced her. "No, it's more than that. You're thinking something. Tell me what it is."

Bodie continued to look out at the crashing waves, lost in their comforting, unrelenting rhythm. "I'm wondering if you could paint easier if you just tried to relax while doing it. You know, not try to control it so much."

"That's not the way I work."

"I know."

"But you think it should be."

"It might be worth a shot." *I'm trying to help. I hate seeing you struggle. Hate seeing you so upset and anxious.*

The sun came out from behind a set of clouds and warmed Bodie's skin. She closed her eyes and allowed her bones to melt into the lounge. It felt wonderful, even if Alora's current demeanor wasn't anywhere close to hers. "Like right now," Bodie said. "You're busy overthinking and worrying when what you should be doing is enjoying the environment around you. Let it seep in and soothe you."

"I—" but she stopped. "We're having a conversation."

"One you're getting all worked up about."

"Because you—you're—"

"Right?"

"Infuriating."

She stood and nearly lost her balance. Bodie reached out and steadied her, but she quickly swatted her away before turning to walk back into the house. Bodie didn't bother to watch her go, but instead sat and relished the warm sunshine. Alora was no doubt going back inside to work, despite her eye pain. The woman was incorrigible and Bodie wondered if she'd ever be able to talk some sense into her. She sensed that there was pain there. Deep pain. But she wasn't sure what it stemmed from, and she seriously doubted that Alora would ever want to talk about it.

So she remained where she was until the sun decided to go back behind the clouds. She gathered the cooler and the clay and numerous tools and brought those inside, before going back out to retrieve the figurines. She set them on the fireplace mantel to finish drying, along with Alora's clay face. She wasn't going to allow her to just get rid of it. She liked it and wanted to keep it safe, hoping against hope, that Alora would someday appreciate it for what it was and want to hang on to it.

"Decided to come in?" Alora said, standing between the kitchen and living room.

"It got cold." Bodie positioned the figurines carefully.

Alora came closer and made a noise of disapproval. "I don't know why you saved that ugly thing," she said, referring to hers.

"I like it."

"Why?"

Bodie looked at her. "Because it's good and because you made it."

The comment seemed to surprise her. Bodie continued. "And because it's the first thing you made with clay. Someday you might appreciate that."

Alora studied her for a moment and then gave a small laugh. "You're a softie, aren't you, Bodie?"

"A softie?"

"Yeah, you know, a romantic, a soft-hearted individual. Sensitive and all that."

"You mean, like an artist?"

Alora shot her a look. Bodie waited.

"We aren't all like that," Alora eventually said. "Some of us have spines."

"Spines?"

"Never mind."

Bodie felt her skin heat. "I don't appreciate the insinuation."

Alora laughed. "Just you saying it like that proves my point."

"Why, because I didn't raise my voice or swear at you?"

"Yes, actually."

Bodie shook her head. "You sure have a funny way of dealing with things, Alora."

"So do you."

"Guess we're just different." Bodie headed for the kitchen, finished with the conversation. Alora liked to act tough, but Bodie suspected there was a soft-hearted woman beneath that tough girl veneer. Bodie had seen slivers of that soft hearted woman and she wondered if she'd ever get a chance to see all of her. She'd sure like to.

"Vastly different." She followed her.

Bodie wanted to head back to the beach, to take a long, peaceful walk, just her and the soft sand and the cold ocean on her feet, but she needed to start dinner. It was her job.

"What would you like for dinner?" She opened the fridge, hoping to find inspiration, hoping to find the will to remain in the same room with Alora. When she was in a mood, she was difficult to endure.

"I don't care. Make something you want for a change."

Bodie turned. "You mean spineless little ol' me?" She regretted saying it the second it came out.

But Alora appeared amused. "That really bothered you, didn't it?"

Bodie shut the fridge, keyed up. "Yes, as a matter of fact it did, Alora. You know, you're not always right about everything. And your ways of doing things and handling things, aren't always right either. They're actually, if I'm being honest, mostly rude."

Alora blinked. "I see."

"Now, what do you want for dinner so I can start making it?"

"I told you, make what you want, I'm not hungry."

"Why not?"

"Because I'm just not."

"Alora, what is going on? You're—cranky—and impossible—and now you've resorted to insulting me. Did you hear from Peter?"

She burned a stare into her. "Why, you assuming it's going to be bad news?"

"No, but it seems like maybe you heard something along the lines of bad news, with the way you're behaving. Now, please tell me what's going on with you, so I can try to help. Talk to me."

Alora continued to stare at her, but her gaze softened and then nearly crumbled as she buried her head in her arms on the counter.

Bodie went to her at once and placed a hand on her shoulder. She felt her trembling and she knew she was crying.

"Did Peter call?"

She raised her head and wiped her eyes. "He doesn't like the painting. The impasto style. No one does."

Bodie gave her shoulder a squeeze. "No one?"

"Well, one person."

Bodie's heart lifted. "You said you only needed one person and the rest would follow."

She shook her head. "You don't understand. The person only bought it because they are a new investor and they wanted it because—because—it's not like my others and not in demand and he thinks maybe someday it will be worth something—as proof of my downfall."

"Jesus, Peter told you that?"

"In so many words."

"Oh, Alora." She embraced her and let her cry. How awful. How terrible. And just who was this Peter? He sounded like a horrible excuse for a human being.

"The guy didn't even pay a lot for it," Alora said, drawing back. "A couple hundred dollars."

Bodie held onto her shoulders and smoothed a tear from her cheek. She couldn't bear to see her cry. It was killing her. "Well, fuck them then."

"No, not fuck them. I need them to buy my work. Otherwise, what am I going to do, Bodie?" She motioned back toward the fireplace. "For God's sake, I can't even play around with a little clay because I can't fucking see anything."

Bodie pulled her in for another tight hug. "Shh. It's going to be okay."

"I don't think it is."

"It will. You'll see."

But Alora continued to cry. "That's just it, Bodie. I can't."

CHAPTER NINETEEN

Alora used the wall for support as she trudged down the hallway to the kitchen. The house was already open, allowing the cool sea breeze to blow through. She inhaled deeply and tried to let the salty air soothe her sad soul, but it did little to combat her heavy mood.

"Good morning," Bodie said from her position on the sofa. She had a mug of coffee in hand and her legs crossed, looking like she'd awoken on the very right side of the bed, as opposed to Alora, who definitely did not.

"Ugh. Morning." She rested against the kitchen island, trying to get her bearings. She glanced at the analog clock hanging just beyond Bodie in the living room. She squinted and made out the time. It was past ten. She'd been sleeping later and later, completely unmotivated to do much of anything since Peter's phone call.

Bodie set her coffee mug aside and stood. "Coffee?"

"Mm, yes, please."

She poured her a cup and Alora joined her in the living room, settling into the chair across from her. The soft cushions felt like clouds and threatened to lull her back to sleep. She blinked and forced herself awake to sip her coffee. "I miss the good coffee from home."

"We should've brought some," Bodie said. "I can ask Tabby to send some."

"No, I don't want her to go to the trouble. She's already doing enough as it is."

She'd spoken to her the day before about the house hunting. She had a few in mind that Alora might like, though they were much smaller and more modest than what she was used to. And as far as her home? She'd had some interest. There was a couple coming back in a couple of days for another walk through. Alora knew she'd have to return home soon to handle it all, and she was not looking forward to it. Not in the least. She'd prefer it if she could just curl up there at the beach house with Bodie and hide away from the world for forever, and she'd actually considered it.

But she'd miss Tabby too much and the kids and Fatima. And she'd miss the Phoenix area. Her life was there in Paradise Valley. She thought of Fatima and grew even more morose. Would she have to let her go? What would Fatima do? She was like family and it broke her heart to even consider the thought of having to let her go.

"Something wrong?" Bodie asked. "You look upset."

"I was just thinking about Fatima and how I'll probably have to let her go." She gripped her hot ceramic mug, needing to feel the sharp heat against her skin. "It's something I don't want to do. She's…very dear to me."

"I understand."

"But I can't afford to pay her and she needs to make money. So, she'll probably have to go work for someone else."

Bodie was quiet, seemingly thinking. "You could always give her a really good reference and visit with her often. There's nothing saying you can't see her anymore."

"Thanks, but that really doesn't help at the moment."

"Well, you could always get rid of me."

"You? Why would I do that?"

"So Fatima can do my job. You know her better and obviously care for her. It just makes sense."

"Fatima can't work for me full-time like you do. Nor can she live with me. She has her grandkids to care for." A sudden rush of panic came over her. "You don't…want to go, do you?"

Bodie's eyes widened. "No, of course not. I was just trying to find a solution to your problem."

Alora fought breathing a sigh of relief. She couldn't totally explain it, but she really liked having Bodie around. She felt safe and cared for. Something she'd only ever felt with Tabby.

"Good. Just…don't leave, okay?" She didn't think she could handle losing one more thing. Tears threatened and she cleared her throat to swallow them down. Bodie was studying her, but remained quiet.

Alora spoke. "We might have to return home soon. Tabby has some interested buyers in the house and I have to find a new home." Her voice cracked as she finished the sentence. A new home. Jesus, would this nightmare ever end? They'd only been in Mexico for a couple of weeks.

"Should I start packing us up?"

"Not quite yet. But be ready."

Bodie nodded but appeared solemn.

"You don't want to go, do you?" Alora asked.

Bodie offered a soft smile. "No, not really."

"The beach life suits you, Bodie Banks." Her flawless skin was sun kissed and glowing and she had a calm about her here that seemed to help soothe Alora's recent distress.

Bodie stared out the open French doors. "Yes, it does."

"I wish I could tell you that we'd come back, but that's not likely to happen."

"Maybe you won't have to sell it," Bodie said, her voice high with hope. "Maybe you can keep it somehow."

Alora didn't think it possible, but she let her hang on to that hope regardless. Everyone needed a little hope in their life. Even if she didn't currently have any.

"Would you like some breakfast?" Bodie asked.

Alora again glanced at the time. "I'll just wait for lunch."

"You really should eat a little something. You've lost more weight."

"Nothing I couldn't stand to lose."

"I disagree. You looked good the way you were. Very—fit."

Alora's heart skipped a beat. "Fit?"

"Yeah—you know—healthy."

She'd covered nicely, but Alora could tell by her stammering that she'd touched on some nervousness.

"And now?"

Bodie blushed and looked away. "You still look good…"

"But?"

"But you don't look as healthy."

"Ah."

She knew she'd seen better days. Right now her hair was mussed and she was aware of the dark circles beneath her eyes. She definitely was not looking her best, but for the past week or so she just didn't care.

Bodie continued to blush, and she looked regretful, as if she shouldn't have said anything.

"Thank you for your honesty," Alora said. "You know I always appreciate that."

"Sometimes silence is for the best," Bodie said.

"Like now? With me?"

Bodie shifted her gaze back to her. "Yes."

"And why is that?"

"Because you seem so down. So sad."

"I am, Bodie. I've lost my entire way of life."

"I know. Which is why I shouldn't rub salt in your wounds."

"I appreciate that. But I really don't think there's much that can help me right now. So, if you feel the need to say something, you go right ahead."

"Okay." She repositioned herself on the sofa and set down her mug. "I think we should go for a walk. We've been here two weeks and you've yet to walk on the beach."

Alora almost argued, but then she realized she was right. She hadn't enjoyed a walk on the beach or really much of anything that she usually did when staying at the beach house.

"So, what do you say we go?" Bodie asked as she stood and held out her hand.

"What, now?"

"Sure, why not?"

"Because I'm a mess."

"So? I doubt the ocean will care. But if it bothers you, I can help you change and get ready."

"If you'll just lay things out for me, I think I can manage the rest." Bodie helped her up and they headed for the bedroom where Bodie set out her clothes and toiletry items and then left her to tend to herself. As Alora studied herself in the mirror, she realized that she really didn't want to go, but she knew deep in her heart that she should. That a walk in the fresh air would be good for her, cleansing. It was just making herself do it that felt so challenging. Thankfully, Bodie was there with her to encourage her. What would she do without her? Funny how things had changed in just a few short weeks.

She left the bedroom and joined Bodie at the French doors and slid her arm into the crook of hers. They crossed the patio to step into the soft sand and the wind whipped their hair. Alora wondered why she'd even bothered to try to tame it.

"Feels great, right?" Bodie said with a smile as her dark hair whipped around her face.

Alora returned the smile but gave a shrug. "I guess."

"It stirs something in me," Bodie said. "I love it. Just inhale that salty air." She took in a big breath and looked for Alora to do the same.

Alora nearly rolled her eyes, thinking she was being a bit overdramatic, but she gave it a try anyway, too moved by her joyful appearance not to. She inhaled deeply and allowed the ocean air to infiltrate her lungs. She exhaled, and damn it if it didn't awaken her a little.

"Again," Bodie said as they bypassed the lounge chairs and edged closer to the surf.

They breathed in together and breathed out and Alora once again felt, well, stirred. Just like Bodie had said.

"Feel nice?"

"Yes, it actually does."

"Good, now keep breathing, nice and deep and close your eyes. I'll guide you."

"But—"

"No, no. Close your eyes. Think of nothing but your surroundings."

Alora closed her eyes and Bodie led her to the sea. She jerked a little as the cold water tickled her toes.

"It's cold," she said.

"I know, isn't it wonderful? Let's go in a little farther."

The water enveloped her feet and drew away, only to come back again seconds later, this time wrapping around her ankles. She shivered with delight at the frigidness and opened her eyes. The water drew away again leaving froth on her feet, sucking the sand from beneath her soles. The strong wind blew against her face, making hollow-like noises in her ears. She inhaled deeply and the saltiness seemed to penetrate her entire body, stirring her mind and soul.

"It's nice, right?" Bodie said, smiling over at her.

God she's beautiful. Like some sort of wild, untamed woman of the sea.

"It is. I—" How could she explain just how nice it really felt? Or just how moved she was by her beauty and care free attitude?

And why in the world didn't I do this sooner? Did I think I wouldn't enjoy it just as much because I can't see very well?

"Yes?" Bodie asked, watching her.

"Thank you." She squeezed her hand, meaning it. "For encouraging me to do this."

"You're welcome."

"You're good for me, Bodie. I—really need you in my life." She croaked out the words as her throat constricted with surprising emotion.

Bodie's smile faltered as a deep seriousness came over her. "I'm here, Alora. Right here."

"Why though? After some of the things I've said and done… why have you stayed?"

"Because of this." She placed her palm on Alora's heart. "It's bigger than you let on and someday you're going to be brave enough to let us all see it."

Alora rested her hand atop Bodie's. "You think so?"

"I know so."

Alora stared into her dark, flashing eyes, searching their depths. "You see me, don't you?"

Bodie swallowed and took a step closer. "I do."

"Then…show me."

Bodie inched ever nearer and Alora's eyes drifted shut. The soft warmth of her lips was a startling contrast to the chill of the water and the strength of the breeze. So much so that Alora fell into it, wanting and needing more. Bodie caught her and they melded, two souls standing ankle-deep in the churning sea, burning with a rising passion for one another.

Alora clung to her and pressed her mouth firmer to hers, loving the taste of her sweet lips and the light tang of the salt from the air. It was a moment she knew she'd remember always and she didn't want it to end. Saw no reason for it to end. God, how she didn't want it to end.

"Alora?"

At first she thought she'd imagined it. But it came again, coming on the sea breeze. "Alora? Is that you?"

Bodie pulled away first and Alora blinked, confused and already feeling a void from the absence of her lips. She followed Bodie's line of sight and saw a couple standing hand in hand smiling at her at the edge of the surf.

"Sorry, we didn't mean to interrupt. We just weren't sure if it was you or not," the woman said.

Alora blinked some more and whisked her hair away from her face. A familiarity came then as she did her best to make out their faces. "Carrie? John?"

"In the flesh," John said.

"Oh, my gosh." Alora couldn't believe it. She even rubbed her eyes briefly just be sure. She ambled as quickly as she could up to them for an embrace, more than surprised to see them. "What are you doing here? It's not even May yet."

"John just retired so we were able to come earlier this year," Carrie said.

"How nice." Alora smiled, truly glad to see them but still frazzled and heated over the kiss. She glanced back at Bodie, longing to feel her close once again. "Oh, I'm sorry. Carrie, John, this is my—friend, Bodie. Bodie Banks."

"Hi, Bodie," Carrie said, followed by John. They shook her hand and Bodie offered them a pleasant smile, but Alora could tell that she felt a little lost and uncomfortable. Alora sidestepped closer to her. She wanted to reach for her hand, but she wasn't sure how Bodie would feel about that. Or even, how she would feel about that. Now that they'd shared a kiss, things felt all askew.

So she kept things simple. "Carrie and John own the house next door. And they're also from Phoenix."

"I'm a dentist," John added. "And my wife here is a hygienist."

"Bodie's a sculptor," Alora said quickly. "She's really quite good."

Bodie looked at her, obviously surprised at her words.

"A sculptor? Wow. So a painter and a sculptor. A perfect match," Carrie said.

Alora gave a nervous laugh.

"Why don't you guys come over for dinner this evening?" John asked. "We just bought some shrimp in town and Carrie makes a mean shrimp scampi."

Alora looked to Bodie who smiled and shrugged a shoulder. She really wanted to spend some more time with Bodie, but she felt pressured and she didn't want to be rude to John and Carrie. She did value their friendship. They were good people and she'd always enjoyed their time together.

"Sure, why not?" Alora said.

"Will you bring the wine?" Carrie asked. "You always have the good stuff."

"Absolutely," Alora said.

"Great. We'll see you about five-thirty then," Carrie said with a smile. They gave a wave and continued down the beach.

"Is that okay with you?" Alora asked Bodie. "If we have dinner with them?"

"Of course." They walked in the opposite direction of Carrie and John, with the wind continuing to whip at their clothes and hair. "But I am somewhat disappointed."

"Oh?" Was she feeling like her? Still completely overwhelmed by the kiss?

"Yes. You've been holding out on me with the wine."

Alora laughed. "I have, haven't I?"

"You gotta secret stash or something?"

"I do."

"And all this time I didn't know."

Alora leaned into her and gripped her fingers. "I'll let you do the choosing of the wine tonight. How's that?"

"Do I get a taste test?"

"You just had one," Alora said, grinning.

Red tinged her cheeks.

"But if you want another, you'll have to wait until tonight."

Bodie laced her fingers into hers. "I can do that."

CHAPTER TWENTY

"How are you feeling about this dinner?" Bodie asked as they left the house to go to the hacienda-style dwelling next door. Alora had grown considerably quiet since running into the couple on the beach. Or maybe since the kiss. Bodie wasn't sure. She just knew how she felt and that was totally awestruck. Alora had felt like heaven itself against her lips and in her arms. She could've drifted away right then and there into the sea to be lost forever and she never would've been happier. It had been that incredible.

"Nervous," Alora finally said.

"Why is that?"

"They aren't aware of my vision loss."

Bodie had gathered as much. Especially when Alora had blurted out that Bodie was a sculptor rather than her helper or assistant. She'd thought it seemed odd, but she understood now that she'd just panicked.

"Do you think you'll tell them?"

Alora glanced over at her. "I don't know. I don't want to, really. It's honestly no one's business."

"No, it's not. But if they're your friends, I'm sure they'd understand." *Come on, Alora, let people in. We're not going to hurt you.*

"I just don't want to have to get into the whole thing. I'm so tired of thinking about it, of having to deal with it constantly. I just would like to have a pleasant meal without the blindness thing even coming up."

Bodie wrapped her arm around her and pulled her close, wanting to comfort her and show her some support. "I get it."

"So, you won't say anything?"

"I would never. That's your story to tell, Alora, not mine."

They entered the cobblestone patio, bypassing a row of queen palms and found John standing at the back door holding an empty wine glass. "There you are," he said with a broad smile. "We've been anxiously awaiting your arrival."

Alora laughed. "I see that. And I can see what you're really anxiously awaiting." She held up the bottle of white wine. It was an Ornellaia Toscana Bianco, 2020, according to Alora.

John came out to kiss her on the cheek and to take the bottle.

"You got me," he said. He turned and called back into the house, "Wine's here. I mean Alora's here, along with her guest."

"Funny," Alora said, and placed her hand on the small of Bodie's back. Bodie warmed at the gesture and they followed John inside. The home was larger than Alora's with a more open floor plan. But it was decorated similarly with custom Mexican furniture and art but with a red tiled floor and bright yellow kitchen. Bodie could smell the butter and garlic sautéing in the pan where Carrie stood pouring in the shrimp.

"Hey, guys," Carrie said, unable to turn to welcome them. "Make yourselves right at home. John, you want to get them a drink?"

"Oh, I don't know if I want to share this wine," he said. But he merely smiled as he popped it open and poured them each a glass. After serving Bodie and Alora, he brought one to Carrie who tasted it and swooned.

"Oh, that is divine," she said.

"I thought it would pair nicely with the shrimp," Alora said, taking a small sip herself.

"That," Carrie said, looking over her shoulder at them, "would pair nicely with anything."

"Agreed," John said. He motioned toward the leather couch. "Please, sit."

"Actually," Carrie said. "Show them to the table. This is just about finished."

"Very well then. To the table it is," John said.

They settled at the round oak table which had been beautifully set, complete with tapered candles and all. Bodie took a hearty sip of her wine, hoping to calm her nerves. She didn't go to dinner parties very often. Well, actually not at all. Especially with people she didn't know. So she was a little anxious and she was also concerned for Alora, wanting, more than anything, for her to open up and enjoy herself with her friends. But she could tell by the soft, hesitant smile on her face, that she was still feeling some nerves.

Carrie finished sautéing the shrimp and John helped carry everything over to the table. Then they settled in and Carrie raised her glass in a toast.

"To friends and neighbors," she said.

"Hear, hear," John said.

"Hear, hear," Alora said and they all clinked glasses and sipped their wine.

"Mm, dig in, guys," Carrie said. "It's shrimp scampi with lemon butter rice and roasted vegetables."

"It looks incredible," Bodie said, waiting for Alora to carefully make her plate before she did her own. "Thank you so much for having us."

"You're quite welcome," Carrie said, forking a bite of shrimp. "We love having Alora over and we're so glad to meet you, Bodie. Tell me, how did you two meet? Was it at some huge art show where you both were the stars of the evening? How exciting." She raised her shoulders and widened her eyes in excitement.

Bodie looked to Alora, who appeared panicked and at a loss for an explanation.

Bodie quickly spoke. "We met through a mutual friend. A fellow artist."

"Oh, how nice. And she just thought you two would be perfect together, didn't she?" Carrie asked.

"Something like that," Bodie said.

"That's how we met," John said. "A mutual friend knew I needed a new hygienist and she introduced me to Carrie. The rest is history."

Carrie reached out and covered his hand with her own. They smiled at one another and Bodie's heart warmed. She looked to Alora who now appeared completely shut down and spaced out.

Suddenly, she spoke. "I'm going blind."

Bodie nearly choked on her shrimp and she brought her napkin up to her mouth to cough it up. Carrie and John merely stared, mouths agape.

"I beg your pardon?" John said.

Alora's gaze was fixed on her plate. "I'm losing my vision."

"But—what? Since when?" Carrie asked, now reaching over to cover Alora's hand.

"It's been a few weeks now since it started," Alora said.

"But you seem fine," Carrie said.

"I'm still able to manage most things. But the process has started, and it most likely will continue."

"You mean you're having trouble seeing right now?" John asked.

Alora looked at him. "I have a black spot in the center of my vision on my right eye. And straight lines appear wavy to me sometimes."

Silence.

"So, how do you paint?" Carrie asked.

Alora's face paled and fell. She shifted, as if uncomfortable in her seat, but couldn't seem to bring herself to speak.

Bodie piped in, the urge to protect her overpowering. "She's taking it slow—"

"I'm not," Alora said.

Carrie was speechless. John cleared his throat. The table was silent for another long moment.

Then Carrie spoke. "Ever?"

Tears filled Alora's eyes and Bodie wanted so badly to stand up and excuse them and leave. She hated seeing her hurt. But she knew she had to let Alora handle this the way she saw fit. Even if it was immensely painful for her.

"Looks that way," Alora choked.

Carrie squeezed her hand. "I'm so sorry."

Alora nodded and wiped her eyes. "I wanted to tell you on the beach, but I just couldn't bring myself to."

"That's a very personal and difficult thing to share," John said. "Thank you for sharing it with us."

"Is there anything we can do?" Carrie asked. "Any way we can help?"

"I have Bodie. She's been a huge help. And I have Tabby, you remember her? She's helping as well."

"What about your work, though?" Carrie asked. "Are you just going to retire?"

"Nothing at all wrong with that," John said with a smile. "I actually recommend it."

Alora tried to smile at his good humor but she failed. "Right now I'm just trying to tighten my purse strings. So that means I'll probably be selling my beach house relatively soon."

"No," Carrie breathed. "You can't. We love having you next door."

"I'm afraid I don't have much of a choice."

"Gosh, Alora. Your whole life, it's just turned on its head, hasn't it?" Carrie said.

Again, Alora wiped away tears.

"She's done remarkably well, considering," Bodie said softly.

"No, I haven't. I've been cranky and snippety and depressed. Bodie's the one who's done remarkably well in putting up with me."

"Alora—" Bodie said.

"No, it's true. You have." Alora forced a smile and inhaled. "But enough with all that. Let's eat, shall we?"

But the rest of the evening felt strained and awkward with Carrie and John doing their best to make small talk. Alora humored them and laughed at their anecdotes and innuendos. But Bodie could tell she was hurting. Her eyes weren't shining and her smile wasn't broad. Nor did her shoulders shake when she laughed like they did when she laughed heartily. Bodie knew these things about her now, and it pained her to see her struggling.

At last, the meal came to an end and Carrie and John bid them both farewell with quick kisses to the cheeks and long embraces.

Alora was quiet on the walk home and as soon as they stepped inside, she headed for the wine stash in the upper kitchen pantry where she pulled out another bottle, this one a burgundy.

She handed it off to Bodie. "Will you open this please?"

"Alora, I thought you said this was your most expensive bottle?"

"It is. That's why I want it."

She crossed to the cabinet and retrieved a wine glass. "You want some?" Alora asked.

"No, thank you," Bodie said. She opened the wine and poured.

"More, please," Alora said softly.

Bodie filled the glass nearly to the brim. That seemed to satisfy her and she sipped heartily.

"Mm, God, yes. That's hitting the spot."

Bodie studied the label. It was a 2009 Chateau Lafite Rothschild Bordeaux Pauillac. Whatever the hell that meant. She set it down and watched as Alora made her way to the sofa facing the fireplace.

"Will you make a fire? It's chilly tonight."

"Sure." Bodie carried in some firewood from the pile against the back of the house and quickly brought the flames to life.

"Come sit next to me," Alora said. "And please, bring the wine."

Bodie got the wine and joined her, placing the bottle on the coffee table. Alora snuggled close to her and intertwined their arms as she tucked her feet up behind her.

"What a night, eh?" Alora said.

"It was. But I'm very proud of you. For being so open with them. I know it was hard."

"They're good friends. I figured they should know that I'm having to sell the house. I didn't want that to come as a surprise."

"You could've given them another reason for that, but you didn't. You told them the truth, as painful as it was." Alora was courageous in ways Bodie never suspected. She really was a strong, thoughtful person.

"Might as well get used to it," Alora said, almost to herself. "People are going to have to know." She scoffed. "People already know." She drank more of her wine and studied the glass. "I should've let this breathe. But…I wanted it right away. Needed it right away."

"You're hurting," Bodie said. *And it's killing me.*

"Yes."

"I'm sorry," Bodie said.

"Please, don't be. I don't want anyone else being sorry for me. Just…be here." Alora snuggled closer and rested her head on Bodie's shoulder to stare at the fire. Outside, behind the closed doors, the ocean churned and the stars pricked through the night sky to shine like diamonds.

"I don't know how to make this hurt go away," Alora whispered, closing her eyes. "I just want it to go away."

Bodie slid her hand into hers. "Just try and relax."

"I am. It's not working. My heart still aches. My head still pounds with worry."

"Just focus on your surroundings. Like you did earlier today. Focus on the sounds and smell of the fire, the distant churning of the ocean, the way the rich taste of that wine floods your mouth."

She opened her eyes. "You're so sensual, Bodie Banks," she said.

"It works."

"That it does." She leaned forward to set her wine glass down on the table. "Know what I like to focus on the most though?" She touched Bodie's face.

"What?"

"The taste and feel of your mouth on mine."

Bodie caught her hand and lightly kissed her fingertips. "Then by all means, focus on that."

CHAPTER TWENTY-ONE

Bodie leaned in and kissed her, delicately tasting her lips by tugging them in and lightly sucking on them one at a time. Alora moaned in sheer delight as she let her, just getting lost in the warm plumpness of her mouth.

"You are the most gentle kisser," Alora said. "Just like I imagined you would be."

"You imagined kissing me?"

"Didn't you, me?"

"I tried not to. But it was difficult."

Alora laughed softly and Bodie kissed her again, this time more urgently, framing her lips, but nibbling on them with her teeth as she drew them in. The sensation caused Alora to gasp and she clung to her shoulders and pulled her in tighter.

"God, you're right. It feels so nice to just forget and *feel.*"

She dug her nails into her as Bodie's hot mouth found the sensitive flesh of her neck.

"Bodie," she breathed, growing dangerously out of control. "Oh, God, Bodie." She pushed her away and stared into her eyes. The irises were so dark she could see the reflection of the orange flames in them.

"What's wrong?" Bodie whispered.

"Nothing. I just—I'm usually the aggressor."

"Oh. Do you want me to stop?"

"No."

Bodie smiled. It appeared soft and heartfelt. And slowly, she took her hand and brought it to her lips where she lightly kissed her fingertips, bringing about a sigh from Alora. Bodie extended her tongue and ran it up and down the insides of her fingers, and Alora's toes curled from the heightened sensation.

"Jesus," she rasped.

"Shh," Bodie said, as she continued to focus on her hand. "Just relax."

"You're making it—hard."

Bodie laughed. "We can stop."

"No. No way."

"Then let me," she said. "Let me love on you."

Alora leaned forward and kissed her vehemently, wrapping her arms tightly around her. Bodie lifted and turned her, carefully easing back down on the couch with Alora atop her lap. She slowly drew her mouth from hers and lowered her head to unbutton her blouse. Alora let her do it herself, but then helped as she slid the fabric from her shoulders and down her arms. The shirt was tossed aside and Bodie, after giving her a long, deep, searing look, began tracing the outline of her bra with her tongue.

Alora hissed and threw her head back. She'd never had a lover so attentive, so sensual and so confident. Then again, she'd never given another woman the chance to be. She'd always been the one in control.

She gasped again as Bodie unclasped her bra and slid it from her arms to breathe upon her aching nipples. Alora tangled her hands in her hair and held her fast to her, needing her fiery kiss on her desperate flesh.

"Suck them," she said.

Bodie complied and she arched her back into her, thoroughly enjoying the feel of her skin inside her mouth. "Fuck," she let out. "Fuck, Bodie, it feels so good."

"Mm," Bodie moaned, releasing one breast to attach to the other. With nimble fingers, she began unfastening Alora's slacks and she parted them quickly to dip her hand inside.

Alora cried out when she found her center and Bodie's eyes slitted and then dilated with desire. "You're so fucking wet," she said.

Alora bucked against her seeking fingers. "Inside me, now."

Bodie gripped her lower back and slid her fingers up into her, causing Alora to stiffen and groan up into the night. "Bodie," she cried. "God, yes, Bodie." She rocked against her and rode her fingers with an increasing frenzy as the fire burned and crackled and sizzled behind them. Heating up the room, along with the growing heat of their passion. Until eventually, Alora clenched her eyes closed, clung to Bodie as hard as she could, and burst forth in a powerful, overwhelming orgasm. One that she saddled for as long as she possibly could, until the heavens seemed to break wide open and rain down upon her, leaving her weak and completely spent. She fell against Bodie and struggled for breath while her heart rate thrummed in her ears.

"You okay?" Bodie asked, whispering into her ear.

"God, yes. I'm more than okay. I'm fucking fabulous." She drew back to hold her face. "You…are the best distraction of all."

"Thanks," Bodie said with a chuckle. "Although I'm not so sure that's a good thing."

"What do you mean?" She looked at her quizzically.

"I'm not used to being a distraction."

Her face contorted. "You think…do you think I'm using you?"

Bodie appeared confused. "I don't—I'm not sure what this is to you."

Alora shook her head. "Bodie, no." She retreated from Bodie's lap and reached for her wine. She took two big gulps and laughed as she looked into the roaring fire. "I just can't seem to find peace, can I?"

"If this means more to you, then just tell me."

"I'm not sure what this is, Bodie. And honestly I don't think you're sure either. So, please don't put this all on me."

"That wasn't my intention."

Alora turned to look at her. "What is your intention? I mean you kissed me, didn't you?"

"You invited it."

Alora pressed her lips together. "This is obviously not going to work." She carried her glass toward the hallway. "I don't know what I was thinking."

"Alora, wait." Bodie stood to go after her. "We should talk about this."

"Why? So we can declare that this—thing between us was pointless?"

"Pointless?"

"I'm your boss, Bodie. We have a working relationship."

"Yes, but we also both want this. Don't we?"

Alora studied her, her heart racing. "We don't always get what we want, Bodie. Take it from me." Her voice cracked with raw emotion and she turned away, not wanting to cry. She'd done enough tearing up for the night.

"I'm right here, Alora." She held her hands out by her side.

Alora forced down a swallow. "I know. But the way I feel at this moment, you might as well be a million miles away." She turned and took a step but paused. "We're going home tomorrow. I won't be able to handle Carrie and John looking at me with pity like they did tonight."

She walked down the hallway to her bedroom, the churning ocean trying to soothe her with its rhythm, but failing miserably. After downing the rest of her wine, she quickly brushed her teeth, stripped down, and pulled back the covers to crawl into her bed. She reached over to her bedside lamp and extinguished the light, needing the blackness to envelop her and take her away. In fact, what she really needed was for all the previous days from the past few weeks to disappear as well, as if they'd never happened. But the darkness, she knew, wasn't that powerful.

❖

When she awoke the next morning after a fitful night of sleep, she could smell coffee and pancakes. Unfortunately, her stomach felt like it was churning battery acid and she didn't have much of an appetite. She blamed the wine she'd drank because she also had a headache and felt like death warmed over, but she relieved herself, dressed, and slowly made her way to the kitchen nonetheless. Bodie was at the stove flipping a flapjack. She welcomed her with a hesitant smile.

"Hey, how are you this morning?"

Still thinking about last night. But you seem to be just fine. "Alive. Barely. How are you?" Alora said.

She glanced at the clock. It was after nine. She'd slept in. Again. She'd forgotten to set her alarm so they could rise early and pack. Her mind was just so overloaded. And now Bodie was added to the list. What was she going to do? She'd thoroughly enjoyed their evening by the fire together. In fact, it had been magnificent. More than magnificent, it had been one of the best moments of her life. Bodie was indeed a very good lover. But where did that leave them now?

"I'm okay," Bodie said, not giving her much else.

"Listen, I'm sorry about last night. I was…upset."

"No need to apologize."

"There is, actually. I was a bear and I'm sorry, Bodie." She, at the very least, needed her to know how sorry she was.

Bodie turned from the stove with the plate of pancakes in hand. "You're going through some major life changes, Alora. That would be hard on anyone."

Okay. Guess she's not going to say much else about it. Did it not mean as much to her? Did she not enjoy it? I should've made love to her. I should've shown her how I'm really feeling about her.

Alora sat at the table and ran her hand through her hair. "Just when I think I'm making a little bit of progress, something else hits me and I'm down again." She looked at Bodie who remained silent. Alora decided not to press her about their moment by the fire. "Having to tell Carrie and John about my vision and then seeing how they pitied me…I don't want to be pitied."

"I don't think they pitied you. I think they showed concern and empathy. They seem to really care about you."

"Whatever it was, I can't bear it. Not right now."

"What would you prefer people do? Ignore the fact that you're losing your vision?"

"Yes, actually. Just everyone go on as is, instead of worrying or offering to help. It makes me feel helpless and…"

"Vulnerable?" Bodie asked

Alora cringed. "Yes."

Bodie forked two pancakes onto Alora's plate and settled in across from her to pour them both some juice and coffee. "And that makes you uncomfortable?"

"Yes, wouldn't it you?"

"If I were in your shoes and as fiercely independent as you are? Yes, probably." She sipped her juice. "But I would have to get used to it. Because people are going to have to know about the vision loss. It's not something you're going to be able to hide for long." She pointed with her fork at Alora's plate. "They're chocolate chip."

Alora looked at the darkly speckled pancakes. Bodie was so kind. So thoughtful. She didn't deserve her. Tears threatened. Why was she crying so much when she never had before? Not even when times were tough when she was younger? Maybe she was feeling more vulnerable than she realized.

"Something wrong?" Bodie asked.

"No. Yes. Everything." She shook her head.

"Hey, why the tears?"

"I don't know. I mean, I'm crying over pancakes, aren't I? Simply because you did something kind for me. It's making me cry."

"Your emotions are raw. Which is understandable, considering all that you're dealing with. I can get that way too."

"Really? Are you…feeling that way now?"

Bodie met her gaze and Alora knew that Bodie understood what she was referring to. Bodie blinked and stared down at her food. "A little," she said.

"Why?"

"I'm not quite sure where we stand."

"Where do you want us to stand?" Alora's heart kicked in her chest.

"I—I'm not sure. I just want what's best for you right now. You're really hurting, Alora. And you're going through so much.

Maybe we moved a little too quickly last night." She held up her palms. "I'm not saying I regret it. I don't. It was—" She blushed. "Really great. But it's probably not a good time to start something. And for the record, I don't feel used. You need to know that."

Alora took in a long breath. "Thank you for being so honest with me." Her chest ached, her heart rate having slowed considerably. Bodie had just confessed her feelings and though they hurt and very nearly crushed her to hear, she knew she was probably right. Her emotions were all over the place and Bodie deserved better than that.

She forced a smile and tried to appear at ease.

Bodie spoke. "You know, when my mother was first diagnosed with cancer I felt very fragile, like the slightest thing would send me over into tears. So I can sort of understand how you're feeling right now."

Alora wiped her eyes, glad they'd moved on in topic. "Please tell me it goes away."

"It does. But it takes time."

"Well, I've got that in spades, don't I? I don't have a job, or much of a life anymore."

"You will," Bodie said softly. "Now, try your pancakes. They're sure to cheer you up."

Alora eyed the food before her and though she wasn't hungry, she forked a bite anyway. They were delicious.

"Good?" Bodie asked.

"Mm-hm."

Bodie smiled.

"Thank you," Alora said, meaning it.

"You're welcome. You better eat up. We've got a big day ahead of us and a long drive."

Alora poured on some warm syrup and took another bite. "We still have to pack and everything."

"I've already done most of it." Bodie motioned behind her to the door that led out to the garage, where a small pile of luggage and boxes sat. "We really just have the perishables in the fridge and your stuff in the bedroom and we're all set."

"You didn't have to do all that by yourself, Bodie. I could've helped."

She shrugged. "I was up anyway and it was no trouble. I also cleaned a bit and put away the furniture on the patio."

"Gosh. You're like Wonder Woman."

Bodie's face clouded and she tried to cover by sipping her coffee. But something had definitely affected her.

"Did I say something wrong?" Alora asked.

She lowered her mug. "It just reminded me of my mother. I used to call her Wonder Woman. She worked two jobs and raised four kids. All on her own. She was amazing."

"She sounds like it."

Alora forked another bite. "You miss her a lot, don't you?"

Bodie played with her pancakes. "I do."

"I'm sorry, Bodie. You obviously loved her very much."

Bodie nodded and finally took a bite. She chewed quietly. Alora let her have the moment, her heart truly aching for her and her loss. Bodie seemed the type who loved very deeply and she knew that losing her mother must've been devastating to her. Not to mention having to watch her suffer with cancer.

She wished she'd known a love like that. But the story of her own mother wasn't quite as remarkable as Bodie's. She still had the memories of the numerous foster homes to remind her.

"What about you?" Bodie asked as if she'd read her thoughts. "You miss your mom?"

Alora grimaced. "No."

Bodie stared. Waiting.

"We didn't exactly see eye to eye."

"Mind if I ask why?" Bodie asked.

"You really want to know?"

"If you don't mind telling me."

Alora sat back in her chair. "I usually avoid the subject like the plague, but since you shared with me, I'll tell you." She crossed her arms. "My mother, my adoptive mother, whom I never really got along with very well to begin with, caught me kissing a girl when I was fourteen."

"Oh, no."

"She decided right then and there to kick me out of the house. No discussion, no second chances, nothing. Just up and told me to get the hell out since I liked playing around with the devil."

Bodie blinked at her. "The devil?"

"She was very religious. Insanely so. Which was one of the reasons why we never really got along. I thought she was crazy and going way overboard, and she tried to push those rigid beliefs on me. But I refused. And, of course, I knew what I was at a pretty young age and I knew there was no way she'd be okay with it. So I hid it. Until that hot summer day when a girl I'd been crushing on came over to swim. I thought no one was home and we, uh…had a great time in the pool together until we were caught with our lips locked on the love seat in the deep end. My mother had apparently come home early and I hadn't heard her. To say we were surprised would be an understatement. We were shocked. And so was my mother. I still remember her face."

Alora laughed as the painful memory flooded her mind. "I've never been able to forget it."

Bodie leaned forward with rapt attention. "So what happened?"

"She freaked and told me to get out. I didn't even have a chance to change or dry off. She threw a towel at me and told me to leave."

"Jesus."

"Yep. So I left with my friend and went to her house. Stayed a couple of nights until the police came knocking. They said I had to go back home to try and work it out with my mom, but I refused. There was no way I was going back to live in that house. Not with her knowing I was gay. So I told them no, told them she didn't want me anyway and that I felt unsafe there and that I'd just run away. They called child protective services and off I went to my first foster home."

"You were in a foster home?"

"I thought my house was bad, but I tell ya, some of the houses I went to…made my house seem like a cakewalk. But that's a whole other story. Eventually, I ran away and moved in with Tabby and her family until I turned eighteen. Then I got a job and went off on my own."

"So you've essentially been on your own since you were fourteen?"

"Yep."

"No wonder why you have such a strong sense of independence."

Alora took another bite of the now cold pancakes and pushed her plate away. "Sorry, but all that kind of made me lose my appetite."

"I guess so."

She pushed away from the table before Bodie could ask her any more questions. She was done discussing it.

"I'm going to go pack."

"Need some help?"

"No, you finish your breakfast. I can manage." She really needed to be alone for the time being and she hoped that having to concentrate on packing would help to get her mind off of her traumatic childhood.

"Okay, just call out if you need me."

Alora carried her plate to the sink. "They really were good, Bodie. I just can't stomach anything at the moment."

"No worries."

Alora gave her a small smile and headed for her bedroom with the image of her mother's angry face still on her mind.

Chapter Twenty-two

Alora slept on the ride home. She'd cried again as they'd left, after saying goodbye to Carrie and John, who'd given them tight hugs and wished them well. Carrie had even mentioned getting together again back in Phoenix and Alora had agreed, but Bodie knew it wouldn't happen anytime soon, seeing as how distant and pained Alora currently was. Plus, she had the task of moving and settling into a new house to look forward to, which would take some time as well as some getting used to. It was going to be a trying few weeks for them all, but especially for Alora, and Bodie dreaded it for her.

They'd called Tabby on speaker phone before they'd left to let her know of their return. She'd seemed a bit surprised, but recovered quickly, and Alora had used her upcoming eye injections as an excuse, though her appointment wasn't for two more weeks. Bodie figured that she hadn't wanted to get into it with Tabby, so she'd just come up with the most practical excuse she could, rather than telling her just how upset and depressed she truly was.

Bodie had to admit that she was disappointed. She'd hoped the trip to the beach would've helped Alora and at least eased her stress level a little. But it hadn't. It had only seemed to worsen it, especially after the phone call from Peter. Bodie really didn't like the guy and if Alora was somehow going to remain in the art world, she definitely needed to get a new art dealer. Preferably someone with a little more tact.

Bodie slowed as she pulled into the Dairy Queen in Ajo. She gently shook Alora awake. “It’s Blizzard time,” she said.

Alora blinked and sat up. “I don’t want anything.”

“Of course you do. It’s Dairy Queen and you hardly touched your breakfast. I’ll even get out and get it. You don’t have to move a muscle.”

Alora propped her head against the window. “I don’t know,” she said.

But Bodie was determined. “You stay put. I’ll be right back.” She left the car running and trotted up to the counter to order. When she returned with the ice cream in hand, she found Alora asleep, cheek pressed to the glass.

“Hey,” she said softly, shaking her once again. “Here’s your Blizzard.”

Alora straightened and took the small Royal New York Cheesecake Blizzard. She took a bite.

“Thank you,” she said.

“You’re welcome.”

“I’m just so tired. I can hardly eat.”

“You’re feeling down. But I was hoping your favorite Blizzard would cheer you up.”

“It’s waking me up, that’s for sure. But cheering me up? I don’t know. Ask me when I’ve eaten it all. *If* I can eat it all.”

“Just eat what you can. There’s no pressure.”

Alora stared out the windshield as she swallowed another bite. “Man, I really crashed, didn’t I?”

“Uh-huh.”

“Thanks for letting me sleep.”

“You must’ve needed it,” Bodie said, smiling softly.

“I think I did. I haven’t been sleeping very well.”

“I know.”

“You do?”

“I hear you sometimes. At night. Moving around.”

“I wake you?”

"I'm a light sleeper," she said swallowing her own bite of ice cream. "And I'm on alert for noises from your room in case you need me."

"Oh. I didn't realize. You must not be sleeping well either."

"I get enough. Besides, I'm used to odd hours from caring for my mother and working at the bakery."

"I meant to ask you about that. Do you think, you know, that you want to stay on and work for me?"

Bodie raised her brow. "I'm not going anywhere, Alora. I thought I told you that." She couldn't leave her now. Not just because she was concerned for her, but because of all the feelings she was now having for her. She couldn't tell her that, though. Not after their discussion at breakfast. They really had moved too quickly, considering all that Alora was dealing with. But that didn't mean that she didn't care for her or have feelings for her.

"You did. I just…wanted to be sure you hadn't changed your mind," Alora said.

"I haven't. Have you?" Bodie swallowed hard as she waited for her response.

"No."

She breathed a small sigh of relief. "Good. Glad we got that settled."

Alora shoved her long red spoon into her ice cream. "I can't eat anymore."

Bodie swallowed another bite of her Peanut Buster Parfait. "I'll throw it out."

Alora reclined in her seat again, barely eaten cup in her lap, and closed her eyes. Bodie finished eating and got out to throw away their trash. Then she climbed back in, buckled her seat belt, and glanced over at Alora.

She was already snoring.

❖

Bodie drove the rest of the way home in silence while Alora slept. Bodie glanced over at her periodically, making sure she was okay and enjoying how peaceful she looked lost in her dreams. At one point she reached behind her for the throw they'd brought and covered her with it. She didn't want her to get cold and wake.

When they arrived at the house, Tabby was there waiting, along with another vehicle, this one an older Chevy Avalanche that Bodie didn't recognize. She pulled into the garage, killed the engine, and shook Alora awake.

"Alora, we're home," she said softly.

Alora groaned and rubbed her eyes. "Already?" She yawned, then unfastened her seat belt and opened her door. Bodie rounded the car to help her out. They'd just about reached the interior door that led into the house when it opened.

"Welcome home!" Tabby said as she enveloped Alora into a big hug.

"Ugh, thanks. Sorry, I'm still not awake," Alora said as they drew apart.

Tabby held her shoulders to examine her. Her face clouded but she said nothing.

"We made good time," Bodie said as they headed inside. An older woman with dark braided hair was standing at the sink, wiping it down. She smiled broadly at Alora.

"Hola, Alora."

"Fatima," Alora breathed. "It is so good to see you, my friend." She hugged her tight and Fatima planted a big kiss on her cheek.

"I miss you," Fatima said with a strong accent.

"I missed you, too. Gosh, it's good to be home."

Alora breathed deeply as she took in her surroundings, then went on to the bathroom. Tabby pulled Bodie aside as Fatima went back to scrubbing the kitchen.

"What's going on?" she asked, her voice a fierce whisper.

"What do you mean?"

"Alora looks like hell and she's acting like she's asleep on her feet."

"She's been in a deep depression ever since that phone call with Peter."

"Peter? Why was she talking to Peter? She left her phone here specifically so she wouldn't talk to people like him."

Bodie was floored. "She didn't tell you about Peter and the painting?"

Tabby appeared lost. Bodie continued, giving her the rundown over the painting Alora sent off and Peter's quick rejection of it. Then she went into more detail about Alora's subsequent depression from all of it.

"My God," Tabby said, massaging her temple. "Just oh, my God."

"What's wrong?" Alora asked as she returned to the room.

Tabby smiled. "Nothing. I just have a bit of a headache. How are you?"

"Tired. I think I'm going to go nap."

Tabby nodded. "Okay. Let us know if you need anything."

Alora walked slowly back down the hall and Tabby collapsed onto the sofa and sighed. "She's in bad shape, isn't she?"

Bodie eased down across from her. "Yes."

"Fucking Peter. How are we going to get her out of this slump?"

"Well, she needs to stop taking his calls, for one thing," Bodie said. "And for another, I think she needs to focus on the things she has, instead of worrying about what she's losing."

"Yeah, she's never been one to stop and smell the roses. She's just always been so driven."

"I tried to get her to focus on her immediate environment, like the sea and the salty air and the sunshine. It worked really well as far as relaxing her, but she couldn't seem to stick with it."

"Damn. I was really hoping the beach would help."

"So was I. But honestly, she rarely spent time enjoying it. She mostly painted and when that ended, she spent most of her time indoors."

Tabby seemed to be deep in thought. "My news, I'm afraid, won't help matters any."

Bodie was quiet, watching her as she thought.

Fatima spoke up from the kitchen. "I am done here," she said.

"Great, thanks so much, Fatima," Tabby said, rising to go to her. She opened her purse and counted out some cash and gave it to her.

"You let me know if I come again?"

"Yes." She hugged her. "Thanks again."

"You take care of her," Fatima said. "She looks skinny and pale."

"I know. And I will. I promise."

Fatima gave a nod, waved at Bodie, and headed for the front door where she exited.

"She's right," Tabby breathed. "I need to take care of her."

"We both do."

"I'm just at a loss as to how. I mean, the woman has lost her whole world. How do you help someone through that? Especially if they don't seem to want the help?"

"We just have to keep trying. And, well, there's always the other alternative."

"Which is?"

"Therapy. And possibly medication."

"Oh, I don't think Alora would ever even consider that."

"She might. If she feels bad enough. And right now she's pretty low. Possibly low enough to consider some help."

"I don't know. But I guess it's worth a shot, isn't it?"

Bodie nodded.

Tabby stood to gather her purse and keys. "I need to run. I'm meeting a Realtor to view another house. This one sounds really promising. It's nearly brand new and it's in a gated neighborhood. It's just so much smaller and more modest than this one, I'm not sure how Alora will react to it. But it looks really nice."

"She'll adjust, Tabby. It's just going to take some time."

"I hope you're right." She touched her arm. "I'll stop back in tomorrow to talk to Alora. Maybe she'll be more awake and ready to discuss some things. Like how she's got an offer on the house to consider."

"Already?"

"Yes."

Bodie's stomach flipped. Things were moving so quickly. What would Alora think? More importantly, how would she react?

"It's going to be a lot for her," Tabby said. "And with her current state, gosh, I'm just really worried."

"Me, too. But we'll get her through it."

Tabby nodded. "I'll see you later, Bodie."

Bodie followed her to the door and saw her out. She turned and faced the interior of the house. The beautiful, grand house that Alora had worked so hard for.

How in the world was she going to handle losing it?

CHAPTER TWENTY-THREE

Are you sure there's an offer?" Alora asked as she glanced over at Tabby in the driver's seat of the BMW SUV. "We just put it on the market."

"It's been on the market for close to three weeks, Alora. And people came to look at it while you were away."

But Alora shook her head. "I'm not ready. It's too soon."

"It's a good offer. Probably the best you'll get in this market and you need to start making some moves to save money."

"Save money. Ha. If only I'd done that all along, I wouldn't be in this mess."

"You'd still need to conserve, Alora. Unfortunately."

Alora stared out the window, wishing she could get lost in the sight of the beautiful blooming desert beyond. "What do you think, Bodie?"

Bodie piped in from the back seat. "About what?"

"About selling the house."

"It's really not my place to say."

"I'm asking you, so say away."

"I think you should seriously consider the offer. It's not going to make it any less painful to put it off."

"That's true," Alora said softly. "It's going to suck no matter when I sell it."

"And if you like this house, the one we're going to see, well, it will all fall into place nicely," Tabby said.

"*If* I like the house."

"True, it's not what you're used to," Tabby said as she slowed and pulled into a gated drive. "It's a lot smaller and it's empty, so you have to imagine your furniture and things in it."

"Will my things even fit in it?"

They pulled in through the opening gate and made a left-hand turn. "Not everything, I don't imagine."

"Great."

"You can always donate what you can't keep. You'd be helping others out."

"Even so, I don't like thinking about choosing what I'm going to keep and what I'm not." Just the thought of having to get rid of things made her anxious. The entire day so far had her stomach in knots.

"Why don't you get a storage facility?" Bodie asked. "And just keep things there for the time being until you're more comfortable and settled."

"That's an excellent idea," Tabby said, smiling over at Alora.

They followed the street around and made a right.

"What about my cars?" Alora said as Tabby stopped at the second to last house on the right with a for sale sign in front. The stuccoed house was a dark beige in color with a cream-colored trim. Several small palms adorned the front Astroturf lawn. But the main thing she noticed, was the two-car garage which was not nearly enough room for her numerous vehicles.

"You can store those too," Bodie said.

"It would probably cost a lot though," Tabby said. "Whereas selling some would free up some cash for you rather quickly."

"I don't want to think about it," Alora said, feeling overwhelmed. "Not right now."

"Let's just focus on the task at hand then," Tabby said, switching off the car. They climbed out of the SUV and followed a brown-stoned pathway up to the front door. A blond woman in a pale green pantsuit greeted them with a wide, perfect smile.

"Hello and welcome," she said as she invited them in. Alora put on a smile and entered the elongated tract house.

"Are you Alora?" the woman asked as she held out her hand. "I'm Bev. Bev Johnston."

"Hello," Alora said, shaking her hand.

"It's lovely to meet you," Bev said. She palmed her chest. "I must tell you, I'm a big fan of yours."

"Oh. Well, thank you." Alora felt herself warm with fear at the mention of her work.

"I actually own one of your earlier works. It's a smaller piece. Bought it back when you first started out. Can't afford one now." She laughed.

Alora prayed she wouldn't ask about her working currently. Prayed nothing along those lines would even come up.

"I hear you're looking to downsize?" Bev asked.

"Something like that."

"Well, let's have a look around, shall we? The house is twenty-three hundred square feet. Three bedrooms and three and a half baths."

Alora tucked her arm into Tabby's and they, along with Bodie, walked into the house a short ways and stopped. "To your left you have a half bath and the garage and laundry room. To your right, over here in this hallway," she said, once again leading the way. "You have your two bedrooms and full bathroom. She showed them the bedrooms, which were medium in size, but much smaller than the rooms at Alora's current house. The bathroom was also smaller with a shower tub, toilet, and two sinks.

"And down here," Bev said, returning them to the center of the house, is the front room or office area if you prefer."

"This is nice," Tabby said. "Don't you think, Alora?"

"It's got great light," Bev said. "For your painting." She winked and Alora felt sick with panic. "But," she said, wagging a finger. "I think you'll find the incredible light is in the great room with the numerous floor to ceiling windows." They left the office and entered into a great room with a full, open kitchen on the left and a large living room on the right. Bright light spilled into the area from the windows, which were actually oversized sliding glass doors, sitting straight ahead. "And how about that backyard, eh? It's completely landscaped with the Astroturf, queen palms, ficus and citrus trees, and rose bushes. Not to mention the 'spool,' which is really just a very large spa."

"Wow," Bodie said, stopping at the window to stare out at the yard. "It's like its own little paradise. And there's a pergola as well." She looked to Alora. "You can put your patio furniture under it."

"And there's ample patio space here too," Bev said, motioning just outside the right sliding glass door.

"What do you think so far?" Tabby asked, lightly grazing Alora's arm.

"It's nice." From what she was able to see anyway. But it wasn't her home. She wasn't going to get excited about it.

"The master bedroom is this way," Bev said. "I think you'll appreciate the size."

Alora headed into the bedroom with Tabby and Bodie and nodded as if she was expected to. It was a lot more spacious than the other bedrooms, but not nearly as big as her own back at her house. Still, it would make do. And so would the roomy bathroom and the walk-in closet. Everything would do. "I like the free-standing tub," she said. She loved a nice long soak in a hot bath. She'd get to continue to enjoy that here at least.

"Oh, the tub is great," Bev said, once again smiling at her. She clasped her well-manicured hands in front of her. "Shall I give you all a moment to talk things over?"

"Please," Tabby said.

"I'll just be right out front." She left them and Tabby led the way back into the great room.

"So?" she said, extending her arms. "Do you like it?"

Alora glanced around, took in the gray kitchen cabinets, the white granite countertops, and the gray ceramic flooring. Then she stared back out at the bright, beautiful backyard. "You said this one is the best you've seen for the price?"

"Yes. But we can always go and look at the others if you prefer."

"It's not going to make much difference. I can't see very well and this one seems nice enough." She looked at Bodie. "You like it?"

Bodie seemed to be surprised she was asked. "I do. It's very nice."

"You think you can live in that small bedroom back there?"

"It's bigger than my bedroom at my house."

"Is it really?"

Bodie laughed. "It is."

"Alora, sweetie, most people don't live like you," Tabby said.

"I guess they don't." She pushed out a long breath. "There'll be less for me to trip over here, and one long walkway through the center of the house. So that means less maneuvering."

"Uh-huh," Tabby said.

Alora threw up her arms. "Okay then. What the hell? Let's get it."

"You sure?"

"Nothing is going to be like where I'm at now, so it's pointless for me to look around expecting that. This place is nice. It works."

Tabby beamed. She came in for a big hug. "I think you'll be happy here, Lor. I really do."

Alora embraced her, hoping she was right.

CHAPTER TWENTY-FOUR

It took a week to pack up Alora's house. And that was with Bodie, Tabby, Fatima, and a handful of movers. Alora helped where she could, but mostly she gave instructions and took private moments alone in her closet where she would emerge a few minutes later with tears in her eyes. But she didn't complain, and she didn't break down in front of anyone. And surprisingly, she didn't snap at anyone either. Overall, she remained relatively calm and patient. Even when they screwed up and boxed something in the storage pile that she wanted in the new house or vice versa.

Bodie was impressed and she told her so on more than one occasion. It wasn't easy leaving the home that you loved behind to start over. And to have to choose between your possessions? Bodie didn't envy her. But then again, Bodie didn't have much in the way of possessions to fret over. So she really couldn't truly empathize with her.

"Do you want the spa?" Alora asked Tabby as they were finishing up with moving the boxes out to the truck.

"What? Alora, the spa was sold with the house."

"Oh."

"You wanted to give it to me?"

"I wanted you to have something, yes. And you always enjoyed the spa."

"You have a giant one at the new place." She pecked her on the cheek. "So I'll just come and use that."

"Did you get the cash for Fatima?" Alora asked.

"I did. And I think it's really nice of you to give her some severance pay. I'm sure she could use it with those grandkids of hers."

"I'm going to miss her."

Tabby embraced her. "I know, hon. Me too. But you just can't afford to keep her on."

Alora drew away from her. "I can't say goodbye to her. It's too—difficult. Will you give her the money for me?"

Tabby touched her face. "No, sweetie, I won't. You need to do it."

She teared up and visibly swallowed. "But I'll—break down."

"That's okay. You go ahead and break down."

Alora turned away and Bodie watched as she tried to gather her composure. Fatima appeared from the laundry room and paused, a concerned look on her face.

"Que pasa?"

Alora gathered her breath. "I have to say goodbye to you, Fatima. And I—can't do it without—crying." Her shoulders shook as she began to silently weep. Fatima hurried to her and enveloped her in a tight hug.

"Ah, mija. It is okay."

"No, it's not. None of this is okay."

"You will be fine." She held her face. "You hear? You will be okay. These two ladies. They will take care of you."

"I'll miss you," Alora said, sniffling and handing her the envelope of cash. "So very much."

"I will miss you too, mija." She didn't open the envelope, just held tightly to it as she continued to comfort Alora.

"Promise you'll visit me?" Alora said.

"I swear." She made the sign of the cross and kissed the rosary she wore around her neck.

They embraced one last time and then Fatima hugged Tabby and said goodbye. She gave Bodie a wave and headed for the door. When she was gone, Alora broke down again.

"Just get me out of here," she said between sobs. "Before I completely lose it."

"Okay, Lor," Tabby whispered, taking her hand.

They led her to the garage where they eased her into the SUV and closed the door. Tabby locked up the house while Bodie tried to comfort Alora from the back seat.

"That was really nice of you," she said. "What you did for Fatima."

More sniffles. "She means a lot to me."

"And you obviously mean a lot to her." Bodie hesitated, but then lightly gripped her shoulder. "I know it doesn't feel like it right now, but things will get better."

Alora didn't respond. She just kept quietly crying. And she did that the entire ride to the new house.

❖

Alora was mostly silent as they moved things into the new house. She'd, of course, answered questions as to where she wanted certain things, but mostly she kept to herself and slowly unpacked her boxes. Bodie kept a close eye on her, worried about her disposition and occasionally she'd see her wipe away a tear or two. She refused to eat when they took a break for lunch, and it was all Bodie and Tabby could do to get her to drink anything.

She was obviously in the throes of a deep depression, so when Bodie followed Tabby back out to the truck for some of the last of the boxes, she shared her concerns.

"She's not okay," Bodie said as she treaded up the ramp into the truck. "I'm really worried."

"I am too."

"Did you look into a therapist?" Bodie lifted a light box and stepped to the edge of the truck to pass it down to Tabby. "She should probably see someone and soon."

"I found a handful that might work for her. They specialize in disabilities and trauma. It's just getting her to agree to see one of them that's going to be tough."

Bodie reached for another box, this one much heavier, and brought it down the ramp to give to Tabby. "I have an idea as to how we might can make that happen."

"Oh?"

"Yes, but I don't want to get your hopes up about it. Let me make some phone calls and see if I can work it out."

Tabby agreed and they finished unloading the rest of the truck, while the movers finished unloading and positioning all the furniture and left. Bodie closed the door behind them and found Alora in her bedroom, lying in the fetal position on her bed, with Tabby sitting next to her, rubbing her leg.

"You okay?" Bodie asked softly. "Can I get you anything?"

"I just want to sleep."

Bodie nodded and Tabby kissed her cheek and stood to cover her with a blanket. They left her alone and closed the door behind them.

"I really feel like I should stay the night with her, but my son has a baseball game this evening and David is working late."

"Go," Bodie said. "I'll take care of her."

"You sure?" She glanced back at the bedroom. "She's in a really bad way."

"She should feel a little better after a good night's rest. And if my phone calls pay off, then she'll definitely have something that'll cheer her up."

"I hope you're right." She grabbed her car keys. "Call me if you need me." She gave her a brief hug and headed for the door while Bodie slid her phone out of her pocket and dialed.

❖

Alora slept well into the next morning and Bodie, who'd slept on the couch to be close to her, only heard her get up twice to use the restroom. So, when she was still in bed at ten o'clock, Bodie knocked softly on her door and entered her room.

"Morning, Alora."

Alora groaned and pulled the blanket up over her head.

"Rise and shine." Bodie opened the curtains and came to sit on her bed. "How you feeling?"

"Tired."

"You slept more than twelve hours."

"So?"

"You'll feel better if you get up and move around some. Come on." She gave her a pat. "Let's go eat some breakfast. I'll make you whatever you want."

"Not hungry."

"You have to eat, Alora. You're getting too thin and it could be contributing to your fatigue."

She didn't respond.

"Come on, we need to get you up and ready. You're going to have some visitors."

She quickly lowered the blanket from her face. "What?"

Bodie smiled. "You're having visitors."

"But I don't want visitors."

"You'll like these visitors."

"Who are they?"

"It's a surprise."

"Oh, God, Bodie, no." She palmed her forehead. "I can't deal with this right now. Please, just cancel whatever craziness you've planned and leave me alone."

"I can't do that, Alora. Now come on, up and at 'em. You'll feel better after a nice long hot shower."

Alora narrowed her eyes at her. "You're not going to leave me alone, are you?"

"Nope."

"And there are really people coming here?"

"Yep."

"Why?"

"I told you, it's a surprise."

"Jesus. And to think I chose you over the others."

Bodie laughed. "Yes, you did."

"You're a pain in the ass."

"I'll wear that title proudly. Now let's get going." She tugged gently at the blanket and Alora groaned again but slowly sat up and slung her legs over the side of the bed. Bodie helped steady her as she stood. Bodie started the shower and turned away as she undressed and climbed inside.

"What would you like to wear?"

"I don't care."

Bodie got her a peach T-shirt and a pair of navy shorts from the closet, along with a pair of panties and a bra from the box next to her dresser. She rummaged through another box to find her deodorant and other toiletries and set those out for her on the counter. She brought her a towel as she finished bathing and switched off the water.

"Thanks," she said as she opened the glass door to take the offered towel.

"Everything you need is on the counter and your clothes are on your bed."

"'Kay."

"Will you need help with anything else?"

"No, I'm good."

"I'll be right outside in the kitchen if you need me."

"'Kay. Thanks."

Bodie left her, gently closed the bedroom door, and strolled into the kitchen to check the clock.

It was almost time.

Chapter Twenty-five

Alora had just finished drying her hair when she heard the doorbell. She quickly coated her fingers with some smoother and then ran them through her locks, styling the salt-and-pepper strands until she was satisfied. She had no idea who could possibly be visiting, and she really wasn't in the mood to get all dolled up, but she didn't want to be caught off guard like she had been when she'd first met Bodie. She lowered her hands and sighed. Her hair looked halfway decent but there was nothing she could do about her face. She was pale and gaunt, her cheekbones appearing sharper than usual. And the dark smears beneath her eyes seemed deeper and more prominent.

She heard Bodie speaking to someone. Heard laughter and what sounded like high-pitched excited gibberish.

"What the hell?"

A knock sounded from her bedroom door.

"Alora? You ready?" Bodie called out.

"Just a sec! Shit." She quickly massaged on some foundation, hoping to give herself some color, and applied some eyeshadow. Lastly, she rubbed on some lip gloss and popped her lips.

She ran her hands over her T-shirt and shorts. They weren't fitting as nicely as they once had. They were a little loose. But they too would have to do. She didn't have time to dredge through her closet and boxes searching for something that would fit. She took one last deep breath and headed for the door. Bodie was waiting for her just inside her room.

"You look nice," Bodie said with a smile.

"Lying doesn't become you. But thanks. It's the best I could do given this surprise of yours."

Her smile widened and she took her hand. "Okay, but before we go out there, please know that this isn't permanent. It's totally up to you."

"Okaay."

What was going on?

"Now, close your eyes."

"Bodie, this isn't the ocean."

"I know. But it's special. Please?"

Alora closed her eyes and allowed Bodie to lead her from the room. There were soft noises and what sounded like a slight metal clanging against itself. And then she heard…breathing. Heavy breathing.

What the fuck?

They came to a stop. "Okay, open your eyes."

Alora opened her eyes and she let out a short laugh. Standing before her was a dog. A large, golden, panting dog.

"What's this?" she asked.

The dog shook and its collar and tag made the clanging noise she'd heard. She looked to Bodie, searching her face for answers.

"His name is Tater," Bodie said, beaming. "Isn't he beautiful?"

"Yes, he is. But what's he doing here?" She looked to the woman holding Tater's leash. "Is he yours?"

"No, I'm a volunteer." She knelt to scratch Tater's head. "Tater here is up for adoption."

Alora nodded, amused at how adorable the dog was and how seemingly well-behaved. But then it hit her.

She again looked to Bodie. "Oh, no," she said. "Nuh-uh."

Bodie help up her hands. "Just hear me out."

"Bodie, I can't have a dog."

"Why not? He's already trained. He went through the seeing eye dog training, but he didn't graduate because he was too friendly with strangers."

"You're telling me he failed?"

Bodie hesitated. "In so many words, yes. But not because he didn't understand the commands or what he was supposed to do. He just…likes people."

"And you what? Want me to take him?" She was so overwhelmed at the prospect that she laughed again and even grew a little lightheaded. She braced herself against the kitchen counter and held her head.

Bodie gripped her arm in alarm. "Here, come sit down." She led her to the couch and Alora sank down into the cushions. Bodie left her briefly and returned with some cold water, which Alora slowly sipped. What was Bodie thinking? Here she was dealing with all these major changes and she thought it was wise to bring in a dog?

Bodie offered the volunteer a seat and she eased down onto the love seat across from Alora with Tater sitting at her feet. His soft gaze was on Alora however and he even yipped once as if to get her attention.

"What's he want?" Alora asked. Did he have to go outside? She didn't want him having an accident on her rug.

"He wants to come to you," the volunteer said.

"Why?"

She smiled. "He likes you."

"He doesn't even know me."

"Dogs have excellent intuition."

Bodie joined Alora on the couch. "I'm sorry, I didn't introduce you to Kimberly. She's a volunteer at a local rescue. The one I used to volunteer at before my mother got sick."

Alora looked over at her. "You used to volunteer at a rescue?"

"I did. And I loved it. So, when I thought of you and your needs, I remembered that we'd get dogs from numerous training programs that couldn't graduate for whatever reason. They're wonderful dogs and highly skilled, they just need a loving home."

"Bodie," Alora breathed. "I can appreciate that, I really can. But this is not the home for a dog." Again, she grew light-headed. And she suddenly felt nauseous. "Oh, God." She covered her mouth. She felt incredibly weak.

"What's wrong?" Bodie slid over to her.

"I feel sick."

"Probably because you haven't eaten. Want me to make you something?"

Alora's stomach growled as if to confirm Bodie's reasoning. She nodded.

"What would you like? Eggs?"

"God no." Just the thought of eggs made the nausea all the worse. "Some oatmeal will be fine."

"Brown sugar?"

"Yes, please." She closed her eyes and prayed for the dizziness to pass. And before she could open them again, she felt a slight nudge against her hand and a cold wet nose. She opened her eyes and saw Tater at her feet, looking up at her with his sweet, soulful brown eyes. He licked her hand.

"Hi," Alora said and hesitantly patted his head. "You're… cute."

"He knows you aren't feeling well," Kimberly said. "So I loosened his rein to allow him to come to you."

"You're saying he's psychic now?"

"Intuitive."

Alora patted his head once again, a little unsure as to how to interact with him. She'd never had a dog before, so she was at a loss. Her adoptive mother had had a cat named Lucifer and he had indeed been the devil, biting and scratching her when she'd tried to pet him. And as for holding him? Forget it.

"I've never had a dog," she confessed. She stopped petting him and he lifted his paw and placed it on her lap.

"He's asking if he can join you on the couch," Kimberly said.

"Up here?" On her furniture? Her expensive furniture?

"He wants to comfort you."

"Here," Bodie said, rounding the couch with a blanket. She spread it out on the cushions and then called Tater. He jumped up and joined Alora and promptly rested his head in her lap, giving his tail a few good swooshes.

Alora poised her hand over his head, a little hesitant still.

"Go ahead, it's okay," Kimberly said. "He loves affection."

Alora stroked his soft fur and Tater let out a deep sigh. Alora laughed, amused. "Well, he seems content."

"He is, now that he's with you."

Alora relaxed back into the cushions as she continued to pet him. She couldn't explain it but his relaxed state and the rhythm of his steady, slow breathing seemed to help calm her. And when Bodie brought her her oatmeal, Tater didn't even raise his head in interest in the food. He just simply closed his eyes, chin resting on her thigh.

"He's so good," Alora said.

"He's very well trained," Kimberly said.

Alora blew on a spoonful of the delicious smelling oatmeal and slipped it into her mouth. At first, her body seemed to reject it and she felt like she couldn't eat any more, not even another single bite. But then, as she sat very still and concentrated on Tater and his breathing and the pressure of his head on her thigh, her stomach seemed to settle and she was able to continue eating.

"How is it?" Bodie asked as she returned to her seat next to her. Tater didn't move, not an inch, even though Bodie was directly next to him.

"Good, thanks."

"Is it helping?"

"Mm." She kept eating, one slow, small bite at a time.

Bodie smiled at her and glanced down at Tater. "He's taken to you."

"I know." Alora looked to Kimberly, who was also smiling. "Is he always like this?"

"You mean well-behaved? Yes."

"Mellow," Alora said.

"He's very laid-back," Kimberly said. "Which is why Bodie thought he might be a good fit."

"I don't know," Alora said. Could she really handle having a dog? Something to care for other than herself when she had all this other crap going on? "I've never had to care for something before."

"He's really not that demanding. He gets fed twice a day, and you have a big yard for him to explore. But mostly he'll want to be with you."

"Me? You mean like go places with me?"

"He can go everywhere with you if you like."

"But he's not a seeing eye dog," Alora stated.

"No. But he's highly skilled and well behaved and will make a wonderful companion."

"So why hasn't he been snatched up already?"

"He went to a home a few weeks ago with four children, all under the age of ten. They were a little rough with him and he withdrew and became stressed. The family thought it best if they returned him to find a more calm, suitable home for him. So we've been looking for someone single, where he can relax and just be with his person."

Alora leaned forward and set her bowl on the coffee table. She stroked Tater's head once again. This time he opened his eyes to lick her palm. Alora chuckled. "He sure is sweet."

"How would you feel about giving him a trial run?" Bodie asked. "Letting him stay a few days?"

Alora scratched beneath his chin and he wagged his tail. "I don't know, Bodie. I just have so much going on."

"Which is precisely why I think he'll be good for you."

Tater rolled onto his side and stuck his paws in the air.

"He wants you to rub his belly," Kimberly said.

Alora rubbed his underside and sighed. Her light-headedness had vanished and she no longer felt sick. And while she knew the oatmeal had probably helped with that, she also knew that Tater's presence had significantly relaxed her and eased her anxiousness. He was like a little furry soother.

"So?" Bodie asked softly. "You willing to give it a few days?"

Alora relished his soft fur and warm body. Got lost in his sweet eyes as he again licked her hand. "Sure."

Bodie grinned. "Wonderful."

"But just for a few days," Alora stressed. She still wasn't sure she could handle the responsibility of owning a dog full time. Especially since lately all she'd wanted to do was sleep.

"A few days," Bodie affirmed. She stood and removed the leash from Tater, and Kimberly came over to kiss him goodbye.

"Be a good boy," she said, giving Alora a playful wink. "Give me a call if you have any questions."

Alora nodded. Tater wagged his tail and licked Kimberly's face before settling back down with Alora. Bodie escorted Kimberly to the door where Alora heard them having a quiet conversation, before they stepped outside.

Alora glanced down at Tater who was studying her curiously. "Looks like it's just you and me, kid," she said. He wagged his tail and she smiled, feeling okay for the first time in weeks.

CHAPTER TWENTY-SIX

Later that evening, Bodie was in the mood to celebrate, so she called Fatima and asked for the recipe for Alora's favorite Mexican dish—sour cream chicken enchiladas. Fatima readily told her how to make them, and Bodie left Alora alone with Tater to run to the grocery store. While she was there, she picked up a bottle of Patron and some margarita mix. She was so proud of Alora for giving Tater a chance and she just had a feeling that things were going to work out. So a little tequila in an icy margarita was called for.

When she returned home, she found Alora slumped to the side on the couch with her ear pods in, fast asleep. Tater was snoozing on her lap and he barked twice at Bodie's entrance but then quickly wagged his tail. The noise woke Alora and she stretched and plucked out her ear pods.

"You back so soon?"

"Yes, indeed. Got everything we need for dinner. Plus"—she held up the Patron—"for margaritas."

"Nice."

Bodie grinned. "You seem to have perked up."

Alora gave Tater a quick pat and stood to stretch again. "I think eating today has really helped."

"And maybe something else has helped too?" Bodie eyed Tater who was doing his own downward dog yoga pose. Then he trotted to the door to be let out. Alora opened the door for him and watched him through the glass.

"Maybe," she said. "He really is great, isn't he?" She faced Bodie. "He hasn't left my side, not even when I fell asleep listening to my audiobook."

"He's bonded with you," Bodie said.

Alora sank onto a barstool. "What are you making?"

"A little something Fatima shared with me."

"Fatima? Really?"

"Uh-huh."

"Oh, my God. Are you making enchiladas?"

"Why? Would that make your day?"

"Are you kidding? That would make my week."

Bodie laughed and Tater pawed at the door and sat and politely waited to be let back in. Alora opened the door and he trotted next to her to the bar where he copped a spot on the cool floor.

Bodie began making the meal and Alora asked if she could help. Bodie gave her doable tasks, like deboning the rotisserie chicken and stirring in the cream of chicken and sour cream, cheese, and green chilis. They worked in tandem and made small talk, mostly about Tater and the numerous dogs Bodie had growing up and how she'd very much enjoyed volunteering at the rescue, which she'd started doing at age twelve.

"So all the dogs you've had were rescues?" Alora asked as she stirred the rest of the contents in with the shredded chicken.

"They were all from the shelter, yes."

"And they were good dogs?"

"They were great dogs. You know, they say that dogs know when they've been saved."

"Really?"

"My dogs seemed to. They just needed a short while to decompress and then they really thrived and we couldn't have been happier with them."

"That's amazing." Alora peeked around the counter at Tater who remained sprawled out on the floor. "Think he's happy here?"

"Oh, definitely. Aren't you, boy?" Bodie asked, coming over to give him pets. He rolled onto his back and swished his tail. "The shelters can be high stress environments for dogs. Especially sensitive ones. So getting them out and giving them a break really helps with their psyche."

"So him staying here with us is going to help him?"

"Absolutely."

"Even if it's only for a little while?"

"Yes."

Alora continued to stir, seemingly deep in thought. "I was just curious." She slid the big mixing bowl over to Bodie who had prepared the tortillas and was ready to spoon in the mixture and roll them. They were silent for a while as Bodie filled and rolled the tortillas and handed them to Alora who placed them side by side in the casserole dish. Then Bodie poured on the remaining mixture, spread it over all the rolled tortillas and Alora doused the final product with a hearty sprinkle of cheese.

"There," Alora said. "It's ready for the oven."

Bodie covered the dish with foil and placed it in the preheated oven and set the timer. When she faced Alora again she found her holding the bottle of tequila. "Margarita time."

"You said it." Bodie got out the blender, the margarita mix, and the limes and rock salt and they set out to blend the drinks.

"I've got margarita glasses somewhere," Alora said.

"Yep, I know where they are." Bodie opened the cabinet next to the refrigerator and retrieved two heavy margarita glasses with blue-and-green rims. "These are nice and big."

"Mm-hm. You want to do the honors?" Alora asked after she wet the rims with tequila and placed them face down in the rock salt for a quick coating.

Bodie poured in the frozen mixture and Alora topped off the glasses with a wedge of lime. She held hers up to Bodie's. "Cheers."

"Cheers."

They were just about to clink glasses when Bodie halted. "And…to better times ahead," she said with a smile. *I want so much for you to be okay, Alora.*

Alora hesitated, but then tapped her glass to Bodie's. "To better times ahead."

Tater barked as if he was joining in on the toast as well. Alora laughed and they sipped their ice-cold drinks.

"Mm, God yes, that's good," Alora said.

"It sure is. I vote this over wine any day."

"Really? You don't like my wine?"

"Not like I do this."

"You must be more of a beer girl."

"Yes, I think I am."

Alora knelt to pet Tater. "And what do you prefer, Tater? Beer or wine?"

He barked and stood, loving the pets Alora was giving him.

"It's really nice having him here," Bodie said as she watched the two of them. "He was just what this house needed."

"What do you mean?" Alora asked, still rubbing on Tater. She straightened when Bodie was silent. "Oh. Right. I have been a bit of a downer lately, haven't I?"

"I didn't mean anything negative. I just meant—"

"I know, Bodie. It's okay. He has lightened the mood, hasn't he?" She cocked her head. "Do we have food for him? I bet he's hungry for his dinner too." Tater wagged his tail and spun in a circle.

"I picked some up at the store. Some of the good stuff." She opened the pantry and pulled out a small bag of dog food. Tater ran to her and slid to a stop on the ceramic floor, tail going wild.

"He is hungry," Alora said.

"I'll say." Bodie opened the bag, got the bowl she'd also purchased, and poured some of the kibble in. Tater dug in, looking up at her as he chewed as if to say thanks.

"He likes it."

"He should. That's top quality right there," Bodie said.

Alora sipped her drink. "Nothing but the best for Tater."

Alora was smiling as she watched him eat. She was really enjoying his presence and Bodie prayed it would continue. It was nice to see her so relaxed and happy. If only for a short while.

But Bodie tried not to think ahead. She was already growing fond of Tater and she knew she'd hate to see him go, so it was just easier to enjoy the moment.

They ate at the kitchen table and laughed over more margaritas. Tater laid at Alora's feet and didn't beg once. When she tried to sneak him a piece of chicken, he looked at her like he was confused and Bodie couldn't help but laugh. He eventually took the small piece of meat very slowly and gently and gave a quick swish of his tail before he once again rested at Alora's feet.

"Dinner was excellent," Alora said as Bodie carried the dishes to the sink. Alora set to rinsing them and handed them to Bodie to place in the dishwasher. "They even rivaled Fatima's."

"Oh?"

"Mm-hm. But they didn't quite have her magic touch."

"I see. Well, I'll have to ask her about that."

They finished cleaning and Tater went outside to explore.

Bodie went to her room and returned with a bucket of clay. She sat next to Alora on the sofa and fished out a hunk of clay and rolled it into a tangerine-size ball.

Alora watched her curiously. "What are you going to make?"

"A teacup."

Alora continued to watch her. "Is it difficult?"

"Not at all." She paused. "Would you like to try?"

She shrugged. "I don't know. I wasn't very good with making the face."

"I love the face."

"Love? As in present tense?"

"I still have it."

"You really kept it? Brought it home and everything?"

"Sure did."

Alora cracked up.

"What? I like it. It's very good."

"If you say so."

"So what do you think? Want to give it another try?"

Come on, Alora. You can do this.

Alora pressed her lips together. "Oh, why not?"

Bodie scooted closer and handed her the ball of clay.

"What do I do now?" Alora asked.

Bodie gently touched her hands. "Press in with your thumb in the center of the ball, like this. About two-thirds of the way down."

Alora did, with Bodie's thumb on top of hers. Bodie heard her breath catch as they worked together, hands touching. Her own heart rate kicked up considerably. Her thoughts went back to that special night in Mexico in front of the fire and the way Alora had danced atop her in the firelight with the ocean churning just beyond the French doors. It had been magical, beautiful, unforgettable. How she longed to get that moment back.

"Now," Bodie said softly, returning to the present moment to look into her beautiful eyes once again. "You simply press outward with your thumbs as you rotate the clay. Like this." She showed her how and Alora did so, sneaking her tongue out in concentration like she'd done in Mexico when making her first sculpture.

"I'm doing it," Alora said. "I'm making a cup."

She sounded thrilled and her face lit up with joy as she studied her work.

"You're doing great," Bodie said. "Keep going until you're satisfied with the thickness of the cup."

Alora nodded and continued. Bodie watched her in silence, smiling at her newfound joy. A few minutes later, Alora stopped and held the cup in the palm of her hand. "How's that?"

"Brilliant."

"We do the handle now?"

"No, next we do the base." Bodie fished out more clay. "You want a coil base or a padded base?"

"I don't care."

Bodie showed her how to roll the clay to form a coil that they wrapped around the base of the cup. "Now we take this sculpting tool and blend the outer edges of the coil into the bottom of the cup. She demonstrated and Alora took the tool and finished the job.

"Now for the handle."

"Can I try?" Alora asked.

"Sure."

Alora pulled out her own hunk of clay and got to work, massaging the clay in her hands, eventually forming a squared-off handle that she stuck to the side of the cup with pride. “Does that work?”

“I think so,” Bodie said, impressed.

Alora held the cup in her palm to examine it.

“Your first teacup,” Bodie said.

Alora smiled. “My first teacup.” She looked at Bodie. “I did it. I made something. And it actually looks good.”

Bodie returned the smile.

CHAPTER TWENTY-SEVEN

Alora kept rotating her teacup in her hands, loving the way she could feel all the different contours and envision the bits she couldn't see in her mind. She couldn't stop smiling.

"Thank you, Bodie," she whispered as tears threatened.

"For what?"

"For coming up with this. I know you did it purposely." Alora looked at her, wanting to study her reaction. Her cheeks reddened. "You knew I could do this, didn't you? Make the teacup?"

"I was hoping."

"Well, it worked."

"I'm glad." She gently took the teacup from Alora to set it on the table. Then she held her hands. "There are things you can still do, Alora. Lots of things. You just have to find them and experiment a little."

"I want to keep making things with the clay," she said. "If you'll help me."

"I'd be honored."

Alora touched her face and Bodie slowly closed her eyes and leaned into her palm.

"Why haven't you found success with your sculpting, Bodie? You're obviously talented, not to mention a wonderful person."

Bodie seemed to think for a moment. "Time. I've never really had it. Between caring for first my family, then my mother, and having to hold down jobs as well, I just have had very little time for my art."

"No," Alora said as she straightened and inched closer to Bodie. She squeezed her hands. "You have to make time, Bodie. If it's important to you."

"But—"

"No excuses. If you want it badly enough you have to make sacrifices. If that means you get very little sleep, then so be it. If that means you don't work the extra shift at your job, then you pinch pennies for a while. But you let nothing stop you. Nothing."

She showed Bodie her inner wrist. "I know you've seen my tattoo, right?"

Bodie nodded.

"Read it," she said, running her finger across her skin.

"Relentless."

"That's right. I got this when I turned eighteen. To remind me that I had to be relentless to get what I wanted. And when it came to my craft, to my art, I would let nothing stop me."

"So, you're saying I need to create more."

"A lot more. You've been with me for weeks now and I've only seen you work with the clay a handful of times."

"Because I need to be caring for you."

Alora adamantly shook her head. "No. That's an excuse. If you have time on your hands, even if you're with me, like right now, you should be creating. And when you're not able to create for some reason, like when you're lying in your bed at night, instead of watching TV, you should be learning about your craft. Studying. Observing others. Like with YouTube videos. Just like how writers read when they're not working. They're studying their craft. Always keeping their minds on the written word."

"And you did this?" Bodie asked.

"Damn right I did. My whole world was art and painting. My life."

"But isn't that obsessive? And unhealthy?"

"Depends on how badly you want it, I guess. If it's not that important to you, then yes, it would probably be unhealthy to devote so much time and thought to it. But if it's in your blood, Bodie, in the deep recesses of your soul, then you need to literally live it. If you do that, you'll find, not only success, but happiness as well. Because you'll be succeeding at what you love to do. It's a win-win."

Bodie's eyes came alive. "I do love it," she said. "More than anything."

"And I bet you've been frustrated with not having enough time to devote to it."

"Yes."

"You gotta change that, Bodie. And only you can do it."

Alora pointed at the bucket of clay. "That clay should rarely leave your side."

"You won't mind, if I create while I'm here with you?"

"Have I ever complained or told you no?"

"No."

"And I never will. Because I get it. I know what it takes and I want you to have it."

"You do?"

"I do."

Bodie smiled. "Thank you."

Alora waved her off. "No need. Just telling you what worked for me and other artists I know."

Bodie was quiet for a moment. "It means a lot to me that you shared that, Alora. I know you were once worried that that kind of advice was all I wanted from you."

"You've helped me a lot. Just thought I'd return the favor."

"So you're no longer concerned about my intentions?"

Alora chuckled. "No."

Bodie smirked. "You sure?"

"Why?"

"No reason."

"Don't get me wrong. You're still a pain in the ass. But yeah, you've really helped me, even when I thought your ideas were ridiculous. Like with Tater, for instance. Had you told me ahead of time that he was coming, I would've shot you down. So not only have you helped me, but you've learned exactly how to do it as well. You're pretty sharp, Bodie Banks. Pretty damn sharp. But…" She wagged a finger. "Don't let that go to your head."

"Never," she teased her.

They both grew quiet and Alora stared into her eyes once again. She wished she could see the full magnetism of them, the full, incredible beauty. But even with what little she could make of them, she could sense the pureness of Bodie's soul. So much so, that she felt like she could reach out and touch it, as if it were tangible and floating all around her.

"Bodie," Alora said as she indeed reached out and touched her, palming her cheek once again. "I'm so glad you came into my life."

Bodie slowly reached up and removed her hand. "You can't keep touching me like that," she said, breathless. "It—does things to me."

"What if I want it to?"

"You said we don't always get what we want."

"I was upset. Angry."

"Inebriated."

"Yes."

"Like you are now."

"A bit."

"So whatever you say, I shouldn't take it to heart."

Alora tried to touch her face again but Bodie held fast to her hand. "We shouldn't," she said.

Alora dropped her hand. "You don't want me to touch you?"

"You've been through a lot, Alora. And last time, in Mexico…"

"Like I said, I was upset."

"You don't trust me," Bodie said and then quickly glanced away.

Alora shook her head. "You're wrong. I—" but she couldn't finish her thought. Bodie was right. She didn't trust her, didn't trust anybody really. Her body went limp and tears threatened. She stood to walk away, the sting of distrust and rejection too much.

"Wait," Bodie said, lightly gripping her wrist. "Alora." She looked up at her. "Tell me why. Tell me what happened to you. Who hurt you."

"I already have," she rasped.

"I know there's more. There has to be. Tell me. Tell me about you. Do you have any other family?"

Alora stood very still, Bodie's warm hand trying desperately to penetrate her desolate heart. "I have a sister. Jasmine. But she—betrayed me too."

"How? Here sit, please." Bodie brought her back down to the couch. Alora perched on the edge as Bodie took her hands in hers.

"She turned her back on me too, when my mother kicked me out. Wouldn't talk to me. Wouldn't see me. And then, later, after I began really doing well in the art world and became well known, someone sold a story about me and my lifestyle. It wasn't complimentary."

"And you believe it was her?"

"I couldn't prove it, but I believe she knew about it, yes."

"Why would she do that?"

"For the money."

Hot tears formed and ran down her face. She wiped at them angrily, but then Bodie stopped her and deftly swept them away with her thumbs. "I'm so sorry, Alora."

"My mother—that's all she seems to want too. She even called me once to ask for some. Said I owed her that."

"She didn't."

"She did."

Bodie inhaled deeply and wiped away her own tears. "So that's why you wanted me to sign the nondisclosure clause?"

"Yes."

"Okay," Bodie said. "I'll sign it. If it makes you feel better."

"No, it's fine. I don't need you to."

"You sure?"

"Not totally, but I'm trying here. Trying to trust."

Bodie smiled and brushed her hair away from her face. "That's a start."

"Why are you tearing up?" Alora asked. "You feeling badly for me again?"

"I just wish I could go back and change things for you. Somehow give you the family that you deserved. A good family. Like the one I have."

"Tabby once told me that family is what you make it."

"She's right."

"So maybe someday—" but she stopped and stood again. "I hope you don't mind, but I'm worn out. I really need to rest." She headed for the bedroom and stopped at the door to wait for Tater who ran right inside.

"Good night, Bodie." She turned to close the door and caught sight of Bodie looking truly crestfallen. Alora had the urge to go to her, to pull her into her arms, to do anything to erase the troubled and sad look from her face. But she didn't budge. She couldn't handle another rejection, regardless of how small the possibility was that Bodie would turn her away. Her heart was pained enough as it was.

"Thank you very much for dinner."

Bodie swallowed and slowly nodded. "You going to be okay with Tater tonight?"

"I'll be fine."

"He might have to go out in the middle of the night."

"I'll let him out the door in my room."

"Okay," Bodie said softly. "Good night then."

"Night."

Alora closed her door, changed into her pajamas, and crawled into bed. Tater sat on the floor looking up at her.

"Oh, alright." She scooted over to make room for him and he joined her on the bed, turning in a circle before settling down against her. She wrapped her arm around him and buried her face in his soft, warm fur. Then she cried herself to sleep.

❖

When she awoke hours later, she was still curled into him, lulled by the cadence of his breathing. A sliver of sunlight shone in through the slit in the curtains and she could hear the early morning chirp of the late April birds. She stroked Tater's head as he stirred.

"Morning," she said.

He angled his head to lick her face, causing her to laugh.

"Morning kisses, huh?" She sat up and he leapt off the bed and ran to the back door. He hadn't woken her once throughout the night needing to go out. He'd let her sleep. She rose and let him out the door. "You're such a good boy," she said as she watched him happily trot around the backyard.

She turned to dress and smelled the fresh brewed scent of coffee. Bodie was up. Alora glanced at the clock. It was after nine. Whatever happened to her getting up early to get started on her day?

She finished dressing and brushed her teeth. Then she went out into the kitchen to join Bodie, who, surprisingly, was sitting at the kitchen table, working on a new sculpture on a small elevated turntable.

"Hi," she said, glancing up briefly at Alora. "Would you like some breakfast?"

"No, you're working. I can manage."

Bodie set down her tool. "I can stop and cook for you."

"I'll just make some cereal." She tried to smile but knew it probably fell flat. She felt bad about the night before and wasn't sure what to say about it. She'd had a little too much to drink and she hadn't handled Bodie's rejection very well. But that wasn't a huge surprise. She hadn't been handling much of anything well lately. Then there was the brief discussion of her past and her mother and sister, Jasmine. Oh, what Bodie must think.

She got herself a mug and carefully poured in some coffee. She burned her finger, but it only stung for a few seconds. Then she retrieved a bowl, some almond milk, and a box of Honey Bunches of Oats and made herself her breakfast. She carried the bowl over to the table to sit across from Bodie.

"What are you working on?"

Bodie halted with her scoring tool and turned the small sculpture around to face her. "I got an idea last night." The piece was of two women, one reaching out to touch the other on the cheek, while the other woman covered her hand with her own. They were gazing into one another's eyes like there was no one else on earth around them.

"Bodie," she breathed. "It's beautiful."

She studied the figures closer. Noted the one with the shorter hair trimmed close on one side, and the other figure with the piercings. "Is that us?"

"Yes."

"I—" She shook her head. "Why?"

"I was torn up after last night. So I wanted to make something that represented how I really feel. And this is it."

"How do you feel, Bodie?"

She visibly swallowed. "I think you know how I feel. Because I think you feel it too. It's just—we're both dealing with a lot right now. Me with my grief over my mother, you with your vision loss and move. I'm afraid if we gave into our feelings for one another right now, it wouldn't end up being as good as it could be. You understand, don't you?"

Alora slowly nodded. "I don't want to necessarily but yeah, I understand."

"Do you hate me?" The corner of her mouth lifted.

"I could never hate you, Bodie."

"And I couldn't you, either."

Alora focused back on the piece as warm tears threatened to fall once again.

"It's wonderful." Her throat tightened.

"Thanks. I think I'm going to make others similar to this. With women. Women in love. You don't see a lot of that in the art world."

"No, I suppose you don't. Not like this." Alora smiled. "You may have just found your niche, Bodie. And you're incredibly good at it." The detail was amazing. Almost impossible looking. "How long have you been working on this?"

"I was up all night. Couldn't sleep."

"Because of me?"

"I couldn't get what you told me from my mind."

"I'm sorry, Bodie. I shouldn't have shared that."

"No, no, no, I'm glad you did. Really glad. In fact, I think you need to talk about it more."

"Oh?"

"How would you feel about talking to someone?"

"You mean like a therapist?" She blinked at her.

"Yes. Someone other than me or Tabby. I think it would really be beneficial for you."

Alora let out a laugh. “Oh, you do, do you?”

“Please don’t take offense.”

“Who’s taking offense? You pretty much just told me I need to see a shrink.”

Bodie held up her hands. “I know how you must feel about it, but, Alora, if it helps any, I’ve been to therapy. Actually, I’m even thinking about starting back up. To help me deal with my grief over my mother. I haven’t exactly been doing well with that and my family has noticed.”

“You’ve—gone to therapy?”

“There’s absolutely nothing wrong with it. It really helps, Alora. It’s self care. And self care is vital. You could take Tater with you to your sessions. He could be moral support.”

“Tater? Really?” It would be nice to have him by her side.

“You could even have the sessions here at the house. There are therapists who work online. Whatever works for you.”

Alora stared out into the backyard at Tater who was lounging in the sunshine. Maybe it wouldn’t hurt to try. Maybe it would actually help. Anything would be better than feeling like she had been feeling lately.

She looked back to Bodie who was watching her closely.

“Okay,” she said. “I’ll do it.”

CHAPTER TWENTY-EIGHT

Tabby paced back and forth in the living room as Bodie put the finishing touches on her sculpture. She'd completed the fine details two days before and now she was working on the finish. When she was done with that, all she had to do was fire it in her kiln, which she'd brought to Alora's. She'd made sure it was okay first and Alora had readily agreed, wanting to fire her own little teacups too. She'd been excited at the prospect of painting one and she was going to just as soon as she was done with her first therapy session.

"God, how much longer?" Tabby asked as she looked at her watch.

"I don't know, but you're going to burn a hole in that rug."

She stopped pacing. "Do you think it's going okay? You know, because she's never done this before and I know how she hates talking about her past."

"I'm sure it's going fine."

Bodie went to dip her brush in more medium gray but realized she didn't have any left. She'd stretched what she'd had far enough. She set down her brush and stood.

"Where are you going?" Tabby asked as if she were going to abandon her.

"I'm just going to go look for my paints. I'll be right back."

She walked through the center of the house back to the rear hallway where she and Alora kept all their art supplies in one of the spare bedrooms. At some point Alora wanted to turn the office area near the living area room into a studio like she'd done at her previous house. But that had been put on the back burner now that she was no longer painting.

Bodie opened the door and switched on the light. She went to the boxes that contained her supplies. She rummaged through a couple, but didn't find her latex paints. She straightened and stared for a moment, hands on hips. Where had the rest of her supplies gone? She rotated slowly, searching the stacks of canvases and boxes and full shelves, but she still didn't see the rest of her boxes, which she'd clearly labeled as her own.

Then she remembered that Alora had been in the room a few days before, searching for something. Maybe she'd moved her boxes.

Bodie rummaged through more supplies, moved other boxes around and searched behind rows of leaning canvases, some of them still wrapped in cellophane. When she found nothing, she turned to face the closet door.

"They've got to be in there."

She opened the door. It was a good-sized walk-in closet and the first thing she noticed was a large wooden easel with a covered canvas on it. She looked back at the canvases lining the wall. Some were painted, some not. Question was, why was this one covered and in the closet?

She faced the easel once again and slowly removed the cover to reveal a beautiful but unfinished painting. A shrill voice came from the bedroom door.

"What are you doing?" It was Alora and her face was twisted into a serious scowl. "Just what the hell do you think you're doing?" She marched in, ripped the cover from Bodie's hand, and slung it back over the painting.

"I'm sorry—I was looking for my box of paints and I—"

"You what? Thought you'd snoop around in my stuff?"

"No, Alora—"

"Well, what do you think, huh? Now that you've seen it."

"Seen what?"

"Don't play coy. The painting. The one I fucked up. The one I'm unable to finish."

"I didn't even really look at it—"

"Right." She laughed. "Just get out."

"What?"

"Leave."

"But Alora—"

"Go!" She backed Bodie out of the room.

"Okay, okay, I'm sorry, I'm going."

Alora slammed the door in her face and Bodie headed back to the living room while Tater remained at the door, looking confused.

"What's going on?" Bodie asked when she found Tabby standing with her head in her hands. "Alora's furious."

"It didn't go well," Tabby said.

"Why not?"

"She wouldn't tell me."

"Well, she has to keep going. It's the only way it will help."

"I know, but the mood she's in right now, there's no way she will agree to do it again."

"I'll talk to her when she calms down." Bodie went to the fridge and cracked open a bottle of water and took a hearty sip. "And what's up with that painting in the studio? The one she said she can't finish?"

Tabby's face paled. "Please tell me you didn't see it."

"Why?"

"Oh, God, Bodie. She doesn't ever want anyone to see it. She's embarrassed by it."

"She has nothing to be embarrassed about. It's just a painting."

"*Just* a painting?" Alora said as she stormed into the room reaching out to brace herself on the counter. "*Just* a painting? That may be all it is to you, but to me it's everything."

"I'm sorry, Alora. I didn't mean anything by that. I just meant—" Bodie tried.

"I thought I told you to get out?"

"Sorry?" She looked to Tabby, thoroughly confused. "I did, Alora."

"No. I mean get out of here. Out of my house."

"Alora," Tabby said. "What are you doing?"

"I mean it. I don't want her here. I don't want anyone here." She looked back to Bodie. "Go. Now."

Bodie swallowed, totally frozen to the floor. Her heart thudded in her ears. She looked to Tabby again who seemed to be as shocked as she was.

"Now," Alora said.

Bodie jerked and went into motion. She headed for the table to pack up her sculpture and supplies.

"No, I mean now," Alora said. "Just take your keys and go. You too, Tabby. I want to be alone."

"You can't be alone."

"The hell I can't." She tossed Tabby her keys and scorched Bodie with a pain-filled look. "And don't come back tonight either."

Bodie tried to speak some sort of reason into her. "Alora, therapy takes time and at first it can be uncomfortable—"

"Don't," she said. "You don't know me, Bodie. What works for you doesn't work for me."

"But if you'll just give it time—"

"Go!" she said, pointing at the front door.

Bodie's skin burned with adrenaline and emotion. She clenched her jaw, more confused than ever and, if she had to admit, more than a little angry. She snatched her keys off the counter. "Fine."

"Bodie, wait," Tabby said, chasing after her. "She doesn't mean it. She's just upset."

"I think she's made herself rather clear." Bodie tugged open the door. How could she do this? After all the talks and feelings they'd shared? She'd really thought Alora had made some progress. She'd thought Alora really cared about her like she did her.

She gave Alora one last look. She was standing between the kitchen and the living room, face buried in her hands with Tater at her side. Bodie's chest ached at the sight and she fought the urge to go to her. But instead, the anger she felt rose and spilled over like a boiling pot of water. "Tell her not to call me. I won't want to talk to her, not even when she's ready to apologize."

"Bodie—"

"No, Tabby," Bodie said as she opened the door and stepped outside. "I've had enough."

"She's hurting—"

"She's an adult, Tabby, and it's time she started acting like one. We all hurt. But we don't all take it out on those around us. Not like she does."

Tabby stammered, still chasing after her as she hurried to her car. "I'm sure she'll cool off. She's just upset over the session—"

"Call me and I'll come get my things when she's not around."

She opened her car door and slid inside. "And, Tabby? Maybe you should do what she wants and leave too. It might be the best thing for her." Bodie closed the door, started her car, and drove away, leaving Alora Anders behind her.

CHAPTER TWENTY-NINE

Alora sat out under the night sky in one of her padded patio chairs. She nursed a glass of wine and reached down to love on Tater, who was sitting in the lounge next to her with his eyes closed.

It was a beautiful evening, even if it was a little warmer than it had been a few weeks before. And the stars? Well, they were there, she just couldn't see many of them due to the city lights of Phoenix. But just knowing they were there and shining down on her was a comfort. Something, she had to admit, she hadn't been feeling much of lately. Save for Tater.

Kimberly from the shelter had called the day before, asking how things were going with him and she'd told her that Tater no longer needed a home. He now had one. Kimberly had been thrilled and she'd said she'd bring over the paper work for his official adoption soon. She'd asked about Bodie, if maybe she'd like her to just bring her to pick up the paperwork, but Alora had told her that wouldn't be doable at the moment. Kimberly had asked no further questions and Alora had been glad.

She slid on her glasses and glanced down at her phone as a text vibrated. It was Tabby, asking how she was. It was the first she'd heard from her in days. Alora stared at the text. Should she answer? If so, what would she say? *Yes, I'm fine, thanks for checking?* Or should she tell her the truth? *I'm alive but I'm miserable and I miss you. Please come over so we can talk?*

She rubbed her temple and spoke into her phone, sending a text back. She told her she was fine and thanked her for checking in. She hesitated however when she tried to say more. She sent the text and lowered the phone, tears stinging her eyes. What was wrong with her? Why was she being like this and pushing everyone away?

Why am I such an ass?

It was that therapy session. Dr. Vega had asked her questions about past trauma. She hadn't dug very deep, but she'd dug enough to upset her. And then when she'd suggested that maybe Alora's trust issues were due to her mother kicking her out at fourteen and that maybe she also had a fear of abandonment, Alora had lost it. What did she know? She didn't. Couldn't. She didn't know her. No one did. Well, with the exception of Tabby.

Dear sweet Tabby, who she'd run off as well.

She looked again to her phone. Tabby hadn't responded. She wondered why.

Because you're still being an insensitive ass.

"Do you think I'm an ass, boy?" she asked Tater, who lifted his head to take her in. "Huh?"

He wagged his tail.

"Great, I'll take that into consideration." She rubbed his head and then lifted her phone. She spoke into it, texting Tabby. She got choked up as she apologized and asked her if they could talk.

It took a few moments, moments in which her heart pounded with the fear of rejection. But eventually a reply came through.

Tabby was on her way over.

Alora breathed a sigh of relief and finished off her wine to stand. Tater followed her into the house and she slipped out of her pajamas and into a pair of soft knit yoga pants and a T-shirt. She hadn't been out of pajamas in days and it felt good to change into something a little more appropriate. She didn't want Tabby to think she'd been up to absolutely nothing since they'd argued. She'd only be more concerned.

Alora spent the next half hour trying to straighten up the house. She loaded the dishwasher, dropped a cereal bowl and had to clean it up, and wiped down the counters. Then she folded the throws and rested them along the back of the couch. She also picked up Tater's numerous toys and chewies, which she'd ordered for him online.

She placed them in a wicker basket in the corner of the living room and took a moment to glance around. It wasn't ideal, but hopefully it didn't look too pathetic either. Then she turned on her wax melter to fill the house with the calming scent of lavender and sage.

Lastly, she eyed the kitchen table, where she'd been working with the clay she'd also ordered online. That and spending time with Tater and downing more than her fair share of wine, was really all she'd been up to. But the clay, the sculpting, had really helped to calm her nerves and she'd even begun experimenting with it beyond the teacups.

The doorbell rang and Tater barked and trotted to her to lead her to the door. She unlocked it, opened it, and smiled at Tabby, who stood looking somber.

"Hi," Alora said, a little confused. Tabby usually always had a smile for her.

Tabby came inside and headed straight for the living room. Only she didn't sit. Alora closed the door and followed her, now more confused than ever.

"Would you like to sit?" she asked, feeling uncomfortable at her scowl and her crossed arms.

"Thank you, no. I just came by to say a few things."

"Oh."

Tabby held up her hands, as if expecting Alora to interrupt her or argue. "Look, Alora, we've been friends for a long time."

"Since we were kids," Alora said softly, her heart already beginning to pound.

"Yes, and in all that time, I think it's safe to say, that I've been there for you, through thick and thin."

"You have."

She paused again as if alarmed that Alora wasn't disagreeing with her. "I think I've more than been there for you. I've been, well, codependent. I've often times put your needs before my own. Before my own children."

Alora gulped. She wanted to argue, to protest, but she couldn't. She couldn't because Tabby was right.

"And I—I can't do it anymore. No—I—won't do it anymore. I won't."

Alora leaned against the counter to steady herself. Her blood pressure was through the roof, she could tell by her fluttering heart, the pounding in her head, and the flushing of her skin. Though Tabby was right and had every right to say what she was saying, each and every word was like a dagger to Alora's insides.

"You need help, Alora. And I won't be around unless you're choosing to get it." She inhaled sharply like she'd said it all in one big breath. "There. That's it. That's what I wanted to say." She looked at Alora, stared at her waiting for her to respond.

But Alora was lost, caught somewhere suspended in time. The present moment null and void to her as if she were on another plane of existence. She couldn't pull herself out of the trance.

"Alora?"

Tabby took a step toward her. "Alora, answer me. You're scaring me." She grabbed her shoulders and shook her. Alora jerked back into the present and nearly toppled over.

"Whoa," Tabby said, supporting her. She led her over to the couch and eased her down. "Are you alright?"

Alora touched her head. "I'm fine." But she felt weak and dizzy. She hadn't been eating very much. Too caught up in her wine and misery.

"You're obviously not fine." She sat next to her. "And this is what I'm talking about. See, now I feel like I need to care for you, to make sure you're alright."

"No," Alora said softly. "Don't. I'll be okay."

Tabby took in the room. "The house needs to be cleaned. You need to eat and bathe. You're not going to be okay."

"But you're right," Alora said. "You can't do it for me, Tabby."

"No, I can't. But I can make sure you find some help. You do want help, don't you?"

Alora closed her eyes. "Yes. If it means you'll stay in my life."

"No," Tabby said, grabbing her hands, forcing her to open her eyes. "You have to do it for you, Alora, and no one else."

Alora opened her mouth to argue but changed her mind. Once again Tabby was right. She had to do it for herself. Problem was, right now, she didn't give a damn about herself. But she did care about Tater and his well-being. And she loved Tabby and the kids and Fatima and…Bodie. Where was Bodie? Was she okay? It had been radio silence from her as well and she'd done her very best not to think of her. It just pained her too much to do so.

Alora nodded. "Okay."

Tabby teared up and held her face. "I love you, you bear. You impossibly stubborn ass bear." She pulled her in for a long hug. "Don't you give up on life, Alora. Please. You have people that care, that love you, that want you to be happy. But you can't treat us the way you do." She drew away. "Understand?"

Alora felt her face crumble as sobs overtook her. Oh, God, she'd treated everyone so unfairly. Been such a moody, angry ass. "I'm sorry," she said. "I'm so sorry. I don't know why I act like I do."

"That's what therapy is for, sweetie. To help you figure that stuff out."

"But—"

"No buts. You have to do it if you want to push through this. I'm not saying it's going to be easy. By any means. But you have to work through the hard stuff so you can enjoy the good. And you've got a lot of good, Alora."

"No, I don't. I've lost everything."

Tabby shook her head. "It's all about perspective. You have a nice home, a wonderful companion in Tater, who I'm assuming you're keeping, and a million opportunities just waiting for you to explore them. Plus, you've got me and the kids, who adore you, and Fatima and—"

"Bodie?"

Tabby's face fell. "I'm not sure about Bodie, Alora."

"What do you mean? How is she?" she asked as she sniffled, feeling a bit panicked.

"She's…okay. I spoke to her a few days ago. She's going back to school to finish her degree. She wants to teach art."

Alora smiled and wiped her eyes. "That's great." She was truly happy for her, happy to hear that she'd be doing something she loved. But her heart fell to her stomach. "That means she won't come back, doesn't it?"

She squeezed her hands. "That doesn't mean that you're on your own here, Alora. I'll give you the numbers to the other candidates we interviewed and you can choose one. You really should have someone here with you."

Alora nodded, knowing she needed the help, but wishing like hell that person could be Bodie. But after the way she'd treated her, she couldn't blame her for leaving and moving on with her life. Just the thought of not seeing her though, sent her mind reeling. "I'm going to miss her," she confessed.

"Me too."

"Do you…think she would talk to me?"

"Honestly? I'm not sure, Lor. She was stung pretty bad when you kicked her out. So if I were you, I'd start out with a big apology and let that soak in before you try anything else."

"Yeah, okay. I really fucked up, didn't I?"

"You did, sweetie. You pushed us all away and you have to find out why so it doesn't keep happening."

Alora squeezed her hand in return. "Okay." She nodded. "I'll do it. No matter how bad it hurts and scares me."

"Good."

"Would you—have dinner with me, Tabby? We can order out."

"You mean you want to eat?"

"I want to try."

"That's great. But unfortunately, I've got to run. The kids have a game."

"Oh, right. Rain check?"

"You bet." She kissed her cheek. "But you should still order out. Get something you love." She headed for the door.

"I'll call you," Alora called out after her.

"See you later, gator." She blew a kiss and closed the door behind her. Alora went to lock it and then stood staring out the window, watching Tabby as she climbed into her car. She drove off quickly, leaving Alora in her wake.

And Alora was once again all alone.

But she supposed she deserved to be.

CHAPTER THIRTY

Bodie put down her pen and rubbed her eyes. She'd been staring at the screen of her laptop for an hour, trying to finish her assignment. And this was after she'd read in her textbook for two hours.

She powered down the laptop and closed the lid. Then she slid from the table and opened the fridge for a cold can of off-brand cola. She cracked it open and settled on the couch. She considered turning on the TV but then remembered that she only had what the antenna she'd bought would pick up and decided against it. She wasn't in the mood for reruns or news. She was in the mood for peace. Peace and quiet.

She rubbed her eyes again as she thought about the history course she'd been working on. While she loved history, the course was intense with a large amount of reading required. And the questions she was required to answer were extensive and detailed, ensuring that she couldn't just skim over the text. It was more work than she'd remembered, even for an elective class, but she was powering through, determined to get her degree so she could teach. She only had a semester left for her bachelor of arts in art history at Arizona State. So, she was taking as many courses as she could online for the summer. Then in the fall, she'd be able to finish up with what was left.

So for now it was Egyptian art and culture, theories of modern sculpture, and revolutionary Europe. Other than having to readjust to the workload, she was enjoying the courses and enjoying the learning. Plus, knowing that she was doing something for herself, for her future, was a satisfying feeling and it gave her hope.

There was a light knock at the door and the knob turned and a tiny face peered in.

"Aunt Bodie?"

She stood. "Hey, you. Come on in."

The door was pushed open and her nephew, Wyatt, scrambled in, carrying a large drink from QT. He brought it to her with two hands and handed it over. "We got this for you."

"Well, thank you."

She took the drink, ruffled his hair, and he took off toward the kitchen where she kept some art supplies for him in a lower cabinet. Kristy followed him inside, carrying a shopping bag from Salad and Go.

"Brought you dinner," she said as she set the bag on the coffee table. "Thought you might be hungry from all that studying."

"I am, thanks."

Kristy headed into the kitchen and returned with two forks and paper towels for napkins.

"Wyatt ate his chicken nuggets in the car," she said, handing Bodie her fork. "He wanted to come right in and color."

Bodie laughed. "He's quite the little artist."

"Takes after you, I suppose."

She settled on the couch next to Bodie and they each retrieved their bowls of salad.

"You got me the barbecue chicken ranch?" Bodie asked.

"Mm-hm. It's what you like, right?"

Bodie popped off the lid and dug in. "Yep. You're an angel."

"Ha, first time I've ever heard you say that."

Bodie smiled. "There's a first time for everything." She chewed and swallowed. "No, but seriously, thank you. You've really been there for me these past few weeks and I appreciate it."

"That's what sisters are for. What family is for. We lift each other up, help when we can. God knows you were always there for us growing up. Christ, you were like a second mother."

"I did what I had to do."

Kristy took a bite and chewed in silence. "It wasn't right," she said. "That you had to do that."

"I'm over it, Kristy. No need to dredge it all up again."

"But it affected you. Your whole life has been put on hold because of the responsibilities you had."

"Yes, but I'm remedying that now. Going back to school and finishing my degree."

"And I'm glad. It's about time, you know? That you focused on you instead of caring for someone else."

Bodie pulled her phone from her pocket as it vibrated with a text. She blinked at it at first, unsure she was reading correctly. But when she read it a second time, it sank in.

Bodie,

I just wanted to say I'm sorry. I'm sorry for the way I treated you and I'm sorry for the way things ended. I was wrong. So very wrong. I hope some day you can forgive me and I hope that you are doing well.

All my best,

Alora

Bodie lowered the phone, her throat tight. She forced a swallow and inhaled sharply as she tucked the phone back into her pocket.

"What is it?" Kristy asked.

"Nothing."

"It's obviously something. You look as though you've seen a ghost."

"Just a text from someone I wasn't expecting to hear from."

"Who? Her? Alora?"

Bodie didn't respond, the words from the text still playing in her mind. She wondered what prompted the apology and why it hadn't come sooner. She also wondered if she should respond and if so, what would she say?

"What she did to you wasn't right, by the way," Kristy said.

"Maybe not, but she has her own issues. I don't hold anything against her." She didn't. Not really. Alora had things she needed to work through. Hell, they all did. And while what she did wasn't right, Bodie wasn't one to hold a grudge. Plus, she cared about her. Really cared about her and that hadn't changed.

"You should," Kristy said.

"What would be the point?" Bodie swallowed another bite and then set the bowl on the coffee table. "She's not a bad person, she's just…lost."

Kristy was quiet for a long moment and Bodie could feel her staring at her.

"Oh my God. You don't have feelings for her, do you?"

Bodie turned to her and felt herself redden. "Why would you think that?" Her feelings for Alora were no one's business. Besides, she knew Kristy would think she was crazy for having them and she didn't want to hear it.

"Oh my God, you do." She pointed her fork at her. "You're so obvious."

"You're being ridiculous."

"No, I'm right. It's written all over your face. You've got a soft spot for her."

Bodie didn't speak. She just stared out the window, thinking of Alora, wondering how she was getting along. Was she okay? Was she managing? How was Tater? Did she keep him? How were her treatments? Was she still doing therapy? Was that what prompted the apology?

"Hello, Earth to Bodie?"

"Hm?"

"Where were you? I've been sitting here talking to you."

"Oh, sorry."

"I asked you if Alora had feelings for you."

Bodie blinked and slowly refocused on her sister. "I think maybe she does. But she's—"

"Too screwed up to know what to do about it?"

Bodie shrugged and took a sip of her big drink.

"I figured," Kristy continued. "With her track record and all."

"She's not a bad person," Bodie said.

"So you've stated." She raised an eyebrow. "But she, what? Has some particularly bad behavior is that what you're afraid to say?"

"I'm not afraid to say anything. I just choose not to. She doesn't deserve that. She's just…lost."

"So you've said." She set down her fork. "You keep repeating the same things. Just what all happened between the two of you? Did you sleep with her? Is that it? And she got pissed over something and kicked you out over some kind of lover's quarrel?"

Bodie shook her head. "It's not like that."

"Then what is it?"

"It's nothing. Nothing that I'm going to share anyway."

"You're always so damn chivalrous. Refusing to say a bad word about anyone, even when you should, for your own well-being."

"That's not who I am."

"Maybe it's who you should be. Because keeping all these things inside can be harmful, Bodes." She stabbed at her salad as if she didn't really want to fork a bite at all. "And I don't like seeing you hurt."

"I'm fine. I'm moving on and moving forward. Alora…well, I wish her the best."

"You're a better woman than I."

Bodie laughed. "I could say so many things to that."

Kristy leaned over and slugged her playfully. "But you won't."

"No, I won't."

Kristy pointed at Bodie's bowl on the coffee table. "You better eat that. You're looking too thin these days."

"I've been living off ramen."

"That stuff is terrible for you."

"I know. But I've got to be careful with my money."

"I thought you were back at the bakery?"

"I work three nights a week."

"Why not work more?"

Bodie sighed, unsure what all she should share, worried about what Kristy would think.

"I need time to study and I need time to…sculpt."

"Sculpt?"

"Yeah."

"Bodie, you need money. You don't have time to be chasing a pipe dream."

"It's not a pipe dream. It's my work. My art."

"But—"

"No buts, Kris. Not anymore. I have to make sacrifices for what I want and I am. So don't try to talk me out of it."

Kristy blinked at her. "Okay, Bodes," she said softly.

"That's one thing I learned from Alora. I need to devote more time to my craft if I really want it and I do. I really want it." She stood. "Come here, I want to show you what I'm working on."

Kristy placed her bowl on the table and followed Bodie into her bedroom where she had her latest sculpture sitting on her desk, covered carefully in plastic to keep it moist. A humidifier blew from the corner of the room to help with the overly dry desert air. Bodie gently removed the plastic and stood aside for Kristy to see.

She reached out to touch it but Bodie stopped her. "Don't. It's a work in progress."

"It's—what is it?"

"It represents what I feel for Mom, now that she's passed."

"Oh." But she looked confused, lost even, and Bodie knew she didn't get it. But she wasn't surprised. Her siblings never understood her creations or even her need to create. To them it was a hobby. A silly, meaningless hobby and she'd only ever got grief from them for doing it.

She re-covered the sculpture and secured the base to keep the air out. Then she turned up the humidifier and went to leave the room. But Kristy remained, staring at the finished sculptures on her dresser and shelves. "Are those…women together?"

"Yes. But I'm no longer making those."

"Why not? They're beautiful."

Bodie shrugged. "I'm just not feeling it."

Kristy ran her fingers over the varying pieces of women embracing. "You really have a thing for this sculpting stuff, don't you?"

Bodie wasn't in the mood to be mocked or made fun of again, so she remained silent.

Kristy glanced at her. "I never really noticed before, but you're very good. Like really good."

"I love doing it."

"Yes, I know."

"Do you?"

"Yes, Bodie. I'm hearing you. For the first time I'm hearing you." She smiled at her. "I'm sorry I didn't before. It's obviously very important to you. I just didn't realize how important."

"It's not a pipe dream."

"No, and I shouldn't have said that." She touched her arm. "I'm sorry." She glanced back at all the sculptures. "You're doing you. And it's beautiful."

Bodie's eyes filled with tears. Kristy wiped a fallen one off her cheek.

"My sister, the sculptor. My sister, the artist. My sister with the huge heart."

Bodie broke with sobs and Kristy enveloped her in a hug and held her tight. Soon she was crying along with her.

"What's wrong with you guys?" Wyatt asked.

They drew apart and wiped their eyes. "Nothing, bud," Bodie said with a short laugh. "These are happy tears."

"Happy tears? I never heard of such a thing." He placed his hands on his hips. "Can I have a pop, Aunt Bodie? I'm thirsty."

"Ask your mom."

"Can I, Mom, please?"

"You've already had one today."

"But I'm thirsty and Aunt Bodie doesn't have anything else in her fridga-dator."

"Then have water."

"Ugh." He crossed his arms. "I don't want water."

"Come on, bud. I'll make you some strawberry lemonade," Bodie said.

"Bodie, that's loaded with sugar."

But Bodie put her finger to her lips. "Not this kind." She led him into the kitchen and opened up one of the single powdered drink packets she'd bought at the dollar store and mixed it with ice water. She brought it to him at the kitchen table where he was playing with Play-Doh. "Whatcha making?"

"I'm cooking," he said, rolling a ball of the smelly clay in his hands. "Pah-sketti."

"Spaghetti? That sounds good. Can I have some?"

He nodded and snuck his tongue out in concentration as he ran the clay through one of the toys to make long strings. The sight shocked her heart as memories of Alora came rushing back into her mind. She braced herself and eased into a chair.

"What's wrong?" he asked her as he paused in his noodle making.

"Hm? Nothing, bud. I'm okay."

"You're probably hungry." He scooped the noodles onto a small toy plate and handed them over. She pretended to eat them and he grinned. "Are they good?"

"Mm-hm. You bet they are."

He clapped. "I love pah-sketti."

"Me too."

He gave her more and then drank heartily from the cup of strawberry lemonade. When he lowered it, he had a dark pink mustache that made her laugh. Then he softly burped and wiped his mouth with the back of his hand and said, "'Scuse me," which made her laugh all the harder.

"What's so funny?" he asked, turning his little head.

"You. You make me so happy."

"I do?"

"Yup."

"How come?"

Bodie thought about that for a second. "Because you're just you, bud." And she realized that she wanted to be just like her nephew. No matter what it took.

CHAPTER THIRTY-ONE

Tater barked just before a knock sounded at the door. Alora checked the peephole with her less affected eye and unlocked the door to pull it open.

"Hey, stranger," Simone Richards said with a crooked smile. The hot breeze teased her red sheer scarf and toyed with the tendrils of her hair. She looked amazing. But then again Simone always looked amazing. The woman was flawless.

"Simone. God, it's good to see you." Alora embraced her and they held each other as Tater wiggled and circled them excitedly.

"Who's this?" Simone asked as she entered the house.

"This is Tater," Alora said as she closed the door.

"Hey, Tater." Simone knelt to love on him. "You're a handsome guy, aren't you?"

"He's a new addition."

"Oh?"

"I decided I needed a furry companion."

"Well, I can see you've made the right choice. He's adorable."

"Would you like me to take your bag?"

She was carrying her unusually large tote, as always. "No, I've got it."

Alora rolled her eyes. "Come on, Simone, I can handle your bag." She held out her hand and Simone slipped off her tote and gave it to her. Alora hung it on the hall tree and they continued into the house.

"So these are the new digs, huh?"

"What do you think? I know it's a lot smaller and not near as nice as the other house, but…"

Simone glanced around and then met her gaze. "What do you think, Alora? Do you like it?"

Alora placed her hands on her hips and exhaled. "I do. I really think I do."

"Then that's wonderful." She spread her arms. "I think it's lovely. And this guy only adds to the charm." She scratched Tater's head.

"Thank you," Alora smiled. "Would you like something to drink? I have wine."

"I'd love some."

Alora retrieved a wine glass and pulled the chilled bottle from the fridge. She poured her a hearty amount and handed the glass over.

"You're not going to have any?"

"I'm cutting back. Turns out it's not so good for my eyes. Or for any part of me for that matter."

Simone kept her gaze as she sipped. "How are you, Alora? You doing okay?"

Alora hesitated, not sure what all she should say. But then she remembered her therapy and how it was okay to be vulnerable. Especially around those that cared for you. "I wasn't for a while, Simone. But I'm doing better now."

"I'm sure it's been a big adjustment."

"It has. And I had, er, *have* a lot of inner work to do still. But I'm trying and that's all I can do."

Simone grew quiet.

Alora unscrewed a bottle of water from the fridge and leaned on the counter to sip from it. "I'm sure you've spoken to Bodie and she's filled you in on me."

"Bodie? No, she hasn't said a word."

"Have you seen her?"

"Yes, of course. But she hasn't said anything about you, good or bad."

Alora pressed her lips together, truly surprised. Maybe Tabby had been right about Bodie after all. Maybe she wasn't the type to spread gossip. Alora's heart flitted as she recalled memories of Bodie and the nice times they'd had. She wished she could go back and change things. She wished for a lot of things.

"Have you spoken to her?" Simone asked.

Alora pushed out a long breath. "I've texted her."

Simone nodded but said nothing further. Alora was glad because she didn't want to have to admit that she'd heard nothing from Bodie in return. She assumed she was still upset with her and rightfully so. She'd behaved unforgivably.

"Is she…well?" Alora asked.

Simone nodded again, but this time smiled softly along with it. "She is."

"I hear she's going back to school."

"You heard correctly. She's finishing up that art history degree."

"Art history?"

"She wants to teach. Not that she has to have a degree in art history to do that. But that's the degree she started years ago and she didn't want the hassle of changing it. Plus, she can do other things with it if she decides against teaching."

"Such as?"

"She can work at a gallery for starters."

"She'd probably really like that."

"I think she'll enjoy teaching more. Kids eat art up and Bodie is a phenomenal teacher."

"Is she still teaching at the rec center?"

"Mm-hm."

"I bet she's a great teacher."

Simone moved toward the kitchen table, glass of wine in hand. "Is this the new work you were telling me about?"

"That's one piece, yes." Alora gently lifted the small pitcher off the wheel and held it out for Simone to examine.

"It's lovely."

"I've really taken to the clay. I can feel my way with it, which helps with the vision issues."

"Right."

"Come on, I'll show you the finished ones."

She led her back through the house to the spare bedroom where she had several of the completed pitchers and teacups on the shelves.

"Alora," Simone breathed, lifting a pitcher. "These are magnificent. I love the composition and the color. The gold streaks throughout really bring the eye in."

"You really like them?"

"Yes, are you kidding?" She replaced the pitcher on the shelf and picked up a teacup. "And look at these! With the little faces on them."

"I do those for fun. Each one represents whatever mood I'm in at that moment."

"They're so whimsical, I love it." She looked at Alora. "These should be shown."

"What? No." She took the teacup from her to return it to the shelf.

"Alora, they're good and unique and I really think people should see them. I've got a friend who's organizing a small, local show here soon and she's got one more spot open."

"It's just me messing around. They aren't show material."

"I'm telling you, they are." She whipped out her phone and began to take photos. "At least let me send her some pics. See what she says."

Alora ran her hand through her hair, her nerves on edge. Should she show her work? Were they really good enough? What if people didn't like them? Could she handle another rejection? But then she once again recalled her therapy sessions and the fact that she needed to take chances in life, regardless of her fears. She also recalled the breathing techniques she'd been taught and inhaled a deep breath, held it for four seconds and then exhaled for four seconds. Thankfully, Simone didn't seem to notice, too busy sending the photos to pay attention. When she finished, she smiled as she took in the rest of the room.

"How's the painting going?" She walked over to a leaning stack of canvases and perused some of the finished work. Work Alora had done prior to her vision problem.

"It's not."

"No?"

"Nope. Those are old. And small."

"They're very good."

"Pick one."

Simone raised her head to look at her. "Don't kid," she said. "You know I love your work."

"I'm not. Go ahead and pick one and take it."

"Alora, you should sell these."

"No. Not after the way everyone has turned on me. I'd rather they go to people who really love them. Who aren't just in it for the investment."

Simone searched through the canvases and Alora continued.

"That's why I've taken to the clay. The painting…I can't seem to do. And what I can do, no one wants."

Simone pulled out a piece done in shades of green. "Did Bodie introduce you to the clay?"

Alora couldn't help but smile. "She did."

Simone studied her. "You smile when you speak of her."

"Do I?"

"Mm. So why isn't she here?"

Alora shook her head. "Because I fucked up. I ran her off."

"And you have no help now?"

"No, I do. She just isn't here right now. She went grocery shopping. But she's…not Bodie."

"Bodie's pretty special."

"Yes, she is."

"Maybe you should tell her that."

"I tried. Well, I apologized and she didn't respond."

"So, you gave up?"

"I don't want to bother her if she's still upset with me."

"What do you have to lose, Alora? Life is short and you want her to know how you feel." She touched her shoulder. "You really care for her, don't you?"

Alora swallowed, fighting tears. "Yeah. And I really miss her."

Simone gave her arm a squeeze. "You don't want any more regrets, Alora." Her phone chimed and she checked her screen.

"You're in, kid."

"No way."

"She wants you. I told you they are good."

Alora held her face, overwhelmed. "Oh, my God. I'm going to be so nervous."

"Welcome back."

Simone held up the canvas. "Can I have this one?"

"Yes. Please. Take it."

"You've got to make more room in here if you're going to continue to sculpt."

"Let's just see how the show goes." She was already nervous enough as it was. She didn't want to plan ahead.

"Don't tell me you're going to quit if the show doesn't go well."

"I don't know, Simone. One thing at a time."

"If you like working with the clay, you should keep doing it, no matter what."

"Yes, I probably should and I most likely will. I just—don't do well with rejection."

They strolled back to the living room. Simone set her painting on the counter, picked up her wine glass once again, and they sat on the couch to talk. Tater jumped up next to Alora and rested his head in her lap.

"Peter really did a number on you, didn't he?" Simone said.

"Let's put it this way, I no longer speak to him."

"I don't blame you." She stared out through the window. "You have a beautiful backyard."

"Thanks. Tater seems to love it."

"And you?"

Alora shrugged. "It's too hot now to really enjoy it much."

"When it cools off that'll change." She sipped her wine. "Do you still do things that give you pleasure, Alora?"

"I—yes. I work with the clay and I play with Tater."

"And?"

"And…" she grew quiet.

"How would you feel about coming down to the rec center to speak to my class?"

Alora laughed. "Are you serious?"

"As a heart attack."

"What on earth for? I'm washed up. I can't paint."

"You're full of knowledge about the craft and you can paint. Peter just got into your head. If you'd just relax and paint for you, and no one else, I think you'd be happy."

"You sound like Bodie."

"Well, maybe she's on to something."

"I don't know, Simone." Her fear of failure was still nearly overwhelming, despite the therapy.

"Oh, come on. My students would absolutely love to meet you. I talk about you all the time, you know and we study your work."

"That only adds to the pressure."

"I think it would be really good for you."

"Can I think about it?"

"Of course. Just give me a jingle to let me know."

Alora gave a nod and craved her own glass of wine. But she refrained. She had to stop pacifying herself with alcohol and just deal with the anxiety she was feeling head on. She inhaled deeply and exhaled. Tater seemed to notice and nudged her hand. She stroked his head and began to calm.

"And you can bring that handsome fella as well."

Alora smiled down at him. "In that case, you just may have yourself a date."

CHAPTER THIRTY-TWO

"And this is the artist, Bodie Banks," Simone said as she introduced an attractive-looking couple to Bodie.

"Your work is incredible," the woman said.

Bodie shook her hand. "Thank you."

"I love the way this piece captures emotion. Like this…. yearning. This reaching. Tell me, what did you use for the finish?"

"Nothing special. I used a medium gray and finished with a clean white."

"It turned out so beautiful," she said, casting her eyes over to one of her larger pieces. "And your inspiration?"

"For these, it was my late mother." Bodie moved closer to the piece in question. "See how the bare branches of the tree reach upward and turn into seeking hands? It's how I feel when I think of her. Like I'm reaching up toward the heavens for her."

The woman touched her heart and looked up at her companion. "How beautiful. I think we may be back to purchase this one."

"Don't wait too long," Simone said. "She's had a lot of interest in this one in particular."

"We'll be back," the woman said, still holding her hand to her chest. The couple walked away in quiet discussion.

"Three pieces sold already," Simone said. "And it looks like this one will be snatched up as well. Not bad for your first show."

"I feel like I'm going to throw up I'm so nervous. Like I can't believe this is really happening."

"It's happening, Bodie. And it's fantastic. So well deserved." She looked at the piece the couple was interested in. It was titled "Heaven." "Your work has really come along here recently. It's far more intense. It holds so much emotion, like she said." She looked back to Bodie. "What's changed?"

"I'm devoting more time to my work. A lot more time."

"Well, it's definitely showing."

"I got some good advice. From Alora, actually."

"Alora?"

"Yes. And those pieces," she pointed to the five pieces of women embracing, "were inspired by her."

"How interesting."

"Why is that interesting?"

"For several reasons. But mainly because," Simone tilted her head toward the front of the gallery, "she's here."

"No," Bodie breathed. "How is she here? Did you tell her about the show?"

"I may have." She grinned. "Alora's actually in the show too. She submitted seven pieces."

Bodie knew she must've looked shocked. "Why didn't you tell me?"

"Would you have still applied for the show?"

"I don't know."

"Then that's why."

"Does she know I'm here?"

"I haven't told her. But you should go say hello. She's sold some pieces as well. You're both doing very well."

"Now I really feel like I'm going to throw up."

Simone grabbed her hand. "Come on, I'll walk with you." She led her through the throng of mingling people to the front of the gallery until they came to a stop in front of Alora, who was chatting politely with a middle-aged man. When she saw Simone she smiled, and when she saw Bodie, she did a double take and paled.

"Would you excuse me a moment?" she said to the man. He nodded and headed toward the refreshments.

"Look, you're both here. What a coincidence," Simone said. "I'm going to go get some wine." She left, giving them both a sly look over her shoulder.

Alora blinked at Bodie. "Hi," she eventually said.

"Hi."

"Simone didn't tell me you would be here," Alora said.

"She didn't tell me about you either."

"Well, you should be here. You're the amazing sculptor."

"From what I hear, you aren't doing so badly yourself."

"I'm nervous as hell."

Bodie chuckled. "You and me both."

She glanced over at her pieces. She had a few of her teacups displayed, only these weren't ones Bodie had seen before, with little faces on them. Then she also had several larger pieces, pitchers with varying lines of color and shimmering gold streaks throughout. They were breathtaking to look at.

"Very nice," Bodie said. "I love how the handles are different on each one."

"Thanks." She shook her head. "I can't believe you're here. Why didn't I think to ask Simone if you would be?"

"I have a feeling she omitted our presence to each other for a reason."

"She has been trying to get me to call you," Alora said.

"Me too."

Alora shifted and pressed her lips together in that way that suggested she was deep in thought. "Did you get my text?"

Bodie nodded.

Alora glanced away as if embarrassed. "I meant every word," she said softly.

"Thank you. It was nice of you to apologize."

"Yeah, well, now I'm thinking that I should've done it in person. But I was too chicken shit." She laughed. "Big surprise there."

"It still took guts to send it. So don't beat yourself up."

More silence. "Why didn't you respond? Are you still upset with me?"

"Honestly? I wasn't sure you meant it. You were kind of up and down there for a while."

She nodded again. "I was, wasn't I?" She sighed. "I'm so sorry, Bodie. For all of it."

"I'm sorry too. I should've answered your text. At the very least to let you know I got it."

"No, you don't owe me anything. So don't apologize."

Bodie watched as Simone tipped her half-full wine glass at them and smiled before disappearing into the crowd.

"You look well," Bodie said, truly taking the time to soak her in. She looked fabulous in a black minidress and matching heels. Her salt-and-pepper hair was slicked back and her lips and eyes were made up. She looked drop-dead gorgeous, but Bodie was careful not to let on.

"I'm actually eating," she said with a smirk. "And I've stopped drinking so much wine."

"It seems to be helping because you look wonderful. Very healthy."

"Thanks. You look good too, Bodie. Really good." Bodie glanced down at her black jeans, white button-down shirt, and maroon crushed velvet blazer that she'd found at a thrift store with Kristy.

"My sister picked out the blazer."

"It works. Sets you apart in a classical way."

Bodie blushed. "Your makeup, I've never seen you this way."

"Tabby," Alora said.

"Ah. Well, she did a beautiful job."

"You're going to make me blush now."

"You blush?" Bodie asked.

"You don't think I'm capable?"

"No, not at all."

"You'd be surprised. Especially when the compliment comes from someone I care about. Like you."

Bodie fell silent and cleared her throat. She was suddenly parched but didn't want to leave Alora's side. Now that she was with her again, she couldn't bear the thought of being without her.

"How about a beer?" Bodie asked.

"You read my mind."

They wove through more people to the bar where Bodie ordered them both an icy bottle of beer. She handed Alora hers and they turned to face the crowd.

"Want to step outside? Get some fresh air?" Alora asked.

"I'll race you to the door."

They hurried through the mass of people to push out the door and into the heavily heated evening, where they leaned against the building to sip their drinks.

"So how have you been, Bodie Banks?"

"Me? I'm good. Busy."

"With school?"

"You heard?"

"How's it going?"

Bodie pushed out a breath. "It's hard. Trying to balance studying with work and my sculpting. But I'm managing."

"You must be if you're here showing your work."

"Your advice, it really helped me."

Alora smiled. "That's nice to hear, Bodie."

"Bodes!" Bodie turned to find Kristy walking out the gallery door toward her. "What are you doing? There are more people who want to meet you."

Bodie hesitated, but then spoke. "Kristy, this is Alora Anders. Alora, this is my sister Kristy."

Kristy stopped dead in her tracks and gave Alora the once-over. She did not look pleased.

"So, you're the infamous Alora Anders?"

Alora pushed off the wall and offered her hand. "Oh, no, I'm not sure I should say yes." She chuckled.

Kristy shook her hand limply and looked back to Bodie. "Come back inside."

"I will in a minute. I'm talking to Alora."

"This is your big night, Bodes. You don't want to waste it."

Bodie's throat tightened at her insinuation. "I'm not."

"She's right," Alora said. "You should go back inside."

"See?" Kristy said. "Listen to her. It's probably the only unselfish thing she'll ever do for you."

Bodie stiffened and Alora clamped her jaw.

Bodie shook her head. "She didn't mean that."

"Yes, I did," Kristy said. "And what are you kissing her ass for? After what she did to you, she should be kissing yours."

"Kristy," Bodie seethed, grabbing her by the arm. "Knock it off."

"No, she's right," Alora said. "I did treat you badly, Bodie. And it's unforgivable."

"From what I hear, you treat everyone badly, like they're disposable. Like all your one-night stands," Kristy said, jerking her arm free from Bodie.

"From what you hear?" Alora looked pained. She stared at Bodie. "What does she mean?"

"Nothing. She's just being rude."

"I'm being truthful," Kristy said. "But it sounds like you can't handle it."

"Have you said things about me?" Alora asked Bodie.

"No, of course not."

"Then how does she—"

The door to the gallery opened again and Simone appeared. "Guys, come on. People are asking for you both." She smiled, but then it fell as she took in the situation. "What's going on?"

"Nothing," Bodie said quickly.

"Everything," Alora added, giving Bodie a hard look.

"Alora, please."

But Alora turned her back on her to walk back inside. Kristy eyed her as she passed her and then spoke to Bodie.

"Forget her," she said. "She's not worth your time."

"You have no right to judge her," Bodie said. "No right."

"I have every right. You're my sister and she hurt you. She hurts everyone."

"Don't you get it? She's working on herself. Trying to change. And now she thinks I've said things about her. Bad things."

"So? It's not like you'd be the only one."

Bodie pushed past her to walk back inside. She tried to find Alora, but she lost her and Simone in the crowd. People began coming up to her, asking her questions about her pieces. She spoke sporadically, all the while standing on her toes to try to locate Alora. Eventually, she gave up and refocused on the interested buyers. Some had already gone however, but she was too upset to care.

"Did you sell anything else?" Kristy asked, joining her.

"I don't know. Nor do I care."

"Well, you should care. This could be your big break."

"All I care about is finding Alora to apologize."

"You can't," a voice said from behind. Bodie turned and saw Simone looking somber. "She just left."

CHAPTER THIRTY-THREE

Alora was sitting in her living room, enjoying a hot cup of coffee when Tater alerted her to someone at the door. She stood to go to the front of the house. Tater ran ahead of her, tail wagging, woofing in his low baritone the way he often did when someone rang the doorbell.

"Good boy," she said, easing him aside to look through the peephole. "What the hell?" She unlocked the door and slowly pulled it open to stand face to face with Bodie's sister, Kristy.

"Yes?" Alora said, truly clueless as to why she'd be on her doorstep. Unless… "Is Bodie okay?"

"She's fine. Actually, she's not. She's pissed at me. Royally pissed and I've come to fix that."

"How do you mean?"

"Look, Bodie never said a bad word about you, okay? It was all me. I know someone, a friend, who told me about you and your dating habits, long before you ever met Bodie."

"A friend, huh?"

"It was stupid and childish, this I know. But Bodie had nothing to do with any of it. She's not like that. She never has an unkind word to say about anybody. And you, even though you may or may not deserve an unkind word, seem to have touched her heart, because she's convinced that you're trying to change for the better. I just hope, for her sake, that she's not wrong."

"I guess only time will tell, right?" Alora said.

"I suppose." She held up her hands. "That's all I wanted to say. Sorry to bother you." She turned to walk away.

"For what it's worth," Alora said. "Thank you."

Kristy didn't turn, she just continued down the path to her car. "Wait!" Alora said. This time Kristy did turn. "Give me one second."

Alora left the door open and made her way into the study where she grabbed a small piece off the shelf. She brought it back to the door and handed it to Kirsty, who looked at it oddly.

"Give it to Bodie," she said. "She'll know what it is. And tell her…tell her she's the one who inspired me."

Kristy closed her fist over the small clay sculpture and nodded. Then she headed off toward her car once again. Alora watched her go in silence. When she'd driven away, she closed the door and leaned against it to cry.

CHAPTER THIRTY-FOUR

Bodie pulled up to the house and killed the engine to her Honda Accord. She sat staring at her steering wheel for a moment, then opened her hand to look at the clay face sitting in her palm. It was Alora's first sculpture, the one she'd made in Mexico all those weeks ago and she'd given it to her, along with a message. One she knew she'd never forget.

Bodie opened the door and walked up to the front stoop and knocked. Her nerves were on edge and her heart was damn near in her throat. She heard Tater bark and heard someone approaching the door. When it opened, just a crack, she saw a woman she didn't recognize.

"Can I help you?" she asked with a heavy eastern European accent.

For an instant, Bodie panicked, thinking she had the wrong house. But then she saw Tater stick his head out and she knew, this must be the new caregiver.

"Is Alora home?"

"She resting."

"Can I speak to her? Please?"

"She had eye treatment. She hurt."

Bodie exhaled. She could walk away, but would she ever have the nerve to come back? "I really need to see her. Can you just please tell her…tell her that her inspiration is at the door?"

The woman scowled. "Inspiration?"

"She'll understand."

"You wait."

Bodie nodded and the door closed. She glanced down at the face in her hand again and remembered the way Alora had looked on the beach that day, wind toying with her hair as she tongued her lip to form the face with her hands. The way she'd been so intensely focused and so overly critical of her work. She'd been so unsure of herself and her talent. But she'd come so far since then. Working the clay on her own and getting good enough to be included in a show. All of it made Bodie warm and she realized just how much she missed her and longed to get to know this new Alora, the one who was trying so hard to better herself in every way.

Tater barked again and the door opened. Alora stood staring at her with watery red eyes and mussed hair. She still took Bodie's breath away.

"Bodie," she whispered.

"Hi." She held out the face. "I got your message."

Alora opened the door farther and stepped to the side. "Natalya, would you excuse us, please."

Natalya grabbed her purse and came to the door. "I go to store."

"Thank you," Alora said. She welcomed Bodie inside. Tater greeted her with heavy licks to her hand.

"Hey, buddy," Bodie said as she stroked his head. "How you been, huh?"

"Wonderful," Alora said. "He's my best guy."

"I'm happy to hear that."

They went into the living room where Alora offered her a seat. "Can I get you a drink?"

"No, thank you." Bodie didn't sit, but rather stood in front of Alora with her heart pounding. It felt like it was lodged in her throat. "I just—"

Alora was staring deep into her eyes as if she were baring her soul to her. Bodie saw it then. All the love and passion she had for her, swirling in her irises like a turbulent sea.

"Yes?" Alora said.

"Ah, hell." Bodie wrapped her hand around the back of her head and pulled her into her for a hot, searing kiss. One that seemed to take them both by surprise with its intensity, leaving them both breathless and moaning for more.

"Wait," Alora said, gently placing her hand on her chest.

"I don't want to wait," Bodie said. "Not anymore."

Alora searched her face. "I don't want you to get hurt, Bodie. Not again."

"So, don't hurt me." She tried to kiss her again, but Alora stopped her.

"I'm still healing," she said. "Processing. Going to therapy."

"That's great."

"And I'm talking with my sister. With Jasmine. It's difficult at times, but I think she's changed, and she swears she wasn't the one who sold the story about me. She thinks it was my mother. But I still get…sad, Bodie. And angry, as I relive my past. The foster homes, they were scary at times. I wasn't abused or anything, but there was one house where I didn't feel safe at all. The man, he kept trying to come in my room at night."

"Jesus, Alora. That's terrible."

"It is, but I'm working on moving past it. On feeling safe within myself. But, like I said, it's difficult at times and I don't always handle the pain of reliving it all very well."

"And you think you might push me away again?"

"No, I'd never do that. I just—I don't want you to take it personally. So how about if we take it slow? That way we can navigate this carefully together."

Bodie held her waist. "How slow?"

"This slow."

Alora lightly kissed her lips, languidly tugging them into her mouth to taste them as if they were the finest of wines.

"You're killing me," Bodie said when Alora drew away, leaving her head spinning.

"It's hard for me too." She smiled. "But I don't want our first time since Mexico to be like this. I'm in physical pain and you've literally just walked back into my life."

Bodie took her hands. "Of course, I should've asked how you were feeling." Alora touched her face.

"I'm okay. Just the treatments, you know? I got home about an hour ago from one and I need to rest."

"Is there anything I can do?" Bodie asked, more than concerned for her.

"There is. You can come lie down with me. Hold me in your arms."

"There's nothing I'd love to do more."

Alora kissed her again, teasing. Then she led them into the bedroom, allowed Tater to enter as well, and closed the door.

CHAPTER THIRTY-FIVE

Alora's palms were sweaty and her head swam with an anxiousness she hadn't felt since the art show. A light hand to her shoulder caused her to nearly jump out of her skin.

"Jesus," she breathed as Simone dropped her hand.

"Sorry, didn't realize you were so jumpy."

Alora bounced on her feet and chewed on a pesky hangnail.

Simone touched her again. "It's going to be okay."

"What if it's not? What if they don't like me?"

"What's not to like?"

Alora gave her a look.

"They're just people, Alora. People who want to paint. And who knows painting better than you?"

"Not anymore."

"That's Peter talking. And fuck him. Seriously. He doesn't know his head from his ass."

Alora stared at her in shock. "You've never spoken that way before."

"Assholes like Peter bring out the best in me. He's not in it for the art, he's in it for the money and that makes me sick. Not to mention what he did to you."

"I'm over him," she said.

"But you're still afraid. We need to fix that."

"Not sure we can."

"Well, this is a good first step."

She smiled down at Tater who was lounging next to her desk. She smiled at the doorway as her students began entering the classroom.

"Welcome, welcome, everyone."

There were all walks of life taking their seats behind their easels. Older, younger, quiet, friendly. Alora began to relax as she studied them, realizing that Simone was right. They were just people.

"Everyone, as promised, we have a guest today." She looked at Alora. "This, my friends, is Alora Anders."

To Alora's surprise the class began to clap, causing her cheeks to heat profusely.

"Thank you," she managed to say when they quietened down. "That was quite a welcome."

"We love you," one woman said from the front row.

"Yeah, thanks for coming to our class."

Simone clasped her hands together beneath her chin. "Why don't we get started so Alora can see what all you're working on?" The students eagerly gathered their supplies and slowly, one by one, began to add brush strokes to their canvases.

"They've been working on these nature scenes for a week now," Simone said, leading Alora around the classroom. They wove in and out of easels, taking in the students' work.

"They're talented," Alora said, truly impressed by the quality of work.

"This is my advanced technique class. Most of them have been with me for a couple of years now."

"You mean they come back to the rec center for your class year after year?"

"Mm-hm."

"That's incredible."

"They're devoted."

"And you're a wonderful teacher," Alora said with a smile. "I know firsthand."

They stopped behind a young man who was sitting idle, shoulders slouched, paintbrush poised and trembling above the canvas.

"Tyrone, is everything okay?" Simone asked.

He forced down a swallow. "I can't paint. I'm too nervous."

"Why are you so nervous?" Simone asked.

"Because I'm not good enough. Look at this." He gestured toward his painting.

Simone looked to Alora. "I think I'll let you talk to him," she said, walking away. Alora almost called out for her, but then clamped her mouth. Tyrone was staring at his canvas, hand still shaking. His work wasn't bad, it was actually quite good from what she could see. But he wasn't as far along as the others in the class.

Alora pulled up a stool and sat next to him. "You know, I feel the same way you do."

His dark eyes widened. "You?"

"Yep. I feel frozen. Like I can't touch that brush to the canvas because I fear that when I do it's going to be complete and utter shit."

He nodded. "That's exactly how I feel."

"But why, Tyrone? From what I can see, you're quite good."

"I—this—it takes me longer. I really have to concentrate whereas everyone else just sits and paints and these amazing scenes come to fruition."

"And that makes you feel inadequate?"

"Big time."

Alora reached out and lowered his hand. "I can relate."

"So, what did you do? You know, to fix it?"

Alora blinked. "I haven't."

His shoulders slumped even more.

"But…" Alora said, standing. "I have an idea." She moved to the back of the classroom and brought back a blank canvas. She traded it out for the other canvas and set it aside. She grabbed a brush and gave Tyrone's forearm an encouraging squeeze. "How about we try together?"

"You mean it?"

"Sure. What do we have to lose?"

"I don't know. Our dignity?"

She laughed. "Tyrone, I've lost so much of that these past few weeks that it doesn't even faze me anymore. Because you know what? I've gained too. And that's what I'm focused on. So we have to work a little differently than other folks? Who cares? I guarantee they don't. In fact, I bet if we ask them, they'll do nothing but encourage us." She called out to the class. "Hey, everyone. Tyrone and I have to paint a lot slower than you. Should that matter?"

A bunch of noes filtered throughout the room.

"See?"

She sat once again and readied her brush. Tyrone licked his lips and readied his.

"Now," Alora said with a smile. "Let's get started, shall we?"

CHAPTER THIRTY-SIX

Bodie stood in the doorway to Simone's classroom looking in on Alora. She was sitting next to a young man and painting with him.

"She's painting," Simone said, coming to stand alongside her.

"I can't believe it. I'm so proud of her," Bodie said.

"She's come a long way?"

"You have no idea."

"My students love her. I think I'm going to ask her to keep coming back for some cameos."

"She'd probably really like that."

"How are things going with the two of you?"

Bodie smiled.

Simone chuckled. "That good, eh?"

"Yeah."

Simone checked her watch. "Shoot, I've got to end class." She clapped her hands as she re-entered the classroom. "That's all for today, guys. Go ahead and clean up and I'll see you next week."

"Will Alora be here?"

"If you ask her, she just might."

They all voiced their encouragement and Alora flushed. She stood. "I'll come back." The class clapped again, and everyone began cleaning up and heading out. Bodie walked in and stood in front of Alora.

"Hi," she said.

"Hi."

"Did you enjoy yourself?" Bodie asked.

"I did."

"I see you painted."

"Uh-huh." She held out her hand. "Would you like to see it?"

Bodie took her hand and rounded the easel. She got goose bumps as she took in the painting.

"You like it?"

"It's Mexico," Bodie said.

"It is. It's our beach."

"Our beach?"

She stared into Bodie's eyes. "Yes. Our beach. And I want to go back. Will you go with me?"

"You didn't sell it?"

"I couldn't bring myself to. After all it's where I fell in love with you."

"You—"

"Yes. I'm in love with you, Bodie Banks. Say you'll go with me and we can do Mexico all over again? This time so, so much better. We can wait until you're done with school. Whatever you need."

Bodie slid her hand beneath her jaw. "Count me in."

Tater barked and wagged his tail. Bodie rubbed his head. "Him too."

Alora laughed and they embraced, Tater standing right at their side.

THE END

About the Author

Ronica Black lives in the desert Southwest with her menagerie of animals and her menagerie of art. When she's not writing, she's still creating, whether drawing, painting, or woodworking. She loves long walks into the sunset, rescuing animals, anything pertaining to art, and spending time with those she loves. When she can, she enjoys returning to her roots in North Carolina where she can sit back on the porch with family and friends, catch up on all the gossip, and relish an ice cold Cheerwine.

Ronica is a two-time Golden Crown Literary Society Goldie Award winner and a three-time finalist for the Lambda Literary Awards.

Books Available from Bold Strokes Books

Behold My Heart by Ronica Black. Alora Anders is a highly successful artist who's losing her vision. Devastated, she hires Bodie Banks, a young struggling sculptor as a live-in assistant. Can Alora open her mind and her heart to accept Bodie into her life? (978-1-63679-810-3)

Fearless Hearts by Radclyffe. One wounded woman, one determined to protect her—and a summertime of risk, danger, and desire. (978-1-63679-837-0)

Forever Family by L.M. Rose. Two friends come together after tragedy to raise a baby, finding love along the way. (978-1-63679-868-4)

Stranger in the Sand by Renee Roman. Grace Langley is haunted by guilt. Fagan Shaw wishes she could remember her past. Will finding each other bring the closure they're looking for in order to have a brighter future? (978-1-63679-802-8)

The Nursing Home Hoax by Shelley Thrasher and Ann Faulkner. In this fresh take for grown-ups on the classic Nancy Drew series, crime-solving duo Taylor and Marilee investigate suspicious activity at a small East Texas nursing home. (978-1-63679-806-6)

The Rise and Fall of Conner Cody by Chelsey Lynford. A successful yet lonely Hollywood starlet must decide if she can let go of old wounds and accept a chance at family, friendship, and the love of a lifetime. (978-1-63679-739-7)

A Conflict of Interest by Morgan Adams. Tensions rise when a one-night stand becomes a major conflict of interest between an up-and-coming senior associate and a dedicated cardiac surgeon. (978-1-63679-870-7)

A Magnificent Disturbance by Lee Lynch. These everyday dykes and their friends will stop at nothing to see the women's clinic thrive and, in the process, their ideals, their wounds, and a steadfast allegiance to one another make them heroes. (978-1-63679-031-2)

A Marvelous Murder by David S. Pederson. When a hated director is found dead in his locked study, movie star Victor Marvel, his boyfriend Griff, and friend Eve seek to uncover what really happened to Orland Orcott. (978-1-63679-798-4)

Big Corpse on Campus by Karis Walsh. When University Police Officer Cappy Flannery investigates what looks like a clear-cut suicide, she discovers that the case—and her feelings for librarian Jazz—are more complicated than she expected. (978-1-63679-852-3)

Charity Case by Jean Copeland. Bad girl Lindsay Chase came home to Connecticut for a fresh start, but an old, risky habit provides the chance to save the day for her new love, Ellie. (978-1-63679-593-5)

Moments to Treasure by Ali Vali. Levi Montbard and Yasmine Hassani have found a vast Templar treasure, but there is much more to the story—and what is left to be found. (978-1-63679-473-0)

The Stolen Girl by Cari Hunter. Detective Inspector Jo Shaw is determined to prove she's fit for work after an injury that almost killed her, but a new case brings her up against people who will do anything to preserve their own interests, putting Jo—and those closest to her—directly in the line of fire. (978-1-63679-822-6)

Discovering Gold by Sam Ledel. In 1920s Colorado, a single mother and a rowdy cowgirl must set aside their fears and initial reservations about one another if they want to find love in the mining town each of them calls home. (978-1-63679-786-1)

Dream a Little Dream by Melissa Brayden. Savanna can't believe it when Dr. Kyle Remington, the woman who left her feeling like a fool, shows up in Dreamer's Bay. Life is too complicated for second chances. Or is it? (978-1-63679-839-4)

Emma by the Sea by Sarah G. Levine. A delightful modern-day romance inspired by Emma, one of Jane Austen's most beloved novels. (978-1-63679-879-0)

Goodbye, Hello by Heather K O'Malley. With so much time apart and the challenges of a long-distance relationship, Kelly and Teresa's second chance at love may end just as awkwardly as the first. (978-1-63679-790-8)

One Measure of Love by Annie McDonald. Vancouver's hit competitive cooking show Recipe for Success has begun filming its second season and two talented young chefs are desperate for more than a winning dish. (978-1-63679-827-1)

The Smallest Day by J.M. Redmann. The first bullet missed—can Micky Knight stop the second bullet from finding its target? (978-1-63679-854-7)

To Please Her by Elena Abbott. A spilled coffee leads Sabrina into a world of erotic BDSM that may just land her the love of her life. (978-1-63679-849-3)

Two Weddings and a Funeral by Claudia Parr. Stella and Theo have spent the last thirteen years pretending they can be just friends, but surely "just friends" don't make out every chance they get. (978-1-63679-820-2)

Coming Up Clutch by Anna Gram. College softball star Kelly "Razor" Mitchell hung up her cleats early, but when former crush, now coach Ashton Sharpe shows up on her doorstep seven years later, beautiful as ever, Razor hopes the longing in her gaze has nothing to do with softball. (978-1-63679-817-2)

Firecamp by Jaycie Morrison. Going their separate ways seemed inevitable for two people as different as Fallon and Nora, while meeting up again is strictly coincidental. (978-1-63679-753-3)

Fixed Up by Aurora Rey. When electrician Jack Barrow and artist Ellie Lancaster get stuck on a job site during a blizzard, close quarters send all sorts of sparks flying. (978-1-63679-788-5)

Stranded by Ronica Black. Can Abigail and Whitley overcome their personal hang-ups and stubbornness to survive not only Alaska, but a dangerous stalker as well? (978-1-63679-761-8)

Whisk Me Away by Georgia Beers. Regan's a gorgeous flake. Ava, a beautiful untouchable ice queen. When they meet again at a retreat for up-and-coming pastry chefs, the competition, and the ovens, heat up. (978-1-63679-796-0)